Dirty TRUTHS

BOSTON BILLIONAIRES

BRITTANÉE NICOLE

Cover Design Mary of Books and Moods
Formatting by Cover to Cover Author Services
Editing by Beth at VB Edits
Beta Editing and Proofreading by Brittni Van of Overbooked Editing

www.brittaneenicole.net

DIRTY TRUTHS PLAYLIST

1. Marry Me by Train
2. Drive by Incubus or Upside Down by Jack Johnson
3. There She Goes by Sixpence None The Richer
4. Everything You Want by Vertical Horizon
5. Closing Time by Semisonic
6. She's So High By Tal Bachman
7. Suddenly I See by KT Tunstall
8. Crash Into Me by Dave Matthews
9. Vogue by Madonna
10. Don't Panic by Coldplay
11. Poker Face By Lady Gaga
12. I Know You Want Me by Pitbull
13. Boston by Augustana
14. The Only Exception by Paramore
15. Slide by The Goo Goo Dolls
16. Amber by 311
17. Love Song By Sara Bareilles
18. Wonderwall by Oasis
19. Friday I'm in Love by The Cure
20. Complicated by Avril Lavigne
21. Don't Dream It's Over by Crowded House
22. Losing My Religion by R.E.M.
23. Fix You by Coldplay
24. Yellow by Coldplay
25. Clocks by Coldplay
26. Chasing Cars by Snow Patrol
27. Look After You by The Fray

28. Chasing Pavements by Adele

29. Bittersweet Symphony by The Verve

30. Everlong by Foo Fighters

31. Mr. Brightside by The Killers

32. Secret by Maroon 5

33. Dancing in the Moonlight by Toploader or Two Princes by Spin Doctors

34. Sunday Morning by Maroon 5

35. Falling for You by Colbie Caillat

36. Only Wanna Be With You by Hootie and the Blowfish

37. I Got You by Jack Johnson

38. The Warmth by Incubus

39. Get Your Number by Mariah Carey and Nelly

40. I Kissed A Girl by Katy Perry

41. Umbrella by Rihanna and Jay-Z

42. Lips on You By Maroon 5

43. Crazy in Love Beyonce & Jay Z

44. Sweet Disposition by The Temper Trap

45. It Had to Be You by Ray Charles

46. Precious Love by James Morrison

47. Bubbly Colbie Caillat

48. Just Got Started Loving You by James Otto

49. You Were Meant For Me by Jewel

50. Warning Sign by Coldplay

51. How To Save A Life by The Fray

52. I Love You Always Forever by Donna Lewis

53. You Are the Best Thing by Ray LaMontagne

54. I Don't Want A Miss A thing by Aerosmith

55. Sparks by Coldplay

56. Only You by Cheat Codes

.

DEDICATION

When I have nothing else, I have music.

And Sara. Thank you, my sweet friend, for all your help.
Jay is yours.

P.S. He's my favorite

XOXO, Brittanee

My only love sprung from my only hate.
Too early seen unknown, and known too late!
Prodigious birth of love is it to me.
That I must love a loathed enemy.

–Shakespeare

PROLOGUE

Jay

I was ten the first time I saw two people fucking. They were in my father's office. His *home* office.

I was excited to tell him about the A I'd gotten on my science fair project. He and I had worked on it together, focusing on whiskey and the fermentation process. That was also the year I fell in love with my father's business.

It was also when I learned that a person can only trust two things in life: themselves and alcohol.

We don't screw ourselves over, and we all know what to expect when it comes to alcohol. Raging headaches when we drink too much.

But it wasn't my father I found in his office that day. It was my mother.

And the man she was fucking wasn't just anyone; he was my father's enemy.

Though I didn't know that at the time.

And because my father's enemies are my enemies, I came up with a brilliant plan to make the man pay. And today I put that plan in motion.

1

MARRY ME BY TRAIN

Cat

September 2009

Deep breaths. I can do this. I'm Catherine Freaking Bouvier. I can make a freaking cup of coffee.

"Any minute now, princess." The man on the other side of the counter scowls.

I bite my tongue, but the death stare I shoot in his direction has him shutting his mouth. As I was saying, I *can* do this. I just have to figure out how to turn these beans into coffee.

I scratch my head and regard them. Mrs. Kearns always made this look so easy. Isn't there a smusher or something? I search the counters for a device that might do just that. God, I really am a fucking princess.

"Seriously, lady, what's taking so long?" the guy asks, annoyance returning to his features. I don't blame him.

"Um." I scan the coffee shop. It's late afternoon. Does this guy really *need* coffee?

I came in to fill out an application and somehow found myself covering for my friend Mia with no training and no idea what the hell to do. She swore she'd only be gone fifteen minutes, and that if anyone did come in—which she swore was doubtful—they'd want a bottle of water, an iced coffee—premade, thank God—or a freaking scone.

Not hot coffee. *Not* a freaking macchiato double spun with an espresso shot and caramel flavoring that I can't locate anywhere in this place.

A line four people deep has formed, and Mia has been gone far longer than fifteen minutes.

I stare at the machine again, taunted by the damn shiny buttons. I lift one of the knobs and go up on my toes so I can peer inside to see if the motion did anything. The machine makes a whooshing noise, and for a second, my heart soars. But as quickly as it started, it stops again.

"Fuck," I whisper to myself.

"Are you new?" A girl with long brown hair steps up next to the annoyed man. She taps one perfectly manicured nail against the counter impatiently.

"It's just…" I start, watching the door.

Where is Mia?

I take in the line again, catching sight of a man at the back. He smirks when he notices my attention, his blond hair falling forward into his eyes. Eyes that melt as soon as they meet mine. They're a glacier blue and impossible to look away from. He glances away first, pulling his phone out of his pocket and tapping on it quickly without looking back up.

"*Hello,* if you don't know how to make coffee, maybe you should have put the closed sign up," the girl suggests, her attention darting back to the mystery man behind her. As soon as she sees him, her entire demeanor shifts. "But I'd be happy to help you," she offers.

Yeah, I've got your number, lady.

"Just a minute," I say, turning back to the machine to focus. I bite my lip as I rack my brain for a plan.

The jingle of the bell above the door is my saving grace. Mia walks in, her long blond hair swaying behind her back as she weaves between tables.

"Finally," I mutter, turning to the counter once more. "How about you all tell me your orders, and we'll go from there?"

The man in the back smirks again, like my ineptitude is entertaining.

16

I twist my lips and glare.

The other customers step up and give me their orders, but my focus keeps slipping back to him. Mia stops when she reaches him, and he gives her his full attention, his smile lifting for her.

He's tall—at least a couple of inches over six feet—and he's wearing a light gray herringbone suit. Versace, if I had to guess. It pulls across his shoulders, hinting at what he's hiding. Strong, broad, muscular shoulders, a tight waist, and an ass worthy of bouncing quarters off.

They say a few words to one another, and she laughs as they both turn in my direction. I glare back.

Mia squeezes his shoulder and walks toward me. Rounding the counter, she smacks my ass. "Sorry, my date took a bit longer than I thought it would," she offers, a flirty smile gracing her lips.

"You were on a date?" I gape. "I thought you had to meet with your professor."

Her eyes dance. "I did."

"Slut," I grumble with a laugh, shaking my head.

"If the name fits," she sings. She turns away from me and claps her hands. "Okay, everyone, your favorite barista is here! Give me five minutes, and I'll give you heaven."

The hottie in the back keeps his eyes on Mia. Or more specifically, her hips.

I sigh. Blondes really do have more fun.

As soon as the rush has passed, Mia leans against the counter and smirks. "Sorry again. I really didn't think anyone would come in this late."

"Can you show me how to work the machine now? I felt like such an idiot."

Mia moves closer and brushes the hair out of my face. "Sorry, gorgeous. You're not an idiot. Just a bit of a princess."

I grimace at the nickname. My father used to call me that, and I hate my father.

"Just teach me, *please*," I beg.

When I turn away, embarrassed by how desperate I sound, I meet those glacier blue eyes again. He's seated across the café, his attention trained on Mia, or maybe on her proximity to my body.

Ugh. She's probably fucked him too. I push away from her in a huff.

Mia follows my gaze and pushes closer to me, her hand cradling my face. "He's just a friend," she murmurs softly, pressing closer to me.

"So am I," I remind her.

It's been a long time since we were anything more.

"You know that's not true," she says as she presses her finger against my lip. And dammit, I don't push her away.

Mia is a user. She's also been my best friend since grade school, the person I've done everything with. And yeah, I mean everything.

I tried to distance myself from her. My grandmother thought it would be good for me. I needed to find my way out of her shadow.

So when we graduated from high school, she went to Providence College, and I went to NYU.

Unlike my older brother, I wasn't interested in going to Brown. It's where my father and grandfather went. And where I was expected to attend.

Jameses go to Brown University.

My grandmother met my grandfather there. And my father met my mother. No one has forgone that school.

Except me. For two years I did.

And then I got the internship at Jolie Magazine. It's my dream job. But their office is in Boston and they're partnered with Brown. So moving back to the area was a necessity.

With Mia still in school here, I thought moving in with her was a no-brainer.

It's been one week, and I'm already questioning the decision.

"You're my only girl," she says, pressing herself closer to me.

I push back against the counter. I'm not going back into that toxic relationship.

"The coffee maker," I say, changing the subject.

She smirks, as if she knows what I'm doing. *Good, be my friend. That's all I want.*

"Fine," she huffs, "I'll teach you how to make a cup of coffee when the next customer comes."

"I'd like a cup," a voice says from behind us. His voice is smooth, deeper than I'm used to. The men at school sound like boys. He is definitely *not* a boy.

When I turn, I'm met with the sky-blue eyes of the man in the herringbone suit. My breath nearly whooshes from my chest. His gaze leaves mine and rakes down my body slowly before moving back up to my arm, where Mia's fingers are stroking seductively. I'm not sure whether she's showing off for him or claiming me.

With her, either is possible.

I pull away from the unwanted contact. "What can we get you?" I ask, offering a smile.

"I'll take a coffee"—he offers me a come-hither smirk—"and your name and number."

I spin away, my hair swinging behind me, and reply, "I'll get you that coffee."

"You're not going to tell me your name?" he asks, the humor in his tone hinting at the smile I can almost guarantee he's wearing.

I examine the confounding piece of equipment in front of me. I have no intention of letting him know I need Mia's help. "Nope," I say. "You have to earn the right to that information."

He chuckles. "And how would one go about doing that?"

Mia's arm brushes against me as she reaches around and hits the switch on the coffee pot. "I got you, babe," she says loudly.

I close my eyes in annoyance and keep my attention fixed on the coffee brewing in front of me.

As soon as it's ready, I pour it into a paper cup, turn around, and hand it to Blue Eyes, although I don't look into them again.

"You never answered my question," he says, his brow arched. "How would I go about earning that information?"

"By being less cliché," I offer.

"Cliché?" he asks, the tone of his voice making it almost impossible to not look up.

"Yes, overused, lack of original thought," I deadpan, finally meeting his gaze.

The right side of his lip raises as he scrutinizes me ruefully.

But before he can respond, Mia calls out, "Hey, Cat, no need to ring him up. He owns the joint."

My face heats with embarrassment as Blue Eyes full-on smiles at me. "Hmm, I had you pegged as more of a kitten," he murmurs before bringing the cup to his lips.

Then, before I die on the spot, he lifts the cup in farewell and walks out of the coffee shop.

2

DRIVE BY INCUBUS

Jay

"I thought you were going to sell the coffee shop," my father says as he studies me over the papers in his hand. "You had your little college experiment. Now it's time to focus on real business."

I prop one ankle on the opposite knee and sip my coffee. That *was* my plan. Likely still will be. But even as I consider it, a vision of the woman with the dark brown hair and bourbon eyes returns to me.

Cat.

She wore exaggerated eyeliner around those mesmerizing eyes. I'd think with her cliché remark, she'd find it almost ironic. Maybe that was the point.

"It's earning a profit. Basically runs itself," I counter.

"And yet you were in there today, because you don't know how to delegate," my father says with a smirk. He's got me there.

"I'll do better," I promise. My plan *was* to put Mia in charge of the shop. She's been there for two years, and as the only female friend I've never fucked, I trust her. *Trusted* her. Until today, when I walked in to find that she'd left the store manned by a nonemployee who didn't even know how to work a fucking coffeepot. I bite back my smile at the memory of the flustered woman behind the counter. "Give me a few weeks. I'll get someone in place."

He shakes his head. "Fine. Now, on to the next order of business. Your brothers will be in town for a few weeks."

Grinding my molars, I grit out, "Why?"

My father puts the paper on his desk and sighs. "It's their right."

"Are you worried that I'm not focused because of the fucking shop? If that's the problem, I'll sell it tomorrow," I say, irritation getting the best of me.

"That's not what this is about. They deserve to be involved in the business too. They aren't your enemies," he says, narrowing his eyes and lacing his fingers on the surface of his desk.

"I'm perfectly aware of who the enemy is, Father."

"Good," he says, a sly grin sliding onto his face. He rises from his chair, tugging on the cuffs of his sleeves. Silently, he moves toward the floor-to-ceiling window and pours two glasses from the decanter that his father passed down to him many years before. He motions for me to join him, and when I accept the lowball glass he holds out, he clinks his against it. "It's time, Jay. You've had years to put this plan in motion. Years to earn their trust. It's fucking time."

3

THERE SHE GOES
BY SIXPENCE NONE THE RICHER

Jay

Mia struts into my apartment and throws me a flirtatious smile as I hold the door for her. "Can I get you a drink?" I offer, guiding her to the kitchen.

Mia, being Mia, ignores my offer completely and strides toward my bedroom.

"Mia," I growl. Dammit, she's already getting the upper hand. The girl can't take a fucking hint. "We aren't going to my bedroom."

"You might not be," she calls, not bothering to turn around, "but that's where I'll be."

I pinch the bridge of my nose and grimace. Why the hell am I still friends with this woman? She fucks everything that walks and listens to nothing I say. But we bonded years ago, and there's no turning my back on her now.

Blowing out a breath, I stomp down the hall and find Mia sprawled out on my bed, her short dress riding up her thighs and exposing her lime green thong. She pats the spot next to her which I ignore, instead dropping into a chair in front of my desk and focusing on the City of Providence out my window.

Just another thing that annoys my father. He wants me to move to

Boston and finish my master's from there. But I can't exactly do what he wants me to do and also fucking move to Boston. I'm being pulled in so many damn directions I can't think straight half the time.

Which is why Mia is here. I need her to grow the fuck up and take over the shop. I can't be worried about a damn coffee shop.

And you don't want to sell it because then you'll have no reason to tease and play with the kitten.

For fuck's sake. I'm demented.

When I was in high school, my father laid out my future. And it wasn't one that involved taking over his whiskey business.

No, the future he created for me revolved around stripping everything that mattered from those who had taken everything away from us. I've focused on nothing but that for the last seven years, and I'm finally close to reaching my goal. Close to making them pay. So I can't be distracted by a fucking pussy. No matter how beautiful she may be.

"I need you to grow up," I say, not bothering to pull my attention away from the city.

There's a rustling of fabric behind me, and I sense her proximity only a second before her hands hit my thighs and she pulls my legs apart.

"Why are you so stressed?" she says in that saccharine voice that scratches at my brain like nails on a chalkboard.

"Don't," I deadpan, not giving her an inch and still not fucking looking at her.

"Don't what?" she asks with feigned, annoying innocence.

"Mia," I finally turn to her. "I swear to fuck, just don't."

She grips the hem of her dress and lifts it over her head, exposing her braless, perky tits. Tits that are just begging to be touched.

I give an exaggerated huff and look out the window again. "Put your fucking dress back on."

She doesn't. Instead, she drops to her knees and reaches for my waistband. "Come on, I'll make it up to you."

"Mia," I growl. "Get the fuck off your knees."

She doesn't listen. In fact, she does the opposite, working to undo the button of my pants. I'm afraid to actually touch her. If I do, I'll probably throw her across the room. So I watch her where she's perched between my thighs and scowl so she knows how fucking pissed I am.

She squeezes my cock—which is, of course, fucking hard—through the fabric of my pants. A naked woman has her hands on me, and she's trying to suck me off. I'd have to be dead in order to not react. Even if I'm uninterested in this particular woman.

"I saw how you looked at her," she murmurs as she slides down my zipper, her eyes burning with defiance. "You want to pretend it's her lips on your cock," she shrugs. "I don't mind."

Just the thought of Cat's mouth full of my cock has me swelling. I groan and squeeze the arms on my chair so I don't strangle this woman. "Mia," I grit, "will you please fucking stop?"

She slides her fingers into the slit of my boxers and pulls out my cock, her eyes going wide in excitement. She's never seen it, and she certainly hasn't fucked it. Her tongue darts out, she licks her lips, then licks her way right up my shaft.

"Fuuuck," I curse as I grab the back of her head and push her down so far that she's choking on it. I wait until she gags, and then I pull her hair and slide back in my chair.

With her blond hair in my fist, she's trapped. Her green eyes water, and she smiles a devious smile. "I can make you come just as hard as I make her come," she says. "I can tell you all about how she tastes."

I clench my jaw, but I don't reply.

"Best pussy I've ever had," she says with a smirk and licks her pouty lips. "I know you want some, but she doesn't swing your way."

Without responding, I let go of her hair, stand up, and fix my pants.

"The only reason I haven't fired you is because you're my best friend. Now fucking get off your knees, put your clothes back on, and act like it."

She sighs as she picks her dress up off the floor and spins in my direction. She watches me for a long moment, forcing me to look at her before she's fully clothed. "I'm your only fucking friend, you ass," she retorts before slipping her dress over her head. "If you didn't call me here to fuck me, then what do you want?"

Mia settles herself against the headboard like nothing happened. We've been friends for two years, and she's never pulled that shit. I can't help but think her friend Cat has something to do with it. Was she jealous because of the way I looked at Cat, or because of the way her friend looked at me?

And does it matter?

"I don't have time to monitor the coffee shop anymore. You need to grow up so I can trust you with it."

Mia smiles as she crosses one leg over the other. "Why didn't you just say that? Duh, that's why I asked Cat to come in for an interview. We need the help."

Looking especially proud of herself, she wears a smug smile, and I can't help but return the expression. I don't like many people. Hell, I don't particularly like Mia, but she almost forces people into her web. She wraps herself around us so we can't help but care about her.

She's just lost. Which is understandable given that, like me, she doesn't have a mother.

I settle myself against the wall, folding my arms and tipping my head back until it meets the surface behind me. "Thank you. But teach her how to make a fucking cup of coffee, okay? I don't need customers complaining about waiting fifteen minutes for a latte because you were giving your professor a blow job."

Mia shrugs, her eyes lighting up. "He went down on me, but whatever."

I shake my head. "You're worth more than this, Mi," I murmur, kicking off the wall and holding my hand out to her.

She takes it and stands next to me. When I pull her in and hug her tight, she sighs against my chest. "I've been in love with her since we were kids," she whispers.

I tip my head back and study the ceiling. That'd be my luck. The first girl to pique my interest in years doesn't like men.

"Have you told her that?" I ask.

Mia pulls back and worries her bottom lip between her teeth. "I'm not good enough for her."

I glower and lift her chin so she's forced to look at me. "Stop sucking cocks and screwing professors and maybe you will be."

She smiles. "But I like cock."

I roll my eyes. "Then let her go."

She raises her brows and bites her bottom lip, this time in a seductive tease. "You could give me your cock, and I could have her. We could be the perfect throuple. I'm sure you wouldn't mind watching."

I shake my head. "Raise your standards, Mi. In the meantime, please don't fuck her in my shop. I need you to take this seriously."

She holds up two fingers. "Scout's honor."

I chuckle and step back. "Do you even know what that means?"

She shrugs. "Nope. But since I gave you a blow job, I deserve a steak!"

Laughter echoes from outside my bedroom door at her declaration. I roll my eyes at Mia and hold out my hand. "Let's grab dinner, you psycho."

In the hall, we're met by my roommate. "You guys having fun in there?" he asks, a knowing smirk on his face.

Mia immediately moves into his arms. "Want to join us for dinner?" she asks.

"No can do," he says to Mia. "Meeting my sister. Wanna join?" he asks, turning to me.

I'm too fucking tired to put on a show for the next two hours, so I shake my head. "Nah, Mia and I need to go over coffee shop business. Don't want to bore you."

He nods and puts his hands in his pockets. "All right, enjoy the *steak*," he says to Mia with a knowing wink.

31

"She didn't," I mutter, though I shouldn't care whether he thinks we fucked.

He bites his lip as he gives Mia a once-over. Her barely there dress shows off the creamy white perfection of her long as fuck legs, and if I didn't know they'd been wrapped around half of the city, maybe I'd have an interest in sliding between them.

"Night, Carter," Mia says with a wink.

4

EVERYTHING YOU WANT BY VERTICAL HORIZON

Cat

"**W**hat time will Cash be here?" I ask Carter while we wait at the bar for our younger brother to arrive. Cash is staying with Carter for the weekend to check out Brown. Which is a waste of time, in my opinion. There's no doubt he'll enroll here when he graduates next year. I'm the only James who's bucked that tradition.

Carter lifts his arm and flicks his wrist to check his watch. "Fuck if I know. He should have been here an hour ago. He said he'd meet me at the apartment, but then he told me he'd be delayed. He and Frank are probably still fucking around in Boston." He huffs out of a breath of annoyance and shrugs. "Fuck 'em. Let's order."

As if we conjured them, my younger brother and his best friend enter the bar, grins on their faces and laughter bursting from them. I jump off my stool and run to Cash. I'll never admit it out loud, but he's my favorite.

"Kit Cat," he murmurs as he hugs me close. After the coffee shop ordeal and the mortification I can't shake after sassing my would-be employer, I crave the extra affection Cash always gives me. Carter can certainly make me laugh and take me out for drinks, but Cash is the serious, affectionate one. He'll sit on the couch and chat with me for hours, watch the movies

I love, and tell me I'm too good for the shit Mia puts me through. Bottom line, he's always been my best friend, and right about now, I don't care that he's only here because he wants to party with Carter.

"How come I never get a welcome like that?" Carter grumbles as he approaches, a hand extended to Frank. I turn to my younger brother's best friend too. He recently buzzed his red hair. He's in ROTC and planning to enlist as soon as he turns eighteen. Unlike us, he won't be handed a college degree on a silver platter. He works for everything he has. He's a good kid, and I've always been thankful for the down-to-earth influence he has on Cash.

Cash lets me go, and he and Carter embrace in one of those man hugs where they shake hands and slap each other's backs, muttering something along the lines of "I missed you, bro" to one another.

I roll my eyes. Boys can be so basic.

I offer Frank a hug as well, and then we grab our drinks from the bar so the hostess can seat us. Once we've ordered and Carter's ordered a round of beer for the guys, even though Cash and Frank aren't old enough to drink legally, we settle into our normal banter like no time has passed since we were sitting around Grandmother's table for Sunday dinner. A meal Frank joined us for more often than not.

"How do you like school?" Cash asks me.

An excited flutter fills my stomach. As much as I loved NYU, I'm thrilled about this program. My family's business has always been whiskey. And while it's probably in my blood, and it most certainly could be in my bank account, I've never been interested in it. I want to pave my own way.

Our grandfather used to take us out on individual dates regularly. When it was my turn, he would tell me about how he built the company from the ground up. The struggles, times when he wasn't sure whether the company would pull through, the long nights. The stress, the blood, sweat, and tears he put into his business. The love he had for the company, the industry, the legacy all made me want to find a career I could be equally passionate about. While there's nothing wrong with furthering one's family legacy, I want to create something of my own instead of being handed the keys to the empire others have worked so hard for.

Which is why, during my senior year of high school, while everyone assumed I'd follow tradition—attend Brown business school, then return to Nashville to learn the ropes with my family—I shocked them all by telling them that I planned to go into marketing and fashion instead.

And then I turned down my grandfather's offer to fund my education.

Instead, I applied for scholarships—merit based, obviously, since I didn't qualify for financial assistance—and I have worked my butt off to keep my grades up and for this literally life-changing internship.

I use my mother's maiden name so I can fly under the radar. Yes, my last name has its perks, and I love my grandparents and my brothers dearly, but that last name brings with it more headache than help. And that is mostly my father's fault. In general, though, I don't want people to think I used my name to get where I am. What I'll do, not who I am, will be the reason that, one day, I'll be senior editor of Jolie.

The dreams are big; I know. But, as they say, if I shoot for the moon and miss, at least I'll land among the stars.

Not even Mia knows my real last name.

We met at boarding school in sixth grade, just after my grandparents agreed to have my name legally changed. Back then, I wanted the change because it made me feel closer to my mom. She died when I was six, and my father lost custody of us a few years later. Changing the name also erased one significant reminder of him.

I begged my grandparents to let me take her last name, and because my grandfather never could say no to me, at the ripe old age of eleven, I became Catherine Hope Bouvier.

I've proudly carried the name since.

"It's good so far. I'm only two weeks in, but everyone is really kind, and all my credits transferred." I smile, giddy about how easy the transition has been.

Carter nods. "When do you start the internship?"

This makes me full-on grin, the excitement almost too much to handle. "I start at the magazine next week. My classes are on Mondays and Thursdays, and I'll intern on the days I don't have class. I'm looking for a job in a bar or something so I can work weekends for extra cash. I applied at the coffee shop where my roommate works."

Carter glares at me. "You can't work, intern, and go to school full time. It's too much."

I flip my hair over my shoulder and sip my vodka drink. "Plenty of people work and still have to take out student loans. I'm lucky I have a scholarship."

Cash smiles, pride shining in his eyes. He may not forgo the family business, but he is certainly no stranger to hard work. Every summer for years, he's chosen to work in the distillery rather than hang out at the beach or on one friend's boat or at another's summer house like most of his friends.

Carter groans. "I hate the idea of my sister scrambling for cash and working herself to death. Especially when she doesn't *need* to."

This time, Frank cuts in. "Looks like she's handling herself just fine."

I smile and hold up my drink in a salute.

"Fine, if no one else sees how ludicrous it is, I'll let it go. But if you need help with money—"

"I know," I cut him off, "my big brother will help me. And I appreciate it. But I need to do this my way."

After dinner, we head back to the bar to continue the festivities. While Carter talks Frank's ear off about his master's program and all the hot women he's banging—*gross*—Cash and I huddle close to really catch up.

"How are things with Mia?" he asks, concern swimming in his eyes. Cash is the only person who knows the details. About who she became to me. About how she broke my heart.

The annoying thing is that I can't quantify the feelings I had for her. Did I love her? Or did I only think I did because she was my first *everything*?

We never discussed what we were doing or what it meant. For us or for ourselves individually. In hindsight, I can see how I assumed a lot of things. Things I never really questioned.

Did I love her? Was I attracted to women?

We went to an all-girls boarding school. I never questioned my feelings or our interactions because that's just what happened there.

But then we left for college, and suddenly the woman I thought I knew turned out to be a stranger.

I thought what we had was real. That what we were doing went beyond experimenting.

Was it more for me? I still don't know.

I don't even notice one sex or another.

People are just people.

Or maybe I'm just screwed up from all the ways she fucked with my mind.

"Oh, she's Mia," I say with a laugh, downplaying my internal freak-out.

Cash puts an arm around my shoulders and pulls me to him, squeezing me tight. "Kit Cat, I'm sorry."

I rest my head on his chest and blow out a breath. "Cash Money, let's not get all emotional about things that literally don't matter. I'm happy. I'm excited. I'm about to start at Jolie! Like…it's a dream come true. I'm not letting anybody get in the way of that."

5

CLOSING TIME BY SEMISONIC

Cat

"**G**ood news, roomie, you got the job!" Mia exclaims, bouncing on my bed.

Pain slices through my head as I open one eye and glare at her. Why does my head feel like it's splitting open?

"What time is it?" I croak.

"Four a.m. I brought a pizza home. Come eat with me." I groan as I pull the pillow over my head. "Go away."

My asshole roommate drags the blankets to the floor and tugs on my arms until I'm practically falling off the bed. "Stop!" I shout, trying to right myself.

"God, don't get your panties in a wad." She smacks my ass and walks to the door. "Come on, you owe me. Pizza. Living room. Now!"

I close my eyes in defeat. My mouth feels like it's stuffed with cotton balls, and I'm pretty sure it's vodka's fault. My brothers had whiskey after dinner, but I refused, instead choosing to down one vodka after another. And here I am, hours later, regretting that last one.

I grab my robe from the back of my door and follow her into the living room.

My brothers would lose it if they saw the size of this apartment. There are no high ceilings, no fireplaces or bars or big-screen televisions. A black futon—with a chenille throw that I splurged on at Home Goods—takes up a larger percentage of space in the tiny living room than it should. Teal boho style lamps brighten up the space from where they sit on black Ikea side tables. There is a small round kitchen table in our eat-in kitchen and a counter that seats two. Barely.

Before I join her, I shuffle to the light switch by the front door and turn down the lights. Mia, unsurprisingly, has every light in the living room on. "Hurts my head," I groan.

The pizza box is open on the living room table, and Mia is perched on the couch, her legs tucked under her as she brings a greasy slice to her mouth. She motions to the box. "Come on, eat while it's hot."

I really shouldn't. One slice is at least three hundred calories of grease and cheese. I hate myself for even thinking like this, but when I look at Mia in her skimpy dress, I can't help but suck in my stomach. She doesn't have an ounce of fat on her. She is literally what men *and women* dream of. Long silky legs, a tiny waist, not a hint of cellulite marring her skin, and perky breasts.

I bite my lip and sit across from her, inhaling the smell of garlic and staring at the pizza longingly.

"Eat, bitch," she coaxes.

I sigh and drop my shoulders. "I'm not hungry."

"Not true. You're worried about the calories. I *know* you," she reminds me, tilting her head and cocking a brow. "You're wondering how long you'll have to work out in order to eat a few bites. Or considering going for it and throwing it up later."

I rear back in response. I wish she didn't know me so well. I wish I didn't think like that. But experimenting sexually wasn't the only secret I kept as a student at an all-girls school.

For most of my life, I was told that women were meant to look a certain way.

And I've tried my hardest over the last few years to fit into that mold.

"Are you going to tell me why I'm awake at this ungodly hour, or are you going to pester me back to sleep?"

Mia raises her eyebrows. "I mean, if we're going to your bed—"

I hold up my hand. "Mia, stop."

She sighs and slumps back against the couch, staring at her pizza with glazed-over eyes. "Fine. Whatever. Anyway, I just wanted to tell you that you got the job."

"How?" I ask seriously.

"Jay was impressed," she says with a flip of her hair.

"Jay?"

"The boss you served the worst coffee ever to."

I laugh. "Why would he want to hire me?" When she bats her eyelashes, I fake a gag. "I take it back. Don't tell me."

She smiles. "Fine. But he's all-in with hiring you. He even gave me a promotion tonight."

That is literally more than I need to hear. Does Mia not realize how she sounds? How everything she says sounds?

I fake a smile. "Great, thank you. Now, if you wouldn't mind, I'm going to bed."

She pouts. "Really? You won't stay up and chat with me?"

"Mia, it's four a.m. I have spin class at eight, and then I'm meeting my brothers for the afternoon."

She looks at me for a long moment, her lips pressed together. "You finally going to introduce me to these infamous brothers?"

I shake my head. "Not a fucking chance."

She huffs in mock offense. "But I'm your best friend."

"Who they know used to be more than that. No, you can't meet them. Cash would…" I shudder at the thought of how my overbearing younger brother would react to meeting Mia. He would not be kind. And Carter? God, Carter cannot know about that.

At least not until I figure myself out.

43

"You shouldn't hide who you are," Mia murmurs.

For a moment, I see my old best friend in there. Not the person who flaunts her sexuality, who teases and flirts with anyone who gives her the time of day. For one second, she's the girl who used to know my every thought. And maybe she still does.

Mia looks up at me, her blue eyes filled with emotion, and I pat her hand, grasping it for a heartbeat. "I'm not hiding. But I'm not the same person I was back then. I'm still finding my way. And you need to let me do that."

She shrugs. Then, in true Mia fashion, she changes the subject. "Can you come to the café on Sunday? Jay wants to go over things with us, and then he's handing over the managing responsibilities to me. You'll like him," she offers.

The memory of his glacier blue eyes surfaces. I *did* like him. And now I have a name to go with the eyes. Jay.

But knowing he's another one of her boys, I'll do my best to keep my distance from him going forward.

6

SHE'S SO HIGH BY TAL BACHMAN

Jay

"**S**o, Catherine Hope Bouvier, tell me about yourself," I say, sitting across from the brunette in my coffee shop while Mia mans the counter. Every now and again, I feel her eyes on us. On Cat. Her possessiveness is obvious, even from ten feet away.

"You mean your knowledge of my killer coffee skills isn't enough?" she asks with a self-deprecating smile.

I almost spit out my coffee. "Yes, I'd prefer you not kill my customers, so be sure to study what Mia does."

She shrinks a bit under my words, which was the opposite of my intention. "I'm just teasing." I hold up my hands. "But yes, aside from your coffee skills, what else should I know?"

She scrutinizes me for several seconds. Probably wondering why the hell I want to know anything other than whether she can make a cup of coffee and what hours she's available. Because those would be appropriate topics for discussion. Eventually, she shrugs and answers. "Not much to tell. I'm in my third year of college, studying marketing and fashion. I just transferred from NYU, and I need these shifts to cover what my scholarship doesn't."

Interesting tidbit. Based on her appearance, I assumed she came from money and just wanted to work to kill time and hang out with Mia. Her manicured nails are classy; she's got perfectly arched eyebrows and tasteful highlights throughout her dark hair that fade perfectly, giving it an almost dark chocolate and swirled caramel look. And her lips? I would have sworn she added filler if they weren't so perfect—the plumpness, the arch of her pout. Not to mention the fucking poise she carries herself with.

She's as natural as they come. I suppose I shouldn't be surprised about her financial standings after all. Money couldn't buy this kind of perfection. Although plenty have certainly tried.

"And your relationship with Mia—" I start, leaving the question hanging while I take a sip of coffee so I can study her reaction.

Her eyebrows shoot into her hairline, and she whips her head back to Mia, who is currently shooting daggers in my direction. I hold my coffee cup up to her and smile.

"What about it?" she stammers.

I look away from Mia and get lost for a moment in the brown eyes that are seriously starting to crumble my well-kept emotions. "I trust it won't affect your job. I don't want—"

She holds up her hand. "I don't know what you think is going on, but she and I are roommates." She's glaring now. Damn, it's hot. "And regardless, I would never act inappropriately in a professional setting," she reprimands.

I deserve it. It's unprofessional to ask about her relationship. I'm pushing buttons that are clearly marked *Warning*. They have warning bells beside them—they should be kept in a metal cage, and my fingers should be electrocuted when I go near them.

But I don't give a fuck. I want answers, and I always get what I want. "Just your roommate?" I ask, leaning across the table on my elbows, a brow cocked in challenge.

Her eyes narrow and she holds my gaze. Then she stands up and stares me down.

Fuck.

The way her eyes ignite, the way she grips the back of the chair so forcefully her knuckles turn white. The fire that consumes her in that moment blazes through me too. "I can work Monday and Thursday mornings and any time on Sundays."

I set my cup on the table and stand as well, holding out my hand. "And what do you do on Saturdays?" I ask, the double meaning clear in my question.

She sticks her hand in mine, and I pull her close. A sweet, flowery scent envelops me, and I have to bite my tongue to keep from inhaling.

Chin tilted up, she watches me, then studies our hands, my large one encasing hers. Her focus shifts again, like she can see something I haven't quite figured out yet. "I sleep," she replies.

I smile, having forgotten the question.

7

SUDDENLY I SEE BY KT TUNSTALL

Cat

With an umbrella above my head and my headphones tucked into my ears, I trudge into the terminal to catch my train to Boston. Today is the day. My first day at the magazine. I readjust the placement of my black bag on my shoulder once I'm out of the rain. The weather and the commute have forced me to wear flats, so I have a pair of heels stashed away in the bag that I can slip them on when I get to the office.

The smell of rain and the end of summer follows me until the stale air of the commuter rail takes over. The possibilities ahead of me keep me from succumbing to the mood a dreary day sometimes puts me in. Around me, the other travelers haven't fared as well. Most wear unfocused gazes and frowns. A few women chat idly, and I can't help but concoct stories about them. Maybe they ride the rails together every day and have formed a friendship because of that. Or maybe they work together and have always been friends. Beside them, a girl about my age sits with her head in a book. Opposite me, a man pulls out his computer and types loudly, as if he's the most important person to ever step foot on the train.

I settle in my seat, my focus on my music. Chris Martin sings about heartache, and I lean my head back and close my eyes.

The ride is only forty minutes, even with the stops we make. When the train stops at Back Bay, I finally disembark. Being back in the city brings a wave of nostalgia. Not all my memories of this place are bad, but they certainly aren't all good either. Instead of focusing on the past, though, I lift my head and smile. The rain has stopped, the sun is breaking through the clouds, and today, I begin my internship at Jolie.

The foyer is lined with black marble that sparkles in the early morning light and accentuates the click-clacking of heels as employees bustle to their offices.

"First day?" the security guard asks as he holds out his hand to me. I have my license in hand already—experience with my family's business over the years makes this interaction almost second nature—and I hand it over to the good-looking security guard. A tattoo peeks out from under his suit at his neckline, and his blue eyes pierce me as they study my face and then my license again.

"Yup. How could you tell?"

"I have photographs of all new hires. Welcome, Ms. Bouvier. Cynthia is expecting you."

I lick my lips while he takes my license and turns his back. When he returns to the counter, he hands me my very own badge. I stare down at it, fighting a grin. Catherine Bouvier is printed at the top, just above my picture.

Where did they get this?

I swallow my questions and regard the man for a long moment.

Before I can ask for directions to Jolie's offices, he says, "Cynthia is on the twelfth floor. Her assistant, Rose, will greet you when you exit the elevator. Have a good day." He smiles at me again, dismissing me.

I study my picture again, holding back the giggle that wants to erupt from within. *I'm at Jolie magazine. Cynthia* is waiting for *me*!

Instead of letting out my girlish squeal in front of the hot security guard, I blow out a big breath, lift my chin, and put one foot in front of the other.

"I'm so nervous," a girl beside me babbles as we enter the elevator with two men.

Her jet-black hair is perfectly styled, and her brown skin glimmers, accentuated by the peach bronzer on her cheeks. Her almond-shaped eyes meet mine anxiously. "It's my first day. I don't usually talk to strangers or freak out like this, but today, I can't help but do both."

I only smile in return, because her stream of consciousness leaves little room for a response. She's too immersed in her own mental gymnastics to wait for one, and I, for one, am happy to focus on someone else's freak-out for a moment.

"I'm about to meet the biggest fashion editor in the country…Oh, shit, do you work for Jolie? You do, don't you?" she asks, giving me a once-over. I swapped my sneakers for my black Louboutins, and her eyes go wide as she homes in on them. "Did you know your shoes cost a thousand dollars? Oh my God, of course you know that. They're on your feet. Fuck. You know Cynthia, don't you? I mean Ms. Caldwell. Fuck, of course you do. Please forget I said fuck." She tips her head back and inspects the ceiling. Her lips move like she's saying a silent prayer, or maybe she's just talking to herself.

The two men look on, lips pressed together like they're holding back their laughter. I glare at them and squeeze her hand. "It's my first day too."

She drops her chin and stares at me, her mouth open in a surprised *O*. "Thank god," she breathes. "I'm Sophie."

I take her proffered hand. "Cat. It's nice to meet you. And everything you're feeling? Yeah, me too."

She laughs, but before we can continue our conversation, the elevator dings and opens to the twelfth floor.

Just outside, a woman wearing a bored expression and a dress cinched tightly around her size-zero waist waits, holding a folder in her hand. She is precisely what I would expect a woman working here to look like.

"Perfect, you're both here. Follow along. We have a lot to get through," she says, turning her back without greeting us or introducing herself.

"I assume this is Rose," I whisper to Sophie, who shrugs and scrunches her nose as we scurry behind the woman.

The sounds of ringing phones and clacking keyboards and a low murmur of voices filter through the office space. Cubicles are set up in what can only be described as a pen, and women glance up at us, one by one, as we walk by. A rack of clothing is set up in the corner, and a woman with a camera watches a man who pushes through each piece, making disgusted sounds as he goes. "None of this works," he grits. "I asked for modern pastels. Not nineties atrocities. What the fuck?"

Sophie giggles beside me, and I clamp my lips shut, trying to keep my own smile from sprouting. This is everything I expected it to be.

Over the next few hours, we're shown to our side-by-side desks inside the pen. Then we're dragged into meeting after meeting where we're told to sit silently and take notes, which will likely never be reviewed. We sit through lectures where we discover we're forbidden from discussing anything we hear within these walls and are told we are not to have an opinion.

By the time six rolls around, I'm dead on my feet, hungry enough to eat an entire pizza, and smiling wider than I have in…well, honestly, I don't know if I've ever smiled this big.

"We made it," I utter as we step out into the Boston evening, a cool chill in the air reminding me that fall will be here and gone in a blink of an eye. Soon I'll be trudging here through snow. But even that thought can't bring me down.

Sophie is wearing an awe-filled expression and the smile of someone who is finally living her dream. "We did," she says, her red lips glistening as she looks back at me. "Want to grab a drink and dinner? I'm fucking famished."

I check my phone and wince at the time. By the time I hoof it to the station, ride the train for forty minutes, then make my way back to my apartment, it'll be almost eight. I can't wait that long to eat. But I hate the idea of taking the train much later than that. "I—uh—I have to take the train back to Providence."

She sighs. "Oh, that sucks. Every day?"

I shrug. "Unfortunately. I live there so I'm close to campus."

She smiles. "You should stash an overnight bag under your desk. Then you can stay at my place the next time we have to work late."

"Really?" I ask, unable to hide my surprise.

She shrugs like it's no big deal. "Why not? Come on, let's get a slice of pizza really quick before we head to the train station."

She takes my arm and pulls me toward the pizza place across the street. "You're walking me to the train station?"

She laughs. "Yes, it's what friends do. We eat pizza, chat, and walk. Does that work for you? Besides, it's on the way to my place."

I sigh. *Friends*. So this is what it's like.

KITTEN'S SONGS

Over slices of pizza and Diet Cokes, Sophie fills me in on her life. "I live with my mom and dad. Pathetic, I know," she says between bites, "but I have the entire basement of our townhouse to myself. Separate entrance and all for the late-night calls," she says with a waggle of her brows. "And since my parents work so much, it's not too crazy."

"Are you guys close?" I ask, tamping down on my envy. Living in one's parents' basement at twenty-one shouldn't bring on jealousy, but I would give just about anything to have even one parent who still wanted me around.

Dramatically, she replies, "Super close. Basically, my mother knew all about my first kiss before I'd left the boy's house." She smiles. "I'm joking. But seriously, they're the best. My parents are both surgeons, so they're super smart and ambitious, but they never put their ambitions on me. They let me find my way, and when I told them I wanted to work in fashion, my mom was all like '*girlll*, finally we'll have someone to help with this wardrobe.' She all but lives in scrubs, so she doesn't need my help, but we have fun."

My heart squeezes at the vision she creates of her perfect family. I have absolutely no idea what that's like.

"Any siblings?" I ask.

She shakes her head and runs her hands up and down her body in a Vanna White way. "They stopped when they reached perfection."

I laugh.

"How 'bout you? Are you close with your parents?" she asks.

I take a sip of my Diet Coke to hide my discomfort and fake a smile. "Nope. But I have three amazing brothers who drive me nuts."

The three brothers bit always distracts from the parental figure line of questioning.

"Wow, *three*? Are they hot?" She shimmies her shoulders.

I laugh at her theatrics yet again. I like this girl. "I guess to other people they are. Carter is twenty-four and kind of an obnoxious asshole, but I love him. Cash is seventeen and far too mature for his age. He's my ride or die. And then there's my youngest brother, Chase. He's fourteen and a bit of a clown."

"Wow, your parents were busy," she laughs.

"Yup," I say, then stuff my face with another bite of pizza.

"Boyfriend?" she asks. I don't know what my face does, but she cringes and blurts, "Or girlfriend? Uh, if that's your thing."

I shrug. "Just me."

"Me too," she replies. "But did you see that photographer? Dexter? He was so hot."

56

Mouth wide open, I gape. "He's like forty!"

"So what? Give me that daddy energy all day long."

Throwing my head back, I let out a cackle, and she joins in. After we've calmed a bit and have continued eating, my phone buzzes on the table. I flip it over and cringe when I catch sight of a message from Mia. After only a few hours with Sophie, I suddenly see exactly how twisted my relationship is with her.

Although it has only been a few hours. Mia didn't show her true self until years into our friendship.

"Who's that?" Sophie asks, and then she shakes her head. "Sorry, that was nosy of me."

"No, it's fine. Mia. She's my roommate." I scan the text. "She wants to know what time I'll be home."

"It's nice of her to check on you," she offers.

Or controlling. But maybe Sophie's right. Maybe this is her way of showing she cares. I pick up the phone and respond.

Having dinner in Boston.
Be home later.

I turn the phone back over and pick up my slice.

It isn't until I'm settling into my seat on the train that I look at my phone again. Five texts.

Mia: Oh. With who?

Mia: Hello?

Mia: Wow, so glad I went through the trouble of making dinner for you to celebrate your first day of work.

Mia: Seriously? No reply?

Mia: Fuck you.

I close my eyes. This can't be normal. The phone pings again, and I sigh, considering ignoring anything more she has to say. But I cave. Like always.

Mia: I'm sorry. I'm just worried about you. Are you okay?

I type out a quick response.

All good. Sorry. Grabbed a slice of pizza with one of my coworkers. I'll be home soon.

As I put the phone down, I can't help but wish I could live at home with parents who loved me.

8

CRASH INTO ME BY DAVE MATTHEWS

Jay

I figured I wouldn't see Cat again unless I stopped in during one of her shifts. Something I'd already decided to avoid. For years, my focus has been locked on one thing, and I'm within inches of my goal. I don't need the distraction. Especially when it comes in the form of a beautiful woman who clearly doesn't even *like* me. And maybe isn't interested in men at all.

Although I'm not entirely sold on Mia's story. There was a spark between Cat and me that first day. One that, based on the way she watched me, she felt as well. Knowing Mia, she was playing with my head.

But I pushed every thought away after the conversation. After I offended her.

Then she sat in front of me on the train, and in seconds, I lost the battle I was so sure would be effortless.

Every day for the past three days, she's gotten on just before the train leaves, grabbing the first available seat—which, so far, hasn't been next to me. I've been intentional about that. I'm not ready to talk to her, so after that first day, I've made a point to sit next to someone else first. And then I use the forty-minute ride to study her.

I'm fascinated by her.

Which makes almost zero sense.

She's no different from any other twenty-something college girl I've met. Don't get me wrong; she's beautiful. But she doesn't flaunt it. She doesn't wear low cut-tops or tight-fitting clothes. She doesn't even notice the attention she garners from both men and women around her. It's like she exists above everyone else.

Not in a cruel or uncaring way. But it's like she walks in and takes the air from the room. With her headphones in her ears and a magazine or book in her hand, she makes it clear she doesn't want to interact with the rest of us.

Which only makes me want to know every fucking thing about her.

What song is she listening to? What kind of books does she like? Where does she go when she gets off the train? What is the status of her relationship with Mia?

The last one is beyond irrelevant, and yet it's the one thing that keeps circling in my mind.

"I can tell you all about how she tastes."

That fucking line is on repeat in my head.

Today, she's right in front of me again.

I drop my newspaper on the floor by my feet and tilt forward, inhaling her floral scent. *Is that how she tastes? Fuck, what is wrong with me?*

I lean back in my seat, the movement pulling the attention of the man beside me. He raises a brow, acknowledging that he knows precisely what I just did. I angle my body toward the aisle. I'm not admitting to anything, fucker.

Fuck this. I'll talk to her when we get off the train.

KITTEN'S SONGS

I take three strides so that I'm beside her, then murmur "hello, Kitten" as I grab her arm.

She jumps, spins, and slams her fist directly into my nose.

"Fuck!" I holler as I slap my hand to my face.

Cat looks at me, her mouth wide in a horrified expression, and cradles her hand. "Ow! You hurt me!" she yells.

I pull my hand away from my face and inspect it. It's covered in blood. Likely because my nose is broken. "I hurt you?" I ask incredulously. "You fucking punched me!"

"Because you scared the shit out of me! Who grabs a woman and purrs in her ear when she's getting off the train in Boston?"

"Who fucking punches people? And I didn't purr; I said your damn name!"

"You called me kitten, asshole." She huffs and studies her hand. Then she rolls her eyes, shakes her head, and strides in the other direction.

I stand there for a minute, dumbfounded. Did she just fucking hit me and walk away without apologizing? What the hell? I storm after her, despite the looks I'm receiving. Yes, I've got blood dripping down my face and I'm probably as red as a fucking tomato. Add in my clenched fists, and I'm sure I look dangerous.

"Hey!" I shout after her. "Catherine Bouvier, turn around this instant!"

Her body stiffens, and her steps falter as she comes to a stop, but she doesn't turn around. Her shoulders rise as she inhales and fall when she blows out a long, steadying breath. Then another. Then she turns, and oh fuck, the look she aims at me would probably knock me dead if we were any closer. I cover my jewels because I honestly don't trust her not to knee me there right about now.

"Excuse me," she says so quietly I have to strain to make out the words. Cars travel past, and people move quickly down the sidewalk on either side of us, but she and I hold firm, locked in a staring contest. I won't fucking blink first.

She stalks closer, and I swear to God, my balls shrivel.

"You are not my grandmother. You do not get to say my name like that," she says as she narrows her eyes.

I blow out a breath. "I'm sorry." I hold up both palms. "I was just trying to get your attention," I explain. The taste of blood on my lips makes me wince.

"Get yourself cleaned up," she says in disgust. "And next time, don't grab women in the train station." With that parting shot, she spins on her toes and disappears into the crowd.

I've got to be honest, even though she probably just broke my nose, I'm still obsessed with her.

Actually, I might be obsessed with her *because* she broke my nose.

I might just be in love.

Yeah, I'm totally fucked.

9

VOGUE BY MADONNA

Cat

It's not until I reach my desk and slam my bag down that I realize that, in my anger, I walked into Jolie with my sneakers on. I can practically hear the walls groaning in distaste. Wincing, I grab my heels from my purse while simultaneously struggling to slip off my shoes.

"You okay?" Sophie asks as she turns her chair in my direction. We share a cubicle, which comes in handy during the day when we want to partake in office gossip. As the new girls, one of us having dark skin and the other wide hips, we don't exactly fit in. Not that we give a shit. Or at least that's what Sophie tells me.

"Why the fuck would we want to fit in?" she said. "I'd rather be me or you any day of the week."

I shake my head and tug at my sneaker. "This prick scared me as I was getting off the train, and I hurt myself punching him."

"Oh my God, did you call the cops?"

I close my eyes and take a deep breath. "No, I mean, I knew who he was."

She gives me a horrified look.

"After the fact…like *after* he scared the shit out of me and *after* I punched him, I realized who he was."

She laughs. "Shit, you must have been mortified. Is he cute?"

I huff. "*Annoyed* is what I was. Who the hell grabs someone and purrs in their ear when they're getting off a train? He should have known he'd get punched."

"He purred in your ear?" she asks, bouncing a little in her seat.

I roll my eyes. "He called me Kitten in a low voice. It sounded like a purr." With both shoes on, I hide my flats under my desk.

When I look back up at Sophie, her lips are pressed together tight, like she's trying to hold back a smile. "He called you Kitten?"

"Why are you repeating everything I say?"

"What does he look like?" she asks, tilting her head and completely ignoring my question.

I throw my hands up in aggravation and then wince in pain. "I don't know. Tall, blond hair, glacier blue eyes, broad shoulders—"

I clamp my mouth shut when I see the smile Sophie can no longer hide lifting her lips.

"Go on," she says.

I scowl. "What's so amusing?"

"*Glacier* blue eyes?"

I huff. "What? They're really light. Like the color of ice."

"Ice doesn't have a color."

"Why are you being so difficult? I had a really shitty morning."

She laughs. "Not as bad as the icicle, apparently. Did you break his nose?"

It's my turn to bite back a smile. "I think I did."

Her laugh turns into an honest-to-God guffaw. "Oh my god, you totally broke the hottie's nose after he called you Kitten. This is too good! How do you know him?"

My face heats. Fuck, I punched my boss in the nose. I sit up straight and spin toward my desk. "Don't we have work to do?"

"You're trying to distract me. How do you know him, Cat?"

I sigh as I turn back to her. Dammit. I know by now she won't let this one go. "He owns the coffee shop."

Her jaw drops. "That's sexual harassment. He can't purr at you and grab you! Good for you for punching him!"

"It wasn't like that. I think he thought he was being cute. Kitten... *Cat*," I explain.

She shakes her head. "Nope. Even worse. Pet names. You're an employee. It's inappropriate."

"It really isn't like that. He scared me is all. He wasn't trying to be inappropriate."

Sophie's straight face cracks, and she laughs again. "Oh my goodness, you should have seen your face. Do you really think I would be upset if a blond God with *glacier* blue eyes called me Kitten?"

I roll my eyes and spin back to my desk. "I'm ignoring you."

She cackles at that. "Don't worry, I'll be over here with my plain ole chocolate brown eyes just hanging out."

I grab a gummy bear from the stash we keep between our desks and chuck it at her. She giggles and dives out of the way, but it lands in her lap. She then picks it up and pops it into her mouth.

This is the most annoying morning ever.

Also, I'm probably going to lose my job at the coffee shop.

Excellent.

KITTEN'S SONGS

For the first time since I stepped foot inside Jolie, I find myself in Cynthia's office. It's nothing new to be inspected like this. I grew up with a grandmother who scrutinized my every move and watched every morsel that went into my mouth. She critiqued the way I folded my legs (*at the*

69

ankle), the way I cut my steak (*on an angle*), how I styled my hair, the length of my skirts, and the fit of my clothes.

If there was something to inspect—*and criticize*—my grandmother was up for the challenge, and she relished it.

No one ever braided my hair or looked me in the eye and told me I was beautiful. Sure, I've been told I *look* beautiful, but never that I *am* beautiful. *Just as I am.*

So, as I sit in front of Cynthia, one of the most iconic women in the fashion world, I don't squirm. I hold my chin up and give her a warm smile while I wait for details about why she's called me here and what I can do to make her happy.

"You don't use your last name," she says, surveying me with a keen eye. It's not a question.

I shake my head. "No. I changed it years ago."

"Even though the name would give you every advantage. Including an office of your own rather than a cubicle out there with everyone else," she says, waving toward the pen as if the entire area is beneath her. *Beneath us.*

"I'm not looking for special treatment."

"Obviously. If not for a call from your grandmother, I would have had no idea."

I manage to keep myself from groaning. "If it changes your position on my internship, I understand."

She shakes her head. "No, no. You misunderstand what I'm saying. I'm impressed, Catherine. Very impressed. But that isn't why I called you in here. And after this conversation, I won't bring it up again."

I suck in a breath. "Thank you."

"Anyway, there is a ball at the end of October. A masquerade ball the weekend of Halloween. The Hanson family is hosting it. I imagine you know who they are."

My family's biggest competitor.

I give her a subtle nod. "I'm aware."

"Will that be a problem?"

I have to hold back a laugh. This isn't a soap opera. Our families are business competitors. I've never met the Hansons, but Carter lives with Jonathan Hanson. Rich boys tend to stick together.

"Not at all."

"Excellent. I would like you to help me prepare for the ball. The rest of the staff will be busy getting our Christmas edition ready. I'm sure you're familiar with that," she adds, a hint of a smile gracing her perfect face. There's even a glimmer of excitement in this formidable woman's eye. Who wouldn't be excited? It's the most amazing thing, year in and year out, and she's in charge of curating it.

Every year, every girl at my boarding school, including me, would wait impatiently for December first. Not so we could listen to Christmas music on the local radio station or in anticipation of gifts. But because on December first, Jolie releases their Christmas edition. It's always filled with the hottest trends, must-have outfits, which makeup is favored by celebrities, and hottest vacation spots. During my time at school, if Jolie said it was in, every single student there would be traveling to San Jose with orange bandanas tied around their foreheads and wearing gladiator sandals instead of their Louboutins.

I'm serious. That was the style during my last year.

Deep breaths. "Yes, I'm familiar with the Christmas edition. I was hoping I could help with that. I can make time for both."

She holds up her hand. "Catherine, let me offer you a piece of advice. You'll shine brighter while standing alone than while moving within a crowd."

Pulling in a deep breath, I nod. She's right, of course. While the Christmas edition is something I've always dreamed of being a part of, I can make a name for myself by working on the masquerade ball. "Let me know what you need, and I'll handle it," I offer.

KITTEN'S SONGS

Exhausted from another long day in the city, I grab a protein bar and a Diet Coke at the train station on the way home in hopes of getting to bed quicker. I open the door to our apartment on a yawn, which turns into a groan at the sound of voices. The last thing I want is to make small talk with Mia and God knows who. And if Mia brought home a date, this will be even more exhausting. Mia is *not* quiet when she gets going.

I close my eyes and take a deep breath before I walk through the room, preparing myself to play the part of friendly roommate.

"Hi—" I start, but halt at the sight of Mia and Jay sitting on our couch.

Smiling, Mia jumps to her feet and makes a beeline for me. "Well, if it isn't Rocky Balboa herself," she teases.

I roll my eyes as I put my bag on the table beside the door and slip off my shoes. When I look up, I'm met by Jay's icy stare. The glacial aspect of his irises is highlighted by the sharp contrast to the black circles under his eyes and a hideously bruised nose.

"Shouldn't you have that bandaged?" I ask.

He attempts a smolder, or maybe it's a glare, but his bruised and swollen face isn't cooperating. "I think the words you're looking for are *I'm sorry*."

Without a glance in Mia's direction, I walk to the couch and stand over him. For a moment, I do nothing but survey him, taking in the state of his face. I really got him good. I shake my head. "Just like my brothers, stubborn men. You need to have that nose set."

"Or what?" he asks with a surprising amount of humor in his voice.

"Or you'll have a deformed nose," I say with an exasperated sigh.

"Maybe it'll give me character," he quips.

"It won't. You're too pretty for character. What it'll give you is a deviated septum."

He laughs. I bite my lip and look away from him to keep from smiling. He *is* fun to spar with.

Without thinking, I settle in the spot next to him and place my palms on either side of his face. He winces but doesn't pull back, his attention locked on me. "That hurt?" I ask softly.

He doesn't reply, doesn't move. I'm not sure he's even breathing.

"Jay?" I try again.

"Hm?" he says, the smile still on his face, his eyes still holding mine.

"I asked if that hurt." I lean back and pull my hands away, but he catches them mere millimeters from his face and presses them back to his cheeks.

"It does."

Okay, crazy. Then let go of my hand so I can stop touching your sore face.

His tongue darts out and swipes at his bottom lip, and I can't help but follow the movement.

"Should we take him to the hospital?" Mia interrupts.

I pull back and mentally shake myself out of my stupor, then turn to her, trying to process her words. "Huh?"

"Come on, Jay. I'll take you to the ER. This one looks like she might fall asleep standing up."

He nods, but he hasn't taken his eyes off me. Grasping my hands again, he asks, "Will you be on the train tomorrow?"

I shake my head. "No, I work in the shop."

"The next day?" he asks, his attention still fixated on me, keeping me locked in his stare.

I regard him, wondering what he sees when he looks at me. Why does he want to talk to me so badly? First, I made him awful coffee, then I ignored him, and today, I punched him in the face. And he's here with

Mia. Are they seeing one another? Is this a date? Does he think I'd be interested in being with both of them?

I cringe. *Gross*. I have no time for these games.

"You should go," I say.

He closes his eyes in a way that almost looks like defeat. Like he knows the spell he was trying to cast has been broken. But once he stands, he angles close and whispers "night, Kitten" in my ear, and a shiver runs down my spine.

10

DON'T PANIC BY COLDPLAY

Jay

I slide the SIM card over to Dean and wait for him to download it like he does every week. Only a few more months of this, and then I'll be done.

"Get everything you need?" I ask, tapping my foot against the cement floor in his office. Everything about this space is as seedy as his job. Located in the basement, the room is lit with a lone desk lamp, and a scar ripples through the wall where it meets the ceiling, indicating water damage. One would think he could afford a nicer office on the obscene amount of money we pay him alone. His silence and the type of work he completes for us don't come cheap.

He doesn't take his eyes off his computer screen when he replies, "Yup." His fingers on the keys don't even slow.

"Anything I should know?" I ask, taking the SIM card back from him once he's ejected it and held it out to me.

I ask the same question every week, and every week, I get the same bored expression. My father doesn't pay him to speak. In fact, I'm pretty sure he pays him specifically to keep the details from me.

I have my part to play in my father's revenge, but I'll never truly know what his full plan is. Despite my involvement, I've never been privy to what he does with the information I gather through the SIM card from

Carter's phone, or the SD card from his computer. Hell, I don't even know whether we're obtaining information or planting it this way.

For so long, I've been blinded by my need for retribution. From the vengeance that floods my veins at the memory of what happened to my father. For what that family cost me.

Any semblance of my own family.

My mother.

My father claims it's better that I don't know the details of the plan. With every passing day, I feel less certain of that. Regardless, I won't be getting the answers from Dean.

"I have a question. How hard is it to hack into an iPod?"

Dean finally looks at me, but he doesn't reply.

"There's this girl…" I clamp my mouth shut and shake my head. "Never mind."

What the fuck am I thinking?

"If you know the handle for her iTunes account, it's pretty easy. What's her name?"

A lump of dread forms in my gut at his question. I don't want to share Cat's information with this guy. I wouldn't put it past him to tell my father about her, and right now, I want just this one thing for myself.

Vacillating, I toss out the first name that comes to mind. "Mia Alves."

He writes her name on a Post-it next to his keyboard. "I'll see what I can do."

I smile and see myself out, blowing out a sigh of relief. Without his help, it'll be tricky, but I'm determined to get Cat to open up to me.

KITTEN'S SONGS

I find my opportunity on Sunday morning. Cat is wiping down tables and humming to herself when I walk into the café. She looks up at me, expression neutral, and then goes back to her task. Burn.

Mia must be in the back because the counter is empty and only one table is occupied. "Your nose looks better," she mutters when I amble over to her, but she keeps her attention fixed on the rag in her hand and the table in front of her.

I stand closer than necessary and watch her, doing my best to force her to interact with me. But she doesn't bite. No friendly greeting, no acknowledgement.

"No iPod today?" Dammit. Clearly, I don't know how to beat around the bush. To be fair, I've never had to work this hard for someone's attention. There is something to be said for the chase, I suppose.

She points to her pocket, drawing my attention to the little silver device peeking out of her jeans. Of course, now I can't help but take in the tanned skin of her stomach she exposes when she leans forward and stretches her arm out to clean the far end of the table. Though I'm spellbound by our proximity and her movements, she has no trouble continuing to ignore me.

"Can I see it?" I ask. "I'm thinking of getting one. How does it work?"

She turns around, amusement dancing in her eyes. A smirk curls her lips, and she tips her chin up to regard me. Even though she's tall, probably five-eight, she's forced to look up to make eye contact, which makes me stupidly satisfied.

With her hand on her hip, she quips, "*You* don't have an iPod?"

"Why do you say it like that?" I ask, folding my arms over my chest and affecting a casual stance.

She shakes her head and closes her eyes for a second. "Nothing. Have at it." She pulls the iPod from her pocket and holds it out.

I smirk as I take it from her, enveloping her hand in mine and holding on for a few beats too many. She raises her brows, her expression screaming *unimpressed*, and I grin right back. She can pretend I don't affect her all she wants, but the way her breath hitches and her lips part tells a different story. She isn't as immune as she'd like me to believe.

"Thanks, Kitten," I murmur, finally letting go of her hand and taking her iPod with me to a table in the corner. "Can you grab me a latte?" I ask, knowing the more complicated drink will keep her attention for a few minutes.

She gives me the most adorable glare. "You know my name is Cat, right?"

I smirk and continue with my task. Connecting to the Wi-Fi in the café, I log into her iTunes account and get to work. By the time she returns with my drink—not a latte but a regular coffee—I've plugged my earbuds in, and I'm scrolling through her music.

"All set with that?" she says, waving at the device with her open hand.

I shake my head like I can't hear her and just smile.

With annoyance and determination, she rips the earbud from my left ear and tips closer. "I said," she grits out, "are you done?"

I smirk. "Never would have pegged you for a Backstreet Boys fan. You seem like an NSYNC girl to me."

She rolls her eyes but doesn't bother to respond, and with one hand propped on a hip, she holds the other out, palm up.

"Thanks for the coffee," I say as I press the iPod to her warm palm, then pick up the paper cup and take a sip.

I wince, garnering a smile from the savage barista. "Taste okay?" she asks with over-the-top concern.

It's disgusting.

"Delicious," I bite back.

Being kind isn't getting me anywhere with her. I grab my coffee, and with a wave, I'm gone.

11

POKER FACE BY LADY GAGA

Cat

I t's officially October, making it one of my favorite days of the year. Fall colors, cooler temperatures, and pumpkin everything. What's not to love? I've got a new burnt-orange cashmere sweater on—I'd wear the color year-round if I could get away with it—paired with a simple black pencil skirt, a black tweed jacket, and a Parisian cap that falls sideways on my head.

I feel like I belong at Jolie today, and with my pumpkin spice latte—which I did not make—I know this month is going to be mine.

The countdown is on for the masquerade ball. We've got four weeks to prepare, and today Cynthia and I are heading to the venue to review everything from the food to drinks to the décor and color scheme. Then I will work with the event planner to make all of Cynthia's wishes come true.

Nothing can spoil my mood.

Not even the sight of Jay sitting next to the only unoccupied seat in the train car. I raise a brow, wondering whether he hired people to sit in every other seat just so he could be close enough to annoy me. I know that's dramatic. Why he bothers going through all the trouble to interact with *me* is a mystery. But the man clearly cannot take a hint. And I can't for the life of me figure out why.

I sigh as I settle in the seat next to him. "Morning," I mumble, because he's my boss and Mia's friend, despite that I find him intolerable.

Without a word, he holds out a hand, those blue eyes pulling me in.

I stare at him in confusion, and when he doesn't speak, I say, "Yes?"

"You didn't bring me a coffee?" he asks.

I laugh as I take another sip and settle into the seat for the trip. Doing my best to ignore him, I bend at the waist and rummage through my bag until I find my iPod. Then I survey him, refusing to look away as I place one earbud in my ear, then the other, a cheeky smirk on my face.

You want to chat, buddy? You can talk to yourself.

He's just another player, and he's only interested in me because I didn't fall at his feet and simper like a fool the first time we met. Despite all the energy he's put into getting my attention, he looks at me like I'm nothing more than a piece on his chessboard. He assumes that, like everyone else in his life, I can be moved around as he sees fit.

I'm not saying I'm the queen, but I'm no one's pawn. I'm not on the board, period.

My focus is fixed, and will remain that way, on school and my job. No man—*or woman*—will distract me. I angle my knees and torso toward him as I hit play and hold his cold blue stare.

After a second or two, Lady Gaga's "Poker Face" blares in my ears. I shake my head—that song is not on my playlist—and hover a finger over the skip button. But when the music starts again, it's the same damn song. *What the...?* I hit pause and gape at the device, dumbfounded.

Jay huffs a laugh, drawing my attention to where he rests his head lazily on the headrest. "Something wrong?" The bastard smirks, holding me hostage with those piercing eyes.

"*You* did this," I say with a huff, setting my coffee cup in my cupholder so I can navigate out of the ridiculous playlist he created and get back to my usual morning music.

He tips forward, resting his elbow on the armrest closest to mine, his chin in his hand. "Is there a problem, Kitten? Happy to help."

I scoff. "Sure you are." I exit the playlist, catching sight of the title. *Kitten's Songs*. I roll my eyes. "You are so insane," I hiss.

He smiles, completely unbothered by my tantrum.

Doing my best to ignore him and his cocky attitude, I focus my attention on my iPod again and attempt to maneuver to another list, but when I try, nothing happens. The screen doesn't change. *This* is the only playlist. And it only has one song.

"What did you do with my music?" I screech.

Jay looks far too delighted by my outburst. He only smiles at me stupidly, not bothered in the slightest by the attention we're drawing from the other passengers.

"Say something," I demand through gritted teeth.

"You're even more beautiful when you're angry, Kitten." He's relaxed as he regards me unabashedly. He denies nothing, and he's not even attempting to avoid the figurative daggers I'm shooting at him.

My tirade comes to an abrupt halt when the angry words swirling in my mind all disappear in a *poof*. He didn't say *you look beautiful when you're angry*. That would be qualifying the beautiful statement.

He said I'm *even more* beautiful.

Naturally, the man who drives me absolutely nuts would be the first person to ever tell me I'm beautiful.

I slump back in my seat and cross my arms, afraid to react and unsure of how I even would.

Keeping my face turned away from him, I inspect the aisle. The scuffed floor, the lights illuminating each side, any detail I can find. And then, because I can't help it, I peek in his direction again. He's settled himself back against the seat, completely at ease.

"Why are you doing this?" I ask, folding one leg over the other and bouncing my foot as I stare him down.

"Doing what?" he asks, a confused frown taking over his face. His blond hair falls across his brow when he tilts his head in question.

I itch to push that lock of hair back. To run my fingers through it. To move closer to him. To be in his space and figure out what's going through his brain.

Is this a game?

I don't even know anymore.

"Why did you wipe my music clean and leave only one song?" I ask, being as specific as I can so he can't feign confusion.

A hint of a smile ghosts his lips, and then he settles back in his seat and closes his eyes. "You refuse to talk to me. I have a lot to say, and since you won't listen…I gave you a song." His smile grows as he crosses his arms over his chest and lets out a slow breath.

He's infuriating.

Now he doesn't want to talk? When I'm forced to be near him and finally have something to say, he's going to tell me to listen to a damn song?

Two can play at this game. I fold my arms over my chest and focus on the seat back in front of me.

Beside me, his seat creaks, and when I look over, he's drinking my coffee. "Pumpkin spice; my favorite. Thanks, Kitten."

I press my lips together and resume my inspection of the pattern on the fabric of the seat ahead. Not going to react.

After several minutes, I can no longer fight the urge to check my iPod, curious now as to why he picked *that* song.

Dammit. I don't want to be curious. That's precisely what he wants. But Poker Face? Really?

12

I KNOW YOU WANT ME BY PITBULL

Jay

For the past two days, it's taken all the strength in me not to reach out to Mia and ask whether Cat mentioned the iPod. I already have the next song cued up, so hopefully she doesn't intentionally leave it at home this morning just to spite me.

As always, I arrive early, but this time I stand outside the train and wait for her. Cat, of course, also has a routine, so she arrives with only moments to spare and looks as beautiful as ever. She's wearing red lipstick today. She's donned her black tweed coat and black tights with thigh-high boots that have one hell of a heel. She still has to look up at me, but she doesn't even slow when she catches sight of me. She simply gets on the train and heads to the back in search of seats.

There's an open one next to a giant of a man and a completely open row. She hesitates almost imperceptibly, waffling between sitting next to the oversized man—thus suffering through the ride in a cramped space— or leaving an open seat beside her where she knows I'll sit. In the end, she turns back to me, glares, and then slides into the seat with the giant. I laugh as I take the aisle opposite her.

"I brought you a coffee," I offer, holding up two cups. "It's the kind thing to do when you know you're going to see a friend on the train in the morning."

She throws daggers in my direction. "We're not friends."

I shrug and set her cup in her cupholder, then lean back in my seat.

"Did you bring your iPod?" I ask before lifting my cup of coffee to my lips and studying her.

Staring straight ahead, she ignores me and her coffee.

"It's a good one today," I promise.

She stays completely silent.

I shrug and prepare to wait her out. Before the doors close, though, a woman boards and stops between us. "Is that taken?" she asks, gesturing with a nod at the seat next to me.

Involuntarily, I peruse the length of her legs, past her luscious curves, and up to her pink pout before meeting a set of blue eyes that offer a warmth the woman across from me never exudes. I smile at her and reply, "It's all yours." Then I stand and allow her to move past me.

I can feel Cat watching, so I turn and wink at her. "Looks like you're off the hook today, Kitten. Enjoy your ride."

As soon as I settle into my seat next to the blonde, she strikes up a mostly one-sided conversation. Although I keep my head turned in her direction, my focus never fully strays from Cat. Her irritation and her curiosity are palpable. And I know precisely when she finally gives in and picks up her iPod. She lets out a loud sigh and then a laugh when Pit Bull's "I know You Want Me" begins to play.

13

BOSTON BY AUGUSTANA

Cat

Friday, I arrive at the train station expecting to see Jay. Secretly, I'm excited to see what song he has planned for today. I found myself laughing more than once at work on Wednesday when, out of habit, I would go to turn on my iPod, only to remember that only Pit Bull currently occupied my playlist. I listened to it more times than I'd like to admit, remembering his cocky smirk and his attentive eyes. Then, over and over, my mind wandered to the blonde who occupied the seat next to him.

Serves me right. I chose to sit next to a middle-aged man rather than Jay, only to have a supermodel sit beside him. The girl talked for the entire forty-minute commute, and when we reached our stop, he followed her off without another glance in my direction.

Even if something came of it, it shouldn't bother me. I wanted him to leave me alone.

So why, then, am I looking forward to seeing him this morning?

I walk onto the train and scan its occupants, but the dreamy blue-eyed boy that has been occupying far too many of my thoughts isn't among them. When I don't spot him, I remind myself that this is exactly what I wanted. The meeting I had scheduled with Cynthia on Monday was canceled—something about the venue needing a new date—so today we're heading there, and I can use the distraction-free commute to focus on my actual job and leave thoughts of the cocky asshole behind.

For once, I get a row to myself and stretch out. I take a sip of my pumpkin spice coffee, my mind immediately drifting to the way Jay sipped from my cup. Like it was an everyday occurrence—something comfortable and easy.

Shit. Why can't I stop thinking about this guy?

I pick up my iPod and sigh when Pitbull's song is still the only one loaded on it. He clearly has access to my iTunes account and could change it if he was so inclined. It seems he's stopped thinking about me right when I can't seem to get him off my mind.

KITTEN'S SONGS

Cynthia, Rose, and I exit the town car, and I stare up at the Beacon Hotel. The place is ornate and absolutely immaculate. It's one of my favorite places to stay in Boston.

"Don't embarrass us," Rose hisses under her breath as she follows after Cynthia.

I tilt my head and offer my best smile. "Of course not."

Rose is wearing all black. Nothing new there. Her long raven hair hangs down her back, and there isn't a curve to be found on her body. But her makeup is flawless, and she exudes money and fashion in a way young girls would kill for, with a Chanel necklace and stiletto heels that make her impossibly long legs somehow *more*.

I hate her.

I blow out a cleansing breath to center myself. I grew up in Chanel. I belong here just as much as she does. In fact, I've stayed here many times throughout my life. With a deep inhale, I remind myself that I'm just as qualified as Rose is. I have every right to walk beside her with my head high, despite the way she looks at me—like I'm a piece of gum stuck to the bottom of her shoe.

Cynthia's blond bob doesn't move as she walks. It's like even her hair knows not to fuck with the queen. I don't just adore her; I want to *be* her.

And not because of the way she does her makeup or the clothes she wears; I want to be feared, respected, and revered the way she is. I want balls to shrivel when I walk into a room. I want power. Not because of money. Not because of status. And not because of my family name. But because of who I am on my own.

"Ms. Caldwell," a thin man with a mustache says as he greets us in the lobby. "They're waiting for you in the tearoom. Is there anything special we can have sent up?"

She shakes her head. "I'm sure what you have planned will be fine. Thank you." She lifts an arm, and like Rose can read her mind, she's on the move before the woman can motion toward the elevator. When it's just the two of us, we make our way after Rose, heels clicking on the marble floor. "I wasn't sure until this morning, but it appears that Mr. Hanson will be able to join us today. I trust that's not a problem," she says, eyeing me with a raised brow that implies that no matter how I really feel, my answer will, of course, be that it's not a problem at all.

What is with her and the Hansons?

"I've never met any of them. I'd appreciate you keeping my relation to the James family to yourself, though."

She smiles. "Perfectly fine with me. I didn't know whether he'd recognize you and blow your cover."

I laugh. "It's not a cover. I choose to use my mother's maiden name out of respect for her."

Cynthia sobers, and her air of superiority is momentarily replaced with genuine appreciation. "I remember her. She always had impeccable taste. You seem to have inherited that," she says.

At her comment, I find myself standing taller. My mother was beautiful. Classically beautiful.

As we exit the elevator and enter the ballroom, there isn't a thing in the world that could bring me down. Not even Rose and her snarky attitude.

Cynthia Caldwell believes I have impeccable taste like my mother. There is no greater compliment.

Gold curtains hang from floor-to-ceiling windows. Warm sunlight pours in, creating a soft glow throughout the space. Round tables with ivory cloths and gold wingback chairs fill the room.

With his back to us, a blond man sits at one of the tables with another woman. When we enter, she stands, but she moves almost imperceptibly closer to the man, almost as if she's not sure who she's more excited to see: Cynthia Caldwell, the most iconic woman in the fashion industry, or Mr. Hanson, a man who, by all accounts, is handsome and well connected—and likely someone she and many other women would love to sleep with.

Okay, maybe that's a generalization. Sex with powerful men isn't a driving factor for all women. Maybe she likes women. Maybe she's not interested in him at all. Perhaps she's just excited about this job.

Her eyes flutter back to him and she blushes before turning in our direction again.

Scrap all that. She wants him.

The man stands and turns slightly, his head down in an almost modest or bashful manner. He's got one hand in the pocket of his gray suit; the action and posture seem familiar. And when he finally raises his head and I'm greeted by his easy smile, my stomach drops.

Jay.

His blue eyes widen as they track my every step until I'm standing before him. But when I wait for him to acknowledge me, he turns to Cynthia and offers her his hand. "Cyn, it's so good to see you."

She pulls him in for a hug, and he kisses her cheek like they're old friends. Then he turns to Rose and smiles. "Jonathan Hanson," he says, hand outstretched.

Jonathan Hanson. Jay is Jonathan *Hanson.*

She blushes, and the first smile I've ever seen from her graces her face.

He turns to me, then, eyes locked on mine, and holds out his hand. "And you are?" he asks, as if we've never met.

My throat has gone dry, and I feel impossibly foolish. He's too good to even acknowledge me? In this space, around people he believes he belongs with, he sees *me* as beneath him.

Fuck that.

I take his hand and squeeze it as hard as I can, which, honestly, is pretty hard. I have three brothers who love to box and taught me how to defend myself. I don't have the grip of a typical woman of my standing. "Catherine Bouvier," I reply.

He raises his brow and then pulls his hand back, his expression void of any reaction.

I despise him.

"Kirsten and I were going over the number of guests and potential layouts for the tables. I'm thinking cocktail tables instead of a sit-down dinner. What do you think, Cyn?" Jay asks as he turns to my boss and places a hand on her back, guiding her toward the table.

I watch the four of them sit, but I'm too shocked by the entire encounter to move.

"Catherine, come over here. I need you to take notes," Cynthia calls in a sharp tone.

I scurry in their direction, catching a slight smirk pass over Jay's face. Asshole.

How is Carter friends with this dickhead? Actually, Carter is also a dickhead. They probably get along great.

I've never been so happy to have trusted my gut. I can't imagine what would have happened if I'd come home with Jay. Carter would have lost his head. *His little sister dating his best friend.* And a *Hanson* at that. It's almost as laughable as the idea of me dating period.

I reach into my purse and grab the pad I brought and proceed to take notes. No one asks my opinion, and no one even glances in my direction, least of all the man who only days ago acted as if he actually wanted my attention.

"You're even more beautiful when you're angry."

With his words echoing in my head, I can't stop myself from peeking up at him, a searing pain squeezing my chest. He was the first person to tell me I'm beautiful, and it was nothing but a line.

14

THE ONLY EXCEPTION BY PARAMORE

Jay

The meeting drags on far longer than I would like. It takes an absurd amount of effort to keep my attention on Cynthia and Kirsten rather than studying Cat like I would prefer.

She mentioned having an internship, but I had no clue it was with Cynthia Caldwell. That's impressive.

And the way she carries herself, without even recognizing the poise she has, is hot as fuck.

Every instinct inside me screamed for me to claim her. I wanted to pull her into my arms, whisper in her ear, and make her squirm like I normally would. But I respect her too much to embarrass her in front of her boss.

Besides, she's not mine. Like a fool, I waited for her to call after the train the other day. I could have sworn we had a moment when she finally laughed at my song choice.

I...*fuck,* I don't know what I thought, because whatever it was, I was clearly wrong. Since then, there's been nothing but radio silence.

"I think that covers everything, Jonathan. Thank you for meeting with us," Cynthia finally says, standing and smoothing out her top.

"I always have time for you," I remind her.

She smiles in appreciation, and with a hand on my shoulder, she leans down and kisses my cheek.

When she steps back, I nod and wait for them to file out of the room, but Kirsten turns to me before they've exited.

"Would you like to grab lunch?" she asks.

A few feet away, Cat turns, and a glare mars her gorgeous face before she can hide it.

"I'm sorry, I have another meeting this afternoon," I say, practically shooting to my feet so I can catch up to the others before they get away. "Cynthia," I say, grabbing their attention.

All three women turn and wait for me.

"If you wouldn't mind," I say, stopping close to Cynthia and lowering my voice so Kirsten doesn't overhear. "I'm having lunch downstairs so I can taste test some of the options for the cocktail hour. I didn't bring my assistant. Could I borrow yours so she can take notes of what I like?"

The woman beside Cynthia, whose name I can't remember, pipes up, "Oh, I'd be happy to have lunch with you, Mr. Hanson."

A smirk crosses Cat's face, and she raises a challenging brow.

"Oh, I meant Catherine. I know your time is invaluable to Cynthia," I pander.

Cat's lips twist mercilessly as she watches the other woman's face fall.

Cynthia smiles. "Oh, that's a wonderful idea. I planned to have Catherine do that herself, but having your input will be invaluable." She turns toward Cat and tilts her head. "Catherine, I trust you'll find your own way back? Feel free to take the rest of the afternoon. Be sure you and Jonathan try everything and take thorough notes."

Before Cat can reply, I interject, "I'll make sure she gets home safe."

At that, Cat shoots me a glare. Shit. What did I say to anger her this time? But she smooths her expression into one of confidence and obedience when Cynthia turns to her again. "I'll be fine. Thank you, Ms. Caldwell. I'll see you Monday." Then she sighs as she looks back at me.

Knowing she won't dare make a scene in front of her boss, I grab her hand in mine. "Shall we, Kitten?" I murmur so only she can hear. She can offer me her icy stares all day; it doesn't hide what I know she feels when I touch her. When I whisper her name, she melts, even if she isn't yet ready to admit it.

She wants to submit. She wants *this*.

"What are you doing?" she hisses as I lead her away from her boss and that nosy assistant.

I don't stop, instead I just enjoy her proximity, her floral scent surrounding me. "Spending time with you like you so obviously want," I tease.

She coughs out a laugh. "An hour ago, I wasn't good enough to be acknowledged, and now you're okay with being seen in public with me?"

We turn a corner, and I tug her hand hard so she ricochets off my body. I grab her other hand, and with both wrists locked above her head, I press her against the wall. "You've wanted nothing to do with me for the last two weeks. Now you find out I'm a Hanson, and you suddenly want me to, what, tell your boss we're friends? Suddenly, *I'm* worth it to you?"

Anger courses through my body as I heave out breath after breath. Her chest rises and falls just as quickly. Brown eyes heat as she glowers at me. And even though I'm angry as fuck, I can't help but fixate on her red lips, the way they've fallen open as she heaves each breath. I ache to run my thumb against her bottom lip, to press my mouth against hers, to tangle our tongues together, to kiss the fucking life out of her.

With her hips, she bucks, trying to escape. "Fuck you. It's *because* you're a Hanson that I want nothing to do with you. Actually, screw that. It's because you're an asshole."

I press into her, our hips aligning as I hold her in place. "How am I the asshole here?"

"Let me go," she demands, turning away from me and tugging her arms, unsuccessfully trying to free her wrists.

I grab her chin and force her to look at me. "Why is it worse that I'm a Hanson? What do you have against my family?"

She lets out an exasperated sigh. "Nothing. I just don't like rich dickheads who think they're God's gift to women."

"I don't care about other women," I admit, my attention once again drifting to her lips, then roaming distractedly to her jawline, her neck. With the back of my finger, I trace that exact line, relishing the way she shudders beneath my touch. "Why are you fighting this?"

She stares at me defiantly, trying like hell to pretend that I don't affect her. I let go of her wrists and back away. "Fine, if that's how you want it, I'll leave you alone."

A flicker of disappointment crosses her face before she manages to school her features again. And that's all I need.

"I thought we were having lunch," she says quietly.

"You think you can bear to sit across from a dickhead for that long?"

She rolls her eyes and lets out a soft laugh, looking past me as she replies, "I can handle it."

Damn.

What I hate more than her assumptions about me is that she automatically assumes everyone's an asshole. What does that say about the people she's been surrounded by her entire life? She clearly hates people with money, she spends far too much time with Mia, who is one of the most toxic people I know, and she's always poised for a fight. She's a living, breathing conundrum. And she wears the best poker face around. I doubt anyone but me even sees her insecurities because she's so adept at masking them with snark and sass. If she'd take a step back, open her eyes, and see *me*, I'd like to think she'd recognize that I'm worth her time. Because for some unknown reason, I want to know everything about her.

Based on our interactions so far, she lives in the *talk is cheap* camp, so I'll have to use my actions to show her the real me instead. She's been tasked with handling the ball. My family is paying for it. Looks like I'll need to be extra involved this year. I hold out my hand to her. "Come on, let's get lunch then."

15

SLIDE BY THE GOO GOO DOLLS

Cat

"**C**hampagne?" Jay asks as the waitress drops a bottle of Dom Pérignon on the table.

He didn't even order it. Am I supposed to be impressed? I imagine many women would be. I grew up around this opulence though, and I would have given just about anything for a glass of iced tea on the porch while sitting with my mother. I'd take one afternoon of that over a lifetime of these lunches any day.

I shrug. "Sure."

The waitress fills my glass and gives Jay a longing look as he ignores her to clink glasses with me. I get minor satisfaction over his attention, and I'm not too proud to admit that.

"Can I get you anything else?" she asks, clearly not ready to let her shot with Jonathan Hanson go.

He finally turns to her. "Ask Fred for the works," he says. Then he turns to me with a grin. "You're going to love this."

Doubtful. He still doesn't get me. He name-dropped the chef like it would impress me. Probably like he thinks his last name does. But if I wanted to live that life, I'd be living as a James.

I take a sip of my champagne, and even I have to admit that it's nice to be sitting in the Beacon Hotel on a Friday afternoon while sipping a glass of Dom. And Cynthia seemed impressed with me this morning. All in all, it hasn't been a terrible day. I take a deep breath and decide to give Jay a break. "So what do you actually do during the day, Jonathan Hanson?"

He rolls his eyes. "Please don't call me that."

I tilt my head in question. "Don't like the last name?"

He sighs. "It comes with a lot of expectations." Then he holds up his hands. "I know, now you're going to say 'oh, poor little rich boy is going to complain about being rich,' but honestly, it's something you can only understand once you've lived this life. I'm fortunate. I know that. But sometimes…"

"It'd be nice to be unrecognizable. To sit and have an iced tea with your mother instead of having to constantly perform."

His eyes shoot up to mine, and he furrows his brow. "Well, yeah…" He pauses. "But I don't have a mother so…"

My hand instantly finds his. "I'm sorry."

Stupid, stupid Cat.

He glances at our clasped hands and then studies my face, his blue eyes dissecting me. "You understand," he whispers.

I nod. "I understand."

We're both silent for a moment, but more is spoken between us in those few quiet seconds than has been said in the entirety of the last few weeks. There's a tenderness in his eyes, a sadness, too, and for an instant, it's like my soul has found a companion. I recognize his pain.

"How?" he asks.

I close my eyes. I'm not prepared to tell him who I really am. But I can share parts of me. "My mom died when I was six," I admit. "And to be honest, I don't think I've felt totally comfortable in my own skin since."

I sigh. It's a truth I've never voiced aloud. Losing a parent takes and takes and takes from a person. Suffering a loss that big so young stole away the idea that things could ever truly be okay. How can anything ever really be okay again?

Jay squeezes my fingers. "I'm so sorry, Kitten."

I offer him a sad smile and am oddly comforted by the nickname.

"You're so different right now," I admit. "This guy…" I smile. "I like spending time with this guy."

A rogue tear slips down my face. Jay immediately reaches across the table to wipe it away. "Better than the dickhead you thought you were having lunch with?"

I cough out a laugh as another tear escapes, and he swipes at that one too. I pull my hand out of his, embarrassed, and grab my napkin to blot my eyes.

The waitress returns with a tray, and I give her my attention, hoping my mascara isn't streaking down my face. "Fred wants you to stop in before you leave," she says as she places two cheeseburgers and french fries in front of us.

The works. I smile to myself.

"Thank you," he says. "Can you grab us two iced teas when you have a chance?"

I fold my lips in to keep from squeaking in surprise.

"Of course, Mr. Hanson."

When the waitress is gone, I smile up at Jay. I don't say anything, though, for fear of more waterworks.

As if he knows I need a minute, he picks up his burger and digs right in. The waitress returns with our iced tea, and Jay holds his up. I raise mine too, and he tips his until they clink. I can't stop the smile that spreads across my face. I don't know why cheeseburgers and iced tea make for a perfect lunch, but it's likely the best one I've had in years.

Maybe ever.

"How did you meet Mia?" he asks, throwing me with the change in topic.

"We went to boarding school together."

He gives me a knowing glance. "So she does come from money," he teases.

"I do," I admit with a smile.

"Should I assume you're an entitled asshole, then?" he says with a smirk.

I shrug. "Certainly could have been."

We both smile, knowing it isn't funny. None of it is, yet what choice do we have but to smile through it? To tease. *To live.*

"I'm sure Mia was a blast in high school," he says before taking another bite.

I laugh. "Yeah, she certainly got us into plenty of trouble."

"And the two of you...?"

He doesn't have to finish the question. I know what he's getting at. And she's likely told him. "It's not that I don't want to answer your question; it's that I honestly don't know how."

He winces. "That complicated, huh?"

"Have you met Mia?" I say with a smile.

He laughs. "Yeah, she certainly is something."

"She means well," I supply. I put my burger down as I struggle for an explanation. "She was my first friend..."

He nods, waiting patiently while I work to put my thoughts into words.

"We were roommates for years...and then, one day, we were more." I slide my napkin from my lap and wipe my hands. "I can't say I ever really thought about her...or anyone, for that matter, in that way. Sometimes I wonder if I'm broken." My cheeks flame at that admission, and I look down at my burger in hopes of hiding the physical evidence of my embarrassment.

"Why do you say that?"

"I just...I don't know. Maybe it's because I never saw my parents together in that way, I've never really put much thought into relationships or sex..." I shrug. "Or any of it, really. The girls at school were obsessed with boys, sure, but there weren't any around. We were literally surrounded by women twenty-four seven, and until we got licenses and could drive, boys just didn't exist in our world. So people… experimented," I say quietly.

Jay grins, and I pick up a fry and throw it at him. It hits its intended target, smacking him on the cheek, then it drops to the table next to his plate.

Laughing, he picks it up and stuffs it into his mouth. "What?"

"I see what your dirty mind is doing."

We stare at one another, stupid smiles on our faces. He's so easy to talk to. I don't think I've spoken this honestly with anyone in years. Or smiled as much.

"Don't stop now. The story was just getting good," he says, eyebrows waggling.

I roll my eyes. "Shut it."

He chuckles. "Come on. Seriously, I want to know this."

"Know what?"

"Honestly?" he asks with a soft smile.

I nod, my chest feeling lighter than I think it's ever felt before.

"Whatever you want to share with me. I don't care whether it's how you like your burger or if you have a to-do list you could read out loud. I like listening to you talk. But I am particularly interested in this conversation, if I'm being honest."

"Somehow," I mutter, still snickering, "you take a totally swoon-worthy sentiment and make it crude."

He shrugs. "What can I say? It's a talent. So go on, tell me about how you experimented."

With a deep breath, I get control over my giggling. "For me, it was more than that. Mia was my best friend. My feelings got tangled up with it all. But you know Mia, so you probably know she's not a one-person woman."

"And you are?" he asks.

"I believe in loyalty. If and when I'm with someone again, they'll be

111

my sole focus."

Honestly, I've never really been with anyone but Mia, yet I can't imagine being anything but all about that *one* person. If I ever find them.

"Me too," he says firmly.

With a tilt of my head, I study him. "Really?"

Jay's jaw goes taut. "I despise cheaters. But I've never really been in a relationship."

"Not even with Mia?" I ask quickly, my jealousy getting the best of me. And it's not over my concern for Mia.

Jay shakes his head. "Never."

"But you've experimented with her?" I ask, almost afraid of the answer.

"No," he says with a firm shake of his head.

I sigh. "She made it seem…"

He grabs my hand. "Kitten, I wouldn't be trying so hard if I'd slept with your friend."

"Why *are* you trying so hard?" I ask, squeezing his hand.

What does he see in me? I've been rude to him, and I've ignored him. The first time we met, I made a fool of myself. And I certainly wasn't dressed up and gorgeous like the women I'm sure he's used to. And since then, he's seen me in business attire, but nothing extravagant. I'm sure women throw themselves at him all the time. He could have anyone. So why me?

He smiles. "Couldn't explain it if I tried."

"Try anyway."

He holds my gaze, his thumb slowly moving back and forth against my hand. "You surprise me. And so few people do. You make me work for your attention. You make *everyone* work for your attention. I'm not sure you even see the way people look at you. You don't have a clue what effect you have on those around you. When you walk into a room, people want to be near you. *I* want to be near you. I can't explain it because the way I feel can't be put into words. If I tried, I'd fall woefully short, but I would say I feel more like myself when I'm beside you than I ever have."

My mouth falls open in a way that would horrify my prim and proper grandmother. I thought he'd comment on my looks. Or how he liked my curves…

"Obviously, you're beautiful," he says, as if it's an afterthought. "But that's not *who* you are; that's just how you're packaged. Which I very much appreciate, by the way," he says with a smile. "Say something, Kitten," he whispers almost desperately.

"I've never kissed a man."

He stares at me, mouth agape, for several moments. And then he blinks.

"Did I break you?" I ask nervously. Shit. Why did I tell him that?

I watch his Adam's apple bob as he swallows.

"What are you thinking?" I beg.

"Kitten, you gotta give me a minute," he says as he swallows again.

"You're regretting this lunch now, aren't you?"

What I wouldn't give to sink under this table and disappear right about now.

"If you think telling me that changed my opinion of you in any way, shape, or form, then let me make myself perfectly clear…I would be fucking *honored* to be your first kiss. Being that I'm a man, the next line, unfortunately, will sound *crude*. But it just dawned on me that if you've never kissed a man, you also likely haven't"—he drops his voice down low—"fucked a man, either."

I lick my bottom lip as I smile and shake my head. "Such a man. You go and ruin a perfectly swoon-worthy response with *that.*"

He laughs and leans back in his seat. "I'm sorry. I think you really did break me. I'll get the check, and we can head out, okay?"

Unable to wipe the smile off my face, I just nod. "Okay."

Jay wanders off to say hello to the chef as promised, and I head to the bathroom. I inspect myself in the mirror, wondering what's going to happen next. Not only have I never kissed a man, but I've never kissed *anyone* besides Mia.

I've never felt a strong enough attraction to another person. That's probably insane. I made it through two years of college in New York City without so much as a peck on the lips. And during my time there, I never once thought about it. I was too focused on proving that I could do things on my own. I could make it without my grandparents and my brothers. I didn't need a driver or a chef. And I could make it without Mia by my side. Because the truth was, her betrayal was soul crushing. I didn't just lose the first person I'd had a relationship with; I lost the trust I had in my best friend. Maybe trust in humanity in general. Mia *hurt* me. So I went to New York and pushed it all aside. I made friends, went to school, and went to parties. I had fun, but I just…I never met anyone who made me feel like Jay does.

I apply ChapStick and fluff my hair a bit. "You don't have to kiss him," I say to my reflection. "But you can if you want to. Neither of those things is untrue. He's not Mia."

I slip a mint into my mouth and take a deep breath before leaving the bathroom. Jay is at the hostess stand. He's angled away from me, but I can see the smile on his face as the hostess flirts with him. But I'm beginning to recognize his smiles. The soft ones he wears when he's listening to me or when he admits how he feels.

The smile he's donning now? That's Jonathan Hanson. With me, he's just Jay. There's no show, and I really like that.

"Ready to go?" I ask as I step up beside him, my hand outstretched.

He turns to me, his eyes soft and his heart on his sleeve. Grasping the hand I've offered, he murmurs, "I'm ready, Kitten."

16

AMBER BY 311

Jay

"Do you have to be home by a certain time?" I ask as we walk out of the Beacon Hotel.

Cat glances at her phone and then looks back up at me. "I'm actually staying in the city tonight. Meeting up with a friend later."

"Ah, Friday night out in Boston. Doing anything exciting?"

She fidgets with the sleeve of her jacket. "Um, we're having dinner at her place. Nothing fancy."

Dinner at her place. That sounds like a date. Normally, I wouldn't be jealous of a woman spending time with the woman I'm *trying* to spend time with, but I'm thrown after our conversation.

"That's nice. Can I drop you somewhere?" I ask.

Her face falls. "Um, sure. But I can just head back to the office myself. You don't have to worry about me."

Did I say something wrong?

The easy conversation we had in the restaurant, even with the heavy topics, has almost evaporated.

"Is it a date?" I ask, getting straight to the point. I avoid relationships because I don't trust women—or people, for that matter—in general, but I want to try with this one. Which means open communication. If she will only ever be a friend, that's fine, but I need to know that now.

She frowns. "Is what a date?"

I sigh and focus on the brick of the hotel's façade just over her shoulder. "The dinner tonight. Is it a date?" I force myself to turn back to her, and before my eyes, her expression softens, and a smile graces her gorgeous face.

She runs a finger between my brows, smoothing out the crease. Then, featherlight, her knuckle dances down my face. I melt against her touch.

"No," she says, pulling her hand back. "It's just dinner with a friend and her parents."

"Oh," I say, a breath of relief whooshing from my lungs. I like that answer a bit too much.

"If you aren't busy, I still have a few hours until I'm supposed to meet her," she offers.

I accept way too quickly.

Fifteen minutes later, we're standing outside James Liquors Headquarters, and I'm feeling a lot less positive. "What are we doing here?"

"I want to show you something," she says, tugging me toward the front doors by my hand.

I dig my heels in. "I'm not going in there."

She rolls her eyes. "Why?"

"You do realize my family is their biggest competitor, right?" I say, holding the bridge of my nose, trying to fight back the migraine I feel coming on. It happens every time I think about this family, which is pretty often, considering Carter believes we're best friends.

"Yeah, I'm not an idiot. We're not going into the corporate offices, crazy. We're going to the roof."

Her surprising aloofness makes me smile. "The roof?"

She grins. "Just trust me?"

I sigh as I follow her inside. Ridiculously, I'm pretty sure I'd follow this girl anywhere...even into my own personal hell.

The foyer is buzzing with activity, as it's a Friday afternoon. "Stay here for one second," she whispers before letting go of my hand and approaching the security desk. The security guard's face lights up when he sees her, and he leans toward her as she speaks to him. He nods and responds, and before I know it, she's heading back toward me, a key card in her hand.

"All set," she says as she grabs my hand again and leads me to the elevators.

My tongue feels too big for my mouth as we step through the sliding doors and I catch sight of the name written in gold. James Liquors. What am I doing here? A man slips in just before the doors close, eyeing Cat like the beautiful woman she is. I grab her hip and pull her into me possessively. She relaxes against me and rests her head against my chest, the actions loosening the tension in my every muscle.

He hits thirty-five, and she hits the P.

P as in penthouse.

Fuck, what did I get myself into? Why does she have a key to the penthouse of James Liquors?

Tipping her head back, she rests her chin against my chest and looks up at me. In a whisper, she says, "Don't worry; it's not occupied. And we're just going to the roof."

All I can do is nod.

The smell of whiskey and wood gets stronger as the elevator ascends. When the door finally opens at the thirty-fifth floor and the man gets off, the scent intensifies. Just outside the doors, decorative whiskey barrels line the entrance of what looks like the actual James Liquors offices. Narrowing my eyes, I scan the space, taking in as much detail as I can, but the elevator door closes before I can get too lost in that world.

With my palms resting on Cat's shoulders, I squeeze, focusing on her warmth, anchoring myself to this moment with her. My entire life has revolved around destroying the James family. But I want this moment to be separate from that. I want Cat nowhere near that world.

As the elevator light indicates that we've reached the penthouse, the doors open, and I find myself inside one of the James family homes.

So much for keeping Cat separate.

"What are we doing here?" I hiss.

She rolls her eyes and drags me out by the arm. "No one lives here. Calm down."

Easy for her to say.

I follow her out a door that leads to a set of steps. She climbs them quickly, only turning around when she hits another door. "Ready?" she says, pressing the door open and illuminating the space with warm light, her face glowing in excitement. Or maybe it's the sun.

I nod and follow her through. The roof is fitted with a large pool and hot tub and boasts an incredible view of the city. I've never looked out over the cityscape from this direction. Boston Harbor glistens in the distance, the *USS Constitution* standing proud in front of the bridge.

"How did you know about this spot?" I mumble, scanning the skyline. *Was my mother ever here?*

"My dad worked here when I was a kid. After my mom died, I'd come here after school. Before he sent me away," she adds quietly.

"He doesn't work here anymore?"

She shakes her head and sighs.

"And the James family didn't mind you coming up here?"

"No one lives here," she replies. "Sal, the guy at the front desk, he lets me come up here whenever I want." She shrugs and moves closer to the edge of the roof. "Come sit with me."

She climbs up onto the stone barrier, sending my heart leaping into my throat. "What are you doing?" I practically shout as I pull her back to my chest.

I fucking despise heights.

She laughs. "I'm sitting down, you weirdo."

"Not up there, you're not!"

Her brown eyes caramelize before me as she smiles softly. "Are you afraid of heights, Mr. Hanson?"

My cock jumps at the way she says my name. But I won't be distracted. "Kitten, if you go up there, I'm going to lose my fucking mind. Please, stay here."

"Do you trust me?" she asks, a teasing glint in her eye.

"Not fucking right now, I don't."

She laughs. "Come on, it's safe. I promise." She pulls away from me and hops up onto the ledge again. Like there's a damn string connecting me to her, my body follows, even as warning bells ring inside my head, screaming that this is a really bloody bad fucking idea.

I throw my leg over the ledge and pull myself up, but I hold desperately to the side that isn't fifty floors above the ground, bile rising in my throat. Meanwhile, Cat dangles her legs over the other side, scaring the shit out of me.

"Will you please turn around? Just look down. I promise it's not as scary as you think," she says with enough sass to make me consider it.

I swallow and force myself to look, my body still straddling the surface of the roof's edge.

She swings her legs again and tips forward, pointing below her. "See, there's a ledge," she says.

My lips fold in on themselves tightly, trying to smother my own scream, but I spot something that looks similar to concrete only a few feet down.

I sigh. "Why didn't you fucking lead with that?"

She laughs as she motions to me. "And miss seeing you straddling a wall and holding on for dear life like some vortex is going to suck you in? Nah, I much prefer this version," she teases.

I right myself on the ledge and dust off my pants. "You're a brat."

She sticks out her tongue, drawing my attention to her plump lips.

"You thinking about kissing me?" she asks.

I shake my head. "I'm not going to kiss you," I say firmly, although I can't help but lick my lips at the very thought of doing so.

"You're not?" she asks with a frown.

"Is that why you brought me here? You want me to kiss you?"

She pushes her tongue into her cheek, then murmurs, "Not if you don't want to kiss me."

"This conversation is going in circles," I say with a smile, all thoughts of our location long forgotten.

"I just thought," she starts, but then she stops and turns away from me, studying the view in front of us. "You…" she tries again, and then she quiets, her shoulders slumping.

I take her hand and lace our fingers together. The simple feel of her long fingers linking with mine makes my stomach somersault. Her skin is soft, and once again, her entire body melts next to mine. My touch alone does that to her. The girl who normally holds herself together, who wears armor during every interaction, protecting a part of her I've only seen glimpses of, softens for *me.*

"You thought correct," I reply, using my other hand to pull her chin so she's looking at me. Her brown eyes search mine, her lashes fluttering as I rub against her jaw. "I want to kiss you. *And I will kiss you.* But not this afternoon."

She opens her eyes and scrutinizes me, her forehead crinkling in confusion. And perhaps disappointment.

I snuff that out right away. "You deserve a perfect first kiss, Kitten. Movie style. Fireworks. Music in the background. Romance."

Surprise dances in her eyes, but she doesn't speak.

"You deserve it all, Catherine Bouvier. And I intend to give it to you."

"See, you are capable of being swoon-worthy without ruining it," she says as a smile plays on her plump red lips.

I lean in close, my lips brushing the shell of her ear and sending shivers rippling through her. "And then I'm going to fuck you, Kitten, and you're going to see stars."

Her resounding laugh leaves us both smiling.

17

LOVE SONG BY SARA BAREILLES

Cat

Before Jay delivered me to Sophie's house, I stole his phone and texted myself from it. "Now I have your number," I said with a smirk.

He beamed at me. "Now I have *your* number. You may regret that, Kitten."

I laughed and slipped out of the car with a wave.

"You spent the afternoon with Jonathan Hanson!" Sophie says for the fifth time as I tuck my feet under me and curl up on her couch with a glass of wine.

"Yes, I spent the afternoon with Jay," I counter.

"Oh, now he's Jay," she says, all posh-like, holding out her finger as she takes a sip of her wine.

I laugh. "No, he was Jay before I knew he was Jonathan Hanson. He's the one who's been stalking me on the train. Jonathan Hanson *is* Jay."

"Wait," she says, holding up her hand, her naturally curly hair shaking as she does. I'm obsessed with her hair and told her so as soon as I walked into the house and watched her remove her wig and brush it out. "Jonathan Hanson is the one who stole your iPod and has been sending you songs?"

I nod, a perma-smile plastered to my face.

"You *punched* Jonathan Hanson in the nose!"

I laugh. "I guess I did."

She falls back against the couch, bringing a hand to her heart. "Oh my God, you're going to date Jonathan Hanson. This is like a Cinderella story."

I narrow my eyes. "Um, excuse me, I'm not in rags." I wave a hand up and down my body. "And I'm not looking for a Prince Charming."

If anything, his name is the *least* attractive thing about him. If I didn't already know him or see glimmers of who I *think* he is when he's not being Jonathan Hanson, then I'd be running in the opposite direction.

He's my brother's best friend, my family's corporate enemy. He's also cocky and entitled—everything I hate about men. He's off limits in every sense of the word. But I like him. *A lot.*

"If you don't want him, send him my way." She waggles her brows. "I'd happily take a Prince Charming any day."

I laugh. "I thought you were obsessed with Dexter."

She smiles dreamily. "Oh, you mean Daddy. Yeah, I'd take him any day too."

"You're hysterical." I wave off her ridiculousness. "How boring was work without me?"

She downs her wine and sets the glass on the table. "Uh, it was horrible. Rose came back from your meeting with a bug up her ass. She was barking orders and making us run circles for the rest of the day."

I wince. "That's probably because of me."

She smiles devilishly, her dark eyes flashing with mischief. "I can imagine how well she took the news when she realized Jonathan Hanson"—she pauses when I roll my eyes at her—"I'm sorry, when she realized *Jay* wanted you for lunch and not her."

I laugh. "Context is important, Soph. He wanted to *have* lunch *with* me."

She shakes her head. "Nah, pretty sure I got it right the first time. He wanted *you* for lunch."

My mind turns to the moment on the roof when he licked his lips and promised me the kiss of a lifetime.

"Can I tell you a secret?" I whisper, taking another sip of wine for courage. Sophie straightens. "Of course. What's up?"

"I've never been with a man," I admit, and God bless Sophie because she tries to hide her gasp with a yawn.

"Well, wow, yes…that's…"

I put my hand over hers to stop her. "I know," I say.

"But you *like* men?" she asks slowly, carefully, like she's trying to find the right words, and I appreciate her honest nature even more in this moment.

"I like Jay," I admit with a shrug.

"But you generally favor women?" she asks, head cocked.

I sigh. This is the part I'm still confused about myself. "Maybe?" I offer. "Honestly?"

She nods but stays silent, scooting forward on the couch and watching me closely.

"I think it depends on the person. Like I don't think about sex that much. Maybe because I've only had sex a few times, and it was a long time ago. And like I said, never with a man."

Sophie blows out a breath. "Man, you must think I'm a dirty whore for all the sex talk."

I huff a laugh. "No, it's been nice. Honestly…I don't know how to say this because I don't want you to get weird on me."

She takes a deep breath. "Okay, if you're attracted to me, I get it. I'm really pretty and awesome, but I like men."

I chortle and swat at her. "Shut up!"

She throws her head back and cackles. "You can tell me anything. Even if it's that you're obscenely attracted to me."

"Yes, well, as attractive as you are, I think I can keep my hands to myself. Don't you worry."

She shrugs, one brow arched. "I know, I know. I'll try not to dress so cute when we go out tonight. Sorry, please go on."

"Thanks, appreciate it. As I was saying, my ex, the last person I was with, the *only* person I've ever been with, was my best friend in high school. She…she made me think things and believe things…and part of me wonders if our relationship, and maybe her influence, messed me up. Like, am I even attracted to women, or did she just make me believe I was? I think I correlate sex with heartbreak now because the closest person to me used my trust in her as a friend to her advantage."

I sigh. I'm making Mia sound like a villain. I do think she loved me, *loves me*, she's just…Mia. Like me, she's never witnessed what love is supposed to be like. Can two broken people ever be right?

Sophie puts a hand on top of mine on the couch cushion and squeezes. "I'm sorry."

I shrug, tired of feeling this way. "My point is, being with Jay, even being attracted to him, has my mind all sorts of messed up." I blow out a breath, giving her the rest of my secrets. "And it's not just because he's a man. It's because *I'm* a James."

Her forehead creases. "You're a what?" she asks, angling closer.

"James Liquors. As in Hanson's biggest competitor."

"You're related to the James family?" Her eyes practically pop out of her head when she asks.

I laugh. "I'm not related to them. I *am* them. Theodore James is my grandfather. My brother Carter, he's Jay's roommate."

"Shut the fuck up!" she says, rearing back.

I shake my head. "I am. Jay and Carter went to college together. I never met Jay because Carter and I have never been that close. I was away at boarding school when they were in college, and then I was in New York and too preoccupied with my own life. So I met Jay as Jay, not as Jonathan Hanson. And no one knows I'm a James, *including him*…I keep that little tidbit of information to myself because it always changes the way people look at me."

"That's…" she shakes her head, "that's a lot."

"I'm still me," I argue with a shrug.

She gives me a small, sympathetic smile. "I know that. I don't care what your last name is. But that's a lot for you. You've been carrying all this around, by yourself, all this time. It can't be easy."

Tension melts from my shoulders as the truth of her words seeps through me. As she *sees* me. Not what she can get from knowing me.

"Honestly, it's okay." I shrug. "I'm happy with my decisions. I'm happy to carry my mother's last name. If I could be anyone in the world, it would be her."

Sophie grabs the wine bottle and refills both our glasses. "I've got to be honest, Cat. I think who you are is pretty awesome too. Don't lose sight of that." She clinks her glass against mine. "Let's go have a home-cooked meal with my mom, okay?"

I nod. "I'll be right there." I grab my phone, feeling lighter and more sure of myself than I have in a long time.

A text from Jay sits waiting.

> Jay: Tell me it's not all in my head, Kitten. Tell me you feel this too.

I feel it. I see it. Hell, it's all I can think about. But I'm not one to give in too easily. And I'm also not 100 percent sure. So I smile as I reply in the only way I know how, and hopefully in a way that will make him smile.

I link the song to the text and hit send.

> "Love Song" by Sara Bareilles.

18

WONDERWALL BY OASIS

Jay

With a rueful smile, I soak in the words of the Sara Bareilles song for the third time. Not two seconds after it ends, my phone rings. The ringtone that blares is the one set specifically for Carter. The calm I felt at the thought of Cat picking out a flirty song is gone, and Jonathan Hanson, the man my father has made me into, returns. "Hey, Carter, what's up?"

"Kev and I are on our way to Boston. We're picking you up and going out. No excuses."

I roll my neck. I'm so not in the fucking mood for this. In front of them, I have to be a different person. Someone I despise. And for one day, I just want to be myself. "I have a migraine. I'm in bed, ready to sleep this off."

"Hanson, we haven't gone out in weeks, and you haven't been home for longer than that. Come on, I know you're busy, but you need a break."

I rub my forehead, trying to ease the inevitable headache that forms each time I have to step into this role. I don't even dislike Carter. It's the immense irony of all of this. His family destroyed mine. But he wasn't involved. Though that doesn't change the facts or what I have to do.

We're not really friends. I can easily disappoint him, and it won't matter to me in the long run.

"I really can't, man," I say again.

"Too late. We're on our way up now. Either let us in, or I'll use my key."

Fucking A. The last thing I want is him here. And how the fuck did he get a key? "Fine. I'll be right down. Give me ten."

"You have five. See you soon."

When he clicks off, I throw my phone.

KITTEN'S SONGS

I'm seated between two blondes in the dark club, with a glass of whiskey in front of me. Carter has a similar drink and one blonde sitting on his lap. Although his whiskey is a James and mine is a Hanson.

In college, fucking idiots that we were, we'd make all our friends do blind taste tests. None of the fools we hung out with knew good whiskey, and we wasted hundred-dollar bottles just to prove a point.

Hanson Whiskey always won.

"Wanna bring the girls back to your place?" Kev asks, leaning over the blonde on my right. Heather, I think her name is. I couldn't give two fucks. This is all a show at this point.

Kelly, the one on my left, who is someone I've taken home from time to time, rubs my leg, her fingers curling against my thigh. "Yeah, let's get out of here. Heidi and I will make it worth it for you, baby."

Heidi. That's her fucking name.

I grimace.

Normally, the idea of two women going at it in front of me, and then letting me do whatever the fuck I want to them, is enough to have me carrying them out of the bar. But it's only ever about sex.

Now, the only thing in my head is Cat. We may not be together, but the potential makes the idea of touching anyone else almost sickening.

And thinking about her out with someone else makes me want to put my fist through a wall. So how could I do that to her?

But we're *not* together. That reminder does nothing to ease the tension pulling every one of my muscles tight. If anything, I find myself gripping my phone, searching for any reason to text her.

"Jay," Kelly whispers in my ear, her fingers gliding up and down my leg. "Take us home."

Carter watches me, waiting for my response.

"Doesn't your family have an apartment here?" I say instead. I don't know why I'm bringing up the penthouse right now.

Carter grimaces. "What?"

That's odd.

I push. "In the James Building. Isn't there a penthouse? Why don't we go there?"

He clenches his jaw and shoots daggers at me, silently signaling for me to shut the fuck up. I bite back a smile. Looks like Cat was right; they really don't use the penthouse.

"I have an early meeting. We aren't going back to my place," I assert, ending this conversation. "I'm going to the bar," I announce, removing Kelly's hand from my leg. I'll have one more drink and then disappear while they get wasted. Then I'll go home and text Cat. I want her to know I'm thinking about her, and hopefully she's doing the same.

19

FRIDAY I'M IN LOVE BY THE CURE

Cat

In a fit of laughter, we stumble out of the cab, Sophie's impression of the men at the last bar leaving us both gasping for air. We booked it out of there and hopped in the first cab we saw when the guys who were buying us drinks realized Sophie was mimicking their accents, and not in a good way.

"It's genuinely not my fault. When I'm drinking, I can't help but adopt the accents I hear," she defends as we walk up to the line for the next bar.

"He was from Australia! You sounded like you were from Georgia, so I kind of understand why he was upset." I guffaw and bring a hand to my mouth to stifle my reaction.

She shakes her head. "I do an amazing Australian accent!"

She's genuinely affronted, but she was awful, and it was absolutely hysterical.

"Whatever you say. What is this place?" I tip my head back to take in the bar's façade. I've never been here.

"Oh, Dexter told me about it."

"Daddy!" I shout as giggles explode from both of us.

"Yes, Daddy! You think he'll be here?" she asks as she peers down the line like she'll be able to spot him through the open door from way out here.

"Did he say he would?" I ask.

She doesn't answer, instead giving me an almost nervous look before heading toward the door.

After a delicious dinner with her mother, where rather than feeling pangs of jealousy over their close relationship, I felt welcomed and included, Sophie and I attacked her closet in search of dresses for tonight. I only had the outfit I'd come in and a pair of sweats. I didn't think we'd go out after dinner. And although we aren't the same size—she has a lot more curves on top—I managed to find a dress that fit me. The black sweater dress hugs my curves in a flattering way and goes well with the boots I wore to work and the red lipstick staining my lips.

Sophie's mother and I convinced her to leave her hair in its natural state, and she's rocking a vibrant purple dress that looks incredible against her dark skin. We hit the front of the line, flash our IDs, and are ushered inside the club.

A red light illuminates the dance floor, where a sea of bodies move in a sensual rhythm. For the first time in I don't know how long, I find myself staring at the way people touch, my skin heating in an unfamiliar excitement.

Maybe it's all the talk of sex this afternoon, or the way Jay licked his lips up on the rooftop. Or maybe it's because I haven't been touched by another person in years. But I have to clench my legs to stave off a bolt of desire just watching people touch.

"Drink?" Sophie shouts over the music, pointing to the bar. With a nod, I follow her. She squeezes her body between people like a pro and orders drinks for us both. I see the moment she spots Dexter, and her eyes flare in excitement. Lucky for her, his reaction tells the same story. His face softens, and his smile grows as he takes her in from head to toe. At his perusal, she lights up and straightens, as if preening for his attention.

They are totally going to fuck.

And I'll let them have their moment. I tap her on the shoulder and point to the ladies' room. "I'll be back. Will you be okay?"

She smiles. "I'll be fine." I don't think the words have even left her mouth before he's pulling her close, elated surprise at seeing her lighting up his face.

I fight my way through the throngs of people to the bathroom. On my way back, I search the bar area for Sophie and Dexter and come up empty. When I turn to the dance floor, I can't help but smile at the sight of her dropping low in front of him. He's *smitten*. Pride emanates from him as he watches her. I love that he recognizes her worth.

It reminds me of the way Jay was with me today. How he acts every time I see him—with the exception of when we were with Cynthia.

I stash that insecurity away, deciding to grab a drink and text Jay.

Taking a page from Sophie's book, I copy her moves from when we first arrived and manage to squeeze my way through to the bar. I order my absolute favorite drink, a dirty martini, and shimmy a little when they have the blue cheese olives I love. I lift up my phone to snap a picture of myself holding my drink when I spot Jay across the bar with a blonde on either side of him.

It takes me a minute to process what I'm seeing. When my brain makes sense of the scene, rage rushes through my veins like hot oil, making me feel like I want to jump out of my skin. My stomach turns, and my heart squeezes, making it hard to breathe.

Fuck him for making me feel this way.

And fuck me for allowing *anyone* to let me feel this way again.

I turn around and take a picture, making sure to capture my drink, my smile, and the evidence of who he really is—a player, just as I suspected— and text it to him before I can chicken out.

I quickly grab the song that's been playing through my mind the last few days as I tried to figure out who he really was. Then I send him a link in another message so he'll understand exactly where we stand.

I down my drink in one gulp, shoot Sophie a text that I had an emergency, and book it out of the club.

So much for being seen.

20

COMPLICATED BY AVRIL LAVIGNE

Jay

I smile when *Kitten* flashes across the screen of my phone where it sits on the bar in front of me. Finally, she's reaching out to me. It's a small gesture, but it confirms what I was feeling this afternoon. We're on the same page. It's not all in my head. She wants this too.

I smile as I see the picture of her drink and those fucking lips that I can't wait to bite down on. Before I can respond, a second message comes in.

"Complicated" by Avril Lavigne.

Squinting, I try to recall the lyrics, but with the beat in the club, I can't conjure them. I excuse myself from Kelly and her friend, promising to return. I have no intention of going back. They followed me to the bar when I tried to ditch them before. They can't seem to take a hint. I'll grab a cab when I get outside and hopefully find out where Cat is.

I hit play on the song and drag it to my ear as soon as I'm outside. The bouncer sees me and motions that he'll flag a cab. I nod in appreciation as the music starts.

It doesn't take long for me to realize this isn't a love song. Fuck. She's clearly pissed off about something.

I'm a fool? How the fuck am I acting like anyone else?

What the fuck?

I scroll back up to the picture, and that's when I see it. Me. Looking like a fucking fool with two blondes hanging all over me.

Fuck.

21

DON'T DREAM IT'S OVER BY CROWDED HOUSE

Jay

I called Cat at least twenty times on Friday night, knowing damn well her phone was turned off. I planned to show up at her apartment Saturday morning, but my father summoned me, citing an emergency that wouldn't keep.

Even the view of the Boston Seaport from my father's apartment doesn't loosen the tension pulling at every one of my muscles. I've never particularly liked this space, and after yesterday, I find myself comparing it to the penthouse owned by the Jameses. Somehow, this apartment is more pretentious. More ostentatious. *Just more.*

And I fucking hate that thought.

Is that how my mother felt? Did the James family entice her more than her own? Was it more than the affair? Was their lifestyle intriguing to her too? Did she long for children who behaved like Carter and Cash? Carter has a sister, too, though I've never met her. But I imagine my mother would have liked having a daughter. Did she compare their picture-perfect life to ours and determine that we didn't measure up?

I didn't measure up.

"Fuck this," I mutter as I undo my tie. I pull at it until it releases completely and ball it in my fist. Carter would never go home in a fucking suit. Why the fuck do I?

My father comes into view, dressed just as formally and standing in the kitchen, sipping what looks like whiskey from a lowball glass.

"Little early, don't you think, Dad?" I mutter, more to myself but not quietly enough.

He raises his gaze to mine, the nearly black stare meant to chastise me. It's a wonder my eyes are as light as they are. I inherited my mother's coloring completely.

"I see someone had a bad night," he snaps, slamming his glass down, the noise clanging loudly in the empty space. It's all windows and bare furniture. No pillows, no pictures, no comfort whatsoever.

Kind of like his heart.

I see my future, and it scares the shit out of me.

Blowing out a long breath, I fight for composure. I can't let him rattle me. Can't let on that I'm *already* rattled. If he finds out I'm hung up on a girl—*a woman*—he'll make sure she disappears. No distractions, no happiness. Nothing but revenge and business. I've lived like this for the last ten years, and suddenly, I can't fathom why.

I'm not sure when I stopped living every moment striving to obtain his goals and instead turned my focus to my own.

Happiness.

I haven't thought of something so trivial in years.

But something about the way Cat challenged me that first day, denying me her name and number, telling me to earn it, made me look at my life and wonder how—*outside of the designer clothes, expensive cars, opulent apartments*—I could be worth someone else's time.

For so long, those material things attracted the kind of attention I wanted. A woman for the night, someone for the now. But who would want to stick around if I have nothing more to offer than work and revenge?

My stomach rolls as I study the liquid in my father's glass. "Just a little hungover," I offer as an excuse. "Carter forced me to go out since I haven't been around much."

"Good, then it won't seem strange when you show up at his apartment to place the next SD card. I told you moving out was fucking idiotic. We're so close, Jonathan. We've worked for this for years."

I avert my attention to the ocean. Anything to avoid his scrutiny. The water is dark and brooding, a formidable opponent that lures us in with its soft waves, lulling us into complacency if we aren't careful. What I wouldn't give to dive in and see where it takes me. I'd rather see the hope from the shore than the despair from this angle.

"I want to speed up the timeline," I say, my attention fixed on the waves. This needs to be over with. Let my father have his revenge. Let James Liquors go bankrupt. Or whatever the mystery plan is. I need to get out of this cycle if I ever want a shot of standing on the shore.

22

LOSING MY RELIGION BY R.E.M.

Cat

The apartment above James Liquors is where my father and mother lived before they had children. After we were born, my mother would bring us here while my dad worked downstairs. I barely remember that time. Or my mother.

With the ache of that loss tugging at my heart, I sink back into the bed in the guest room. The room, my former nursery, is a light pink with a plush white rug to soften the space. All other reminders of my time in this room have been removed.

After she died, my brothers and I remained in Bristol, Rhode Island—a picturesque small town my mother was determined to reside in while she raised us—with our nannies, while my father stayed here. My father never came home on the weekends. He just disappeared.

My grandparents kicked him out of the penthouse after they fired him. So much of the past and details of those events remain a mystery to me. But even back then, when I came home from school for holidays and the summer, this is where I came. I'd sneak up here, though I'm sure my grandfather knew where I was—nothing happens in this building without his knowledge. But if he did, he never said anything.

It's been a long time since I've stayed here overnight, but I can't possibly go back to my apartment. I can't face Mia. She probably knows exactly the kind of person Jay is. Hell, she probably knows he was pursuing me. A sick part of me wonders if she was part of it. She'd get a thrill out of being with both of us.

My stomach sinks at the thought that the words he spoke, that meant so much to me at the time, were nothing more than lines. Probably pulled from a list he kept handy for all his flirtations.

And then it twists at the image of Jay and Mia together. I can't banish it from my mind.

He said he's never been with her, but he's a lying liar, so his words hold no value. He probably saw me on the train and figured he could have us both. I was an opportunity. A game. Nothing more.

I sigh in disgust, hating how I've given a boy the power to make me feel this way. No, not a boy; a man. A man who wears suits and smirks at me as if he knows more about me than I know about myself. As if he knows my thoughts and wants when I haven't even figured them out. A man who promised me a movie-style kiss and then left me out in the cold, wishing for something I'd never even considered until he worked his way under my skin.

A real love story. A chance at happiness. The potential for more.

KITTEN'S SONGS

It's a rarity for the four of us to get together anymore. While Chase is spending the weekend working on a project for school, Cash and Frank attend school close by and jumped at my Sunday brunch invite. For years, the whole family would sit down for this meal once a week. But as we've gotten older, it's become more difficult to get us all in one place. My grandparents are in Nashville for the week, but Carter offered to take the train in to meet us too. And meeting two out of my three brothers plus

Frank is a feat in itself. Honestly, I probably like Frank more than the rest. Except Cash. He'll forever be my number one.

Carter has a reputation for being late, but the one time I'm counting on it, he strolls in right on time. I was hoping to get a few minutes alone with Cash. I want more information on Carter's roommate and best friend, but I'd really like to not bring it up around Carter.

Oh well.

"How come you're in Boston?" Carter asks as he slides into the booth next to me. Frank and Cash sit on the other side, and all eyes turn to me.

"Oh, I stayed with a friend from work," I lie. Sophie didn't end up going back to her house. She and Dexter spent all of Saturday in bed, and although she offered to ditch him Saturday night, I feigned a stomach bug. She deserves the joy, and I'm not ready to spill my guts to her just yet.

"If I'd known, I would have had you meet me on Friday. You should have seen this club. It was amazing." Carter looks over at Cash and Frank. "Sucks you guys aren't old enough. Fuck," he gushes, "the women at this place—" He clamps his mouth shut when I glare at him.

"Can we not?" I say, scrunching my nose and studying the menu.

"Please, you know we're all getting laid. This isn't news," Carter says with a smirk.

I don't dare look up at Cash and Frank. I don't want to think about either of them having sex. Gross.

I blow out a breath. "Just make sure you're wearing a condom, please."

"Okay, mother," Carter crows.

When Cash and Frank burst into laughter, I glower at them all.

"Kit Cat, you're in rare form today," Cash offers quietly once he's settled down.

"I'm fine. I just don't want your dicks to fall off from misuse."

Frank quirks a grin at me. "Misuse?"

"Yeah, from, like, rotten vagina."

This time, we all burst out laughing.

I breathe deeply as the giggles wear off. "Sorry, I'm just in a weird mood."

"Things okay with Mia?" Cash asks, likely thinking my overnight stay in Boston has to do with her.

I smile at my younger brother. "Things are fine." Then I turn, taking the opportunity to ask what I really want to know. "Speaking of roommates, how are things with yours, Carter?"

Cash grins at the change in topic. "Yeah, how's our competition doing?"

Carter laughs. "Only you think like that, Cash. I swear you were meant to run the business. Pa will probably skip right over the problematic man-child," he waves a hand up and down his torso, "and hand the company to you."

"Excuse me!" I hold my hands up and point at myself. "Am I chopped liver?"

"Please," Frank drolls, "like you'd want anything to do with that place."

I shrug. "True."

The waitress stops at our table, and Carter scans her from head to toe before I nudge him. "You are so embarrassing," I scoff quietly.

"I could have her panties in my pocket before she gets our drinks," he says in challenge under his breath.

"We'll have two coffees. She'll have a mimosa, and he'll have your number," Cash offers, pointing at Carter, who doesn't even pretend to be put off by the call-out.

"I will," he says with a wink.

The waitress giggles, and that's the end of that. She was too easy. He'll be over her by morning. *After* she's been under him.

Men.

Hell, women too.

When will these girls realize that the only women these James men will ever take seriously are the ones who don't fall over themselves to be with them? There's no way they'll settle for anything less than women who put them in their place. Someone with a little backbone.

152

"I'll also take an Irish coffee," he adds.

She disappears with a smile. There's no way she won't return with her number on a napkin. So predictable.

"As for my roommate," he adds, giving me a pointed look.

My stomach plummets in response to his scrutiny. Does he know about Jay and me? *Is there a Jay and me?* Maybe there was for about half a second, but not anymore.

"He isn't anymore."

"Huh?" I ask, sure I misunderstood while I was having a mini freak-out.

"What do you mean?" Cash asks.

Carter ogles the waitress as she sets each of our drinks in front of us, leaning over a bit more than necessary. "He has to be in Boston, so he moved out. His stuff is still there and he's still paying rent, but I have the place to myself. It's not terrible," he says with a cocked brow, his attention fixed on the waitress's ass as she walks away.

I nudge him in the arm. "Gross."

He laughs.

"Cool, so Frank and I can stay there next weekend?" Cash asks, already scheming.

Carter nods. "Yeah, he won't mind. I'll text him to check, but he hasn't been back in weeks."

The conversation shifts to the kind of trouble the guys are getting up to at school, but I tune out, my mind spinning. He hasn't stayed in Providence in weeks? But he takes the train to Boston with me every day. From Providence. Where I assumed he lived. Where he did live. Where he *doesn't* live?

If he's staying in Boston, why is he taking the train?

23

FIX YOU BY COLDPLAY

Jay

"**W**here is she?" I say when I stalk into the coffee shop on Sunday morning. I swear to Christ if she isn't here…

"Who?" Mia asks like an idiot. She twirls her hair around her finger and everything, feigning a clueless expression but knowing precisely what she's doing.

"Mia, today is not the day."

I have bags under my eyes, I'm wearing jeans, which is rare as shit, and I'm running on limited sleep. My father forced me to endure hours of discussions about what I need to do this week to ensure the last few steps of his plan succeed.

"So testy this morning," she teases. "Is someone missing his play toy?"

I pinch the bridge of my nose, trying to keep myself from shouting at her in the middle of my café. Maybe I *will* sell this place after all.

"Mia," I warn.

She lifts her chin, eyeing me defiantly. "You're not good enough for her. And I told you how I felt about her. *How could you*?"

I scrub my hands through my hair. "I didn't *do* anything."

"You haven't been pursuing her, despite knowing how I feel?" she asks in a softer voice, her expression almost vulnerable and so unlike the feisty woman who struts around like she doesn't have a care in the world.

I motion toward a table, and she flags down the other barista on the schedule today. Once the register is covered, she plops down across from where I remain standing.

"Where is she?" I ask again, forcing my voice to remain even.

Mia rolls her eyes and crosses her arms over her chest. "She hasn't been back to the apartment since Friday. I have no idea where she is. And whatever's going on obviously involves you because she texted me yesterday to tell me she quit. What did you do?"

I grip the back of the chair before finally taking a seat, feeling restless. "Mia," I urge, dropping my forearms to the tabletop. "I care about her."

"You don't care about anyone," she snaps, biting her quivering lip like she's trying to hide her trepidation. I fucking hate that we're both interested in the same woman, but while Mia isn't any good for her, I could be.

If I haven't already fucked everything up.

"I'll tell her who you really are," she threatens, her eyes narrowing to slits.

With a deep breath, I keep my temper in check. As usual, when it comes to conversations with this woman, my patience is waning. Why did I ever think I could confide in Mia? I'd hoped money could control her mouth, but maybe I was wrong.

Darting a glance at my clenched fists, she drops her hands to the Formica tabletop and relents. "I'm sorry. I wouldn't actually do that," she rushes out.

I sigh. "Any idea where she could be staying?"

She shrugs. "She's not close with her family...not that she's ever introduced me. I think she's embarrassed..." She trails off and looks away.

Grabbing her hand, I lean forward and duck my chin until she's looking at me. "Be her friend, Mi. That's what she wants from you. Be her friend."

Her green eyes soften. "You really care about her, huh?"

I release her hand and scrub at my forehead. "Yeah, I really do."

She doesn't have to ask why. Mia sees Cat just as I do. But she had her chance. Now I want mine.

She sighs. "She used to talk about some apartment in Boston she'd use when she needed to get away. She said it was empty. You could try there," she suggests. I'm on my feet before she finishes her thought. "Wait, you know where it is?" she asks, her brow furrowed.

I shrug. "Think so."

And for the first time ever, heading toward James Headquarters sends a bolt of excitement through me.

24

YELLOW BY COLDPLAY

Cat

I leave brunch stuffed and perfectly confused. Cash gives me a hug and tells me to call him later. Being the incredible brother he is, he knows something is off. And I want to talk to him. I want to confide in him. Just not yet.

I need time to wrap my head around all things Jay first.

I walk down Commonwealth Avenue, pulling my caramel tweed coat tight around me as the wind whips my long dark hair into my face. I push my hair back and stare up at the cloudy October sky. Auburn-colored leaves swirl around my booted feet as I trudge slowly toward the penthouse.

Along with burnt-orange colors and pumpkin flavors ushered in by the fall weather, I love the wardrobe. Boots and cozy jackets, a signature scarf for a pop of color. The cloudy day fits perfectly with my mood. I dig my hands into my pockets, still trying to wrap my head around Jay when I catch sight of a figure hovering outside the James building.

Our building is glass with brick accents. The glass is almost mirror-like, which gives me the opportunity to study the man's face even though he's facing the opposite direction.

Frown lines, downcast eyes, and a furrowed brow. Blond hair falling forward that he doesn't bother to brush out of his line of sight. Jeans, a black wool coat, and loafers.

"Jay," I gasp into the wind.

He looks up but doesn't turn, instead choosing to study me in the mirrored glass in the same way I studied him. As if he wants a moment to prepare himself for what he'll find when he turns around. I keep my face devoid of emotion, building barriers to keep my thoughts locked up tight. The truth is, I have no idea what I'm thinking other than *he's here. He came for me.*

And I swear to God when he turns, his face relaxes in relief. The tension around his eyes softens, and his shoulders drop, like he's been holding on to unease the same way I have. Like maybe his thoughts mirror mine, and he's thinking *she's here. She came for me.*

The wind whips again, as if signaling that *this* is the moment, the leaves lifting, caught in a vortex and blowing around me.

"You don't live in Providence anymore." It isn't a question.

His blue eyes hold mine as he shakes his head.

"But you ride the train every day."

He nods, a sigh escaping his frowning lips.

"You take the train from Boston, *where you live*, to Providence, *where I live*, to take the train back with me every day," I whisper, my head tilted in question, searching for clarification.

His lips lift in a half smile. "I'd ride the train all day if I could spend just a few minutes sparring with you."

A whoosh of air leaves my lungs. "Fuck the movies," I mutter as I walk straight into his arms.

Jay's eyes register pure surprise as I take his face in my palms. Up close, the stress the past few days has caused him is obvious. It's in the light blond scruff that tickles my fingers, the dark circles under his eyes, the red of his irises—which likely matches mine from lack of sleep. The way his hair looks like he's been running his hands through it, stressed and waiting for me to appear.

"Kitten, what are you doing?" he whispers, his attention dipping from my eyes to my lips and back again. He mimics my stance, gripping my cheeks as if he's afraid I'll pull away.

As if I would try.

I lick my lips. "Testing a theory," I reply. Then I press my mouth to his.

For a moment, neither of us moves, the fusion of our lips more than enough. But then I get curious, and I swipe against his lips with my tongue, wanting more. He groans as he opens his mouth and tilts my head for better access. Then his hands are in my hair and my arms are looped around his neck, my fingers gripping at his blond locks. Champagne flutters dance through me, and I can't help the smile that forms on my lips. Jay pulls away for a moment and studies me. "Perfect," he whispers.

My smile expands. "Hollywood style," I murmur, pulling him closer so I can kiss him again. And again. His kiss is magic. Tender. Meant for me.

Jay pulls back again, the corners of his lips turned up. "Give me a second." With that, he pulls his phone out of his pocket and presses a few buttons. Then the opening strains of a song filter through the crisp air.

The leaves swirl around us while we make out on Commonwealth Avenue on this perfectly grumpy fall day, the wind whipping at our feet. It's grays and burnt oranges. Mimosas and pumpkin lattes. It's Coldplay singing "Yellow" just for us.

25

CLOCKS BY COLDPLAY

Cat

"**S**pend the day with me," Jay says, examining me, his hands still lost in my hair, our bodies pressed together.

I smile as I soak in the sight of him, loving how his hold has me angled up so I can't get away. As if I would try. "And what does Jonathan Hanson do on Sundays?"

"Sleep," he teases, echoing my retort from weeks ago when he asked what I did on the weekends.

"Doesn't sound terrible," I admit. We could probably both use a nap.

"There will be no sleeping if I get you anywhere near a bed," he murmurs, dragging his lips against mine again in a tender kiss.

Shivers drag across my chest with that whispered promise. "While I may sleep next to you," I say, "I am not sleeping *with* you."

Jay guffaws, his breath tickling my skin. "Wouldn't dream of it." He presses his lips together and studies me, his eyes full of heat. "Okay," he finally says, "I would dream of it. In fact, I have, but if you think I made you wait forever for this kiss, just wait until you see how long I make you wait for everything else."

My eyes grow wide. "Oh, you think you'll be the one making me wait, Mr. Hanson?" I tease in response.

His smile falls a bit. "Don't call me that. Please. Just let me be Jay when I'm with you."

I understand probably better than anyone how he feels about his last name. "Sure, if you agree to stop calling me Kitten."

He laughs and shakes his head. "Never." He rakes his fingers through my hair and then drops them to my shoulders. "Where to?"

Biting my bottom lip, I look up at the tall building beside us.

He shakes his head, his eyes going round. "No fucking way."

"My stuff is inside," I say with a laugh. "Come on. Let's take a nap. Then we can pick up groceries and cook dinner together."

"You want me to spend the afternoon in the Jameses' penthouse?" he says incredulously.

I shrug with a smile. "Why not? Afraid we'll get caught?"

His eyes dance with humor, and he's holding back a grin.

"Never pegged you for a scaredy cat, Jay," I tease, tugging him by the hand and striding toward the building.

He catches up to me and wraps his arm around my shoulders before dropping a kiss to my temple. "The things I'll do for you," he mutters under his breath.

Joy bursts from somewhere deep inside me, radiating to the tips of my fingers and down to my toes. His admission and the desperation in his tone and his actions make me feel like I'm walking on air.

Sal is stationed at the desk and stands as we approach. There's no doubt he knows who Jonathan Hanson is, so I'm not surprised when he gives me a warning look, his brows creasing in concern when he catches the way Jay keeps my body tucked close to his. I send up a silent prayer that he doesn't give away who I am just yet. Jay needs to know. *Today.* I just want to be the one to tell him.

"Ms. Catherine," he says with a nod. "Heading up to the penthouse?"

I smile warmly. "Yes. Thanks, Sal. I'll see you in a bit."

He nods, and we continue on through the lobby, but before we get to the elevator, he calls, "I trust brunch with your brothers went well?"

I shoot him a scowl. He *definitely* knows who Jay is. "Perfectly," I reply, then step into the waiting elevator.

"Brothers?" Jay asks.

I nod as I press the card against the screen, and the elevator door shuts. "Three," I reply without looking at him.

He practically chokes on his surprise. "Three?" He coughs. "Geez, why did I have you pegged as an only child?"

I smirk. "Must be my bitchiness. Seemed like an entitled princess to you?" I tease.

He laughs. "I shoulda known with that right hook of yours that you had brothers."

"They do like to box," I admit before realizing my error. I'm giving away too much information too soon.

He hums thoughtfully beside me. I have a pretty good idea what he's thinking.

When the elevator doors open to the penthouse, I stroll in like I own the joint. *Newsflash, I kinda do.* "Want to watch a movie?" I ask over my shoulder, heading for the couch.

Jay doesn't follow me, instead wandering through the space, taking in all the details. "Want to go up to the roof again?" he asks, his low tone full of both hope and hesitation.

"It's a little too chilly for that today," I reply. "You're being weird."

He sighs, his shoulders slumping. "I'm trying not to be, but this isn't the easiest space to be in."

I huff out a frustrated breath. Shit. If he's uncomfortable now, I can only imagine how he'll feel when I tell him I'm Carter's younger sister. Will that be a deal breaker? On our way up, I was determined to divulge that connection, but after this reaction, I'm warring with myself about whether to rip off the Band-Aid now or wait until we've spent more time together. But keeping my true identity from him isn't fair. I have all the facts and so should he. And if it's a deal breaker, it's better I know now so

I don't get too invested.

As if I'm not already there.

That kiss left my head spinning. I still feel like I'm on cloud nine, though his mood is dangerously close to bringing me down.

"Jay, please," I hedge. "Will you sit with me for a minute? You're freaking me out."

He spins around and meets my eyes. Whatever he sees on my face has him moving my way without hesitation. Without question. Warm hands and his strong embrace comfort me. He tilts my face so I'm forced to look at him, his fingers holding me in place. "I'm sorry. This is my hang-up. I'll stop." He angles closer, his palm still flat against my cheeks, and presses his lips to mine, and I swear I see stars.

We tumble onto the couch and laugh through our kiss. I straddle him and pull back, marveling at him. "Is it always like this?" I ask, genuinely curious. Is this what it feels like to be attracted to someone? Easy and charged with emotion. Fun and heavy at the same time. I want to lick up his neck, bite his lip, rub against him until there isn't a space I haven't touched. I want to do nothing but kiss this man for the rest of the day, and I don't understand it at all.

He rakes his hands through my hair and shakes his head. "God, this is going to be fun," he murmurs as he rests his hands on either side of my neck and pulls me close, claiming my mouth again.

I lean back. "You didn't answer the question."

"Kitten, the power you're giving me is going to my head. No, it's not always like this. It's *never* like this. What I feel for you, this insane attraction, it goes so much further than wanting you. You're asking me questions as if I have all the answers, but when it comes to the way I feel for you, I'm even more inexperienced."

Talk about things going to one's head. Shit. The goofy smile on my face can't be hidden. "And what is this you feel for me?"

He leans back on the couch and rubs his hands up and down my arms.

"Fuck…" He grins. "You make me want to be someone worth knowing." He studies me, his irises blue flames of desire. "None of this impresses you?" he asks, his hands lifting and motioning around us.

I shrug. "It wasn't earned. My grandfather built this company from the ground up, but my father," I sigh in disgust, "he never had to work for it. This was his," I say softly, holding my arms out wide, still balanced on his lap. "He was given everything, and he destroyed it all. I don't want to be like that. If I ever decide to be part of this organization, I'll make my way through hard work. I want to do it on my own."

Jay's eyes cloud in confusion. "What?"

I bite my lip. "This is my father's apartment. Was. Years ago."

"And your father is…?" Jay asks with a frown, the confusion turning into a look of concern.

"Edward James."

Every molecule of air is sucked from the room as Jay freezes. Statue still, all he does is gape at me.

"Say something," I whisper.

Finally thawing, he shakes his head. "I don't understand."

"I'm Carter's sister." I swallow thickly. "This is my family's building," I say, infusing cheer into my tone, then I spell it out for him. "I'm a James."

"You're a James," he parrots, running his hands through his hair again and then staring at something over my shoulder, his face taking on a faraway expression. Then he focuses on me again, his hands landing on my hips. "You're Carter's sister? And you didn't tell me?"

I nod. "I didn't know who you were until Friday. I wasn't hiding it from you."

His jaw clenches. "You said your name was Catherine Bouvier. That sounds an awful lot like hiding the truth."

I slide off him in agitation at his implication that I intentionally withheld my identity from him. "I am Catherine Bouvier. I haven't gone by James since I was a kid. Like you, I don't want the attention the name brings."

He shakes his head. "Don't do that. Don't put this on me. Don't act like we're the same."

My skin heats as anger courses through me. I huff out an annoyed laugh. "How are we different? We both hate the attention our names garner. You never told me your last name. Not until you were forced to when we found ourselves at the same business meeting. I didn't immediately blurt out who I was because I was shocked. And then I was thrown by our lunch and the way you looked at me. And then I saw you with those women." Taking a step closer so I can glare down at him, I put my hands on my hips and ask, "*Who were they, by the way?*" The second I laid eyes on him this morning, I forgot all about Friday night and why I was angry with him to begin with.

"No one, Cat. But that really isn't the point now, is it?"

"Oh, now I'm Cat?" I ask, my heart splintering.

He heaves himself off the couch and stalks to the window, sighing heavily. "I can't do this." When he's halfway to the elevator, the image of us I'd pieced together in my mind shatters. Before we even had a chance.

"If you walk out that door, then you're right—we can't do this. Take a minute and think this through before you leave," I say with more confidence than I feel.

He stops in front of the stainless-steel door and plants one hand on the cool surface, his head hanging. Wearily, he breathes in and out several times, his chest heaving with each breath. Will he step onto the elevator and end things for good? If he walks away right now, I'm done. I won't put myself through another toxic relationship, no matter how confused he is. If we have any shot of making this work, we have to talk things out now.

"I just—" He hesitates as he slumps against the closed elevator doors. "I need a minute to wrap my head around this. Can you give me that?"

"Stay here then," I plead, tears welling in my eyes. "Take your minute here. I'll go. Just please, don't leave like this. Don't leave me here wondering what you're thinking. Wondering what you want."

He turns around and watches me, his hardened expression cracking. I don't mean to be so upset. I don't want to be so vulnerable, and I hate that he's standing witness to these damn tears. I'm so thrown by how we went from kissing each other to this. *It's just a last name.*

"If I knew what I wanted, I would tell you," he says with an edge of despair. "What I want is for you not to be a James. What I want..." He looks away from me.

"So that's it. My last name—that's a deal breaker?" I purse my lips, trying hard to control the desperation pouring from me.

He stares at me, and his shoulders sag. "I don't know."

26

CHASING CARS BY SNOW PATROL

Jay

This is a fucking nightmare. At a complete loss, I can do nothing but stare at Cat. The thoughts swirling around in my head are fucked up. This entire situation is fucked up.

How could I have not seen the writing on the wall? Why else would she hang out at the James family penthouse?

But how? How is it possible that this woman, the one I want more than I've ever wanted *anything*, is the one person I *can't* have?

There's only one thing to do right now. Be honest. Let her see my demons. Let her push me away. Because I can't walk away. I'm in too fucking deep.

But we'll never work.

This will *never* work.

"You want to know what I'm thinking?" I sneer, dreading what I'm about to do.

She stands tall and tips her chin up. This beautiful woman who doesn't rely upon her family name, who works in a coffee shop and lives in a tiny apartment with the friend who broke her heart. The woman who's trying to make it on her own laurels. She stands tall. She doesn't break before me. She's a fucking goddess.

Storming across the room, I force myself close even though being near her makes me want to take her in my arms. "I'm thinking," I say, running the backs of my fingers down her arm, watching as she shivers beneath my touch, "that you'd give me your virginity if I asked, wouldn't you, Kitten? That I want to fuck Edward James's only daughter, and you'd let me."

"Then do it," she whispers, the repulsion I expected nowhere to be found.

I scowl in disgust. "You deserve *so* much better than that."

I turn my back and heave out a long breath.

Cat grabs at my arm, but I don't turn. I can't look at her. She presses her forehead against the middle of my back, and we stand there, frozen, her heat seeping through my shirt, warming me in a way I shouldn't let it.

"You think you hate my father, but you have no idea," she says almost inaudibly. "My feelings for you have nothing to do with him, though."

I spin back, grinding my molars and staring her down. "That's my point. My feelings are now jumbled together with my *hate* for him." I put a hand to her cheek, the gentle movement in direct opposition with the anger coursing through me. "Kitten, you have no idea what you're asking of me."

She tips her chin up, those soft, sad brown eyes pleading, and my heart cracks. "You have no problem being friends with Carter, but you can't be with me?"

"I don't want to be your friend," I answer honestly. "I couldn't *just* be your friend."

Cat's face falls. She knows it too. "Please, just…" she pulls in a shaky breath, "God, I hate sounding so desperate. Just spend the day with me. If you still feel the same way in a few hours, I won't push. I'll let you go. Just…give me today?"

Every cell in my body screams at me to leave. My mind knows the right answer.

"Okay," I say, ignoring every rational thought.

"Okay?" she asks, her eyes going wide. She's just as shocked as I am by my response.

"Okay," I reply, pulling her against my chest and stealing another moment of happiness. She melts into me and exhales. How could having this woman in my arms ever be wrong?

"Let's go to the farmers' market. I think we could use the fresh air," she offers.

I nod but don't let go. Instead, I take her hand, clasping it tightly, and let her lead me out of the apartment.

KITTEN'S SONGS

We meander by every booth at the farmers' market. We share homemade waffles with powdered sugar and fresh fruit while sipping coffee and kissing between bites. Waffles, I now know, are her absolute favorite breakfast food, but she never eats them because her grandmother always told her they were messy and loaded with calories. I want to have waffles delivered to her every day just to see the smile on her face when she takes a bite. It's magic. *She's magic.*

Now the sun is dipping from the sky, reminding me that our time is almost up. We walk hand in hand, enjoying a comfortable silence unlike any I've ever had with another person.

Cat breaks the silence. "We still have to figure out the food for the ball," she reminds me.

I smile down at her. "I'll take care of it." Her shoulders droop a bit, and I wrap an arm around her and pull her close. "*With you.*" I kiss her temple. "I'll take care of it with you. Promise."

She sighs. "Okay."

"Tell me something I don't know about you," I insist, trying like hell to focus on her and not our circumstance.

Looking up, she surveys me closely, like she's memorizing my face, her lips turned to the side in thought.

"I don't like peanut butter," she says with a forceful nod.

I laugh. "*What?*"

"I think it's the texture. Or the consistency. I don't know, I'm not a fan," she says with a smile.

I can't explain why that was the perfect answer, or why I have a goofy grin on my face, but she makes the gloomy, sunless day vibrant.

"I'd have to agree with you, Kitten. Peanut butter does have a strange texture."

Her eyes dance. "Thank you!"

We continue hand in hand, wearing matching smiles. "Favorite meal?" she asks.

"Cheeseburger and iced tea," I reply easily.

She smirks. "Oh yeah, why?"

"Reminds me of a beautiful girl I shared a perfect lunch with."

"So it was about the company, not the food?" she challenges.

"Probably both. Best lunch I ever had."

We grin at one another stupidly.

"Favorite singer?" I ask.

She folds her lips, holding back a smile before she admits, "Definitely Mariah Carey."

I raise both brows at that. "Really?"

She nods. "What about you?"

"I shared the best kiss of my life while listening to Coldplay, so I'd have to say Chris Martin will forever be a favorite now."

Cat stops in her tracks, the abrupt halt yanking me back. "Really?" she asks softly, her eyes so warm and full of vulnerability.

I run my hands through her long locks, pressing closer until our bodies are flush. Spellbound by the way she's looking at me, all I can do is stare back as I reply, "Really." Then I press my lips to hers again, savoring her taste, memorizing her soft moans, the way she feels in my arms.

We kiss as if we have all the time in the world. As if there is no one in the city but us. No one exists outside this moment. If I could will this moment into forever, I would.

It's the ultimate irony that the two of us would meet in the way we did, only to be kept apart because of the actions of our parents decades ago.

Cat loops her arms around my neck and hugs me close. "Thank you for today," she whispers into my shoulder.

"A million todays would never be enough," I concede. "I don't want to say goodbye."

She smiles sadly. "Then don't. Just…you go that way, and I'll go this way," she says, pointing us in opposite directions. She leans in one more time and brushes a kiss against my lips, then she lets go and walks away.

27

LOOK AFTER YOU BY THE FRAY

Cat

Like an insane person, I show up at Carter's apartment on Sunday night. "Can I stay here?"

He takes one look at me and ushers me inside. "Sure, you can stay in Hanson's room. I'll text him and make sure he's not coming back."

With a grateful nod, I follow him into the kitchen. Jay won't be back. I don't know the reasons behind his hatred for my father, but I can't imagine he'd come back here after the way we left things today. And because I can't be with him, I'm going to lie in his bed and sleep on his pillow like a damn creep. Pathetic.

"What's going on with you and your roommate?" Carter asks after he pockets his phone. "He says it's fine, by the way. He's not coming back to Providence. Stay as long as you need."

I should be embarrassed. Now Jay knows precisely where I am, and he probably knows why I came. But I don't even care.

I shrug. "I don't know. Just need a little space."

"Want me to order food?" he offers.

I shake my head. "Nah, I'm tired." I point to the hallway with a thumb. "I'm just going to get some rest."

And lie in the bed of my would-be boyfriend. The one man I want, but the man I can't have.

I hate our father and we share DNA. I can only imagine what my father did to the Hanson family. Likely a business deal gone wrong. Nothing would surprise me. Edward James is a scab.

Carter hesitates. "I know I'm not generally who you would turn to, but if you need someone to talk to, I'm here." He regards me carefully, seriously, his eyes soft but full of worry, a small frown marring his face. I don't think I've seen him wear such a pensive expression since we were kids. Our mother's death affected us all differently. Carter hides his pain behind a flippant personality. After we lost her, everything became surface level for him. His heart broke so thoroughly from her loss that he couldn't handle letting anyone else in.

I offer him a small smile. "I appreciate it. But I just need sleep. I promise."

"It's the first door on the left," he offers, holding an arm out, palm open.

Nodding, I hoist my overnight bag higher on my shoulder and take a deep breath before trudging down the hall and pushing open Jay's door. This may be the most ridiculous thing I've ever done, but I refuse to overthink it. Instead, I slip off my clothes, slide under his covers, and snuggle into his pillow.

And then I cry myself to sleep.

KITTEN'S SONGS

Monday morning, I foolishly scour the train platform for a blond man in a suit with a smirk and an extra coffee in hand.

He's not here.

Why would he be?

With my headphones on and iPod in hand, I click on Kitten's Songs and listen to the four he uploaded over the last two weeks on repeat.

DIRTY TRUTHS

At the office, Dexter is propped up against Sophie's desk while the two of them have their heads tipped close and talk in low voices, smiling at one another. It's adorable and, oddly, not as heartbreaking as one would expect after yesterday's events.

"Good morning, beautiful Cat," Sophie singsongs.

Dexter straightens. "I'll let you catch up. Have a good day." His eyes heat as they roam over her once more, and then he walks off.

I squeal. "That looked promising."

Sophie tries hard to school her smile, but her elation is so intense it can't be contained. "He is something else. How was your weekend?" she asks, studying me with a hip propped against her desk.

So much has happened since I left her standing at the bar with Dexter on Friday. For all she knows, I spent the weekend in bed with Jay. If only that alternate reality were true.

I shake my head. "We ended it." It sounds so foolish out loud. There was nothing to end. *We were nothing.* But nothing doesn't keep a person up at night. Nothing doesn't haunt every thought. One doesn't curl into nothing's bed and dream of only him.

We were everything and yet nothing at all.

Sophie jumps up and pulls me into her arms. "What? Why?"

I hug her close, happy to have someone to fall apart against. "I'm a James, and he's a Hanson. In the end, it was just too much to move past."

She pulls back, keeping hold of my upper arms. "But he's your brother's friend."

"It's not the same as dating. I think we both know this could be the real deal. Why start something if it can go nowhere?"

I understand Jay's reasoning. I've distanced myself from my father's name, but I'll always be his daughter.

"That's ridiculous. Why can't Jameses and Hansons be together? This isn't *Romeo and Juliet.*"

With an eye roll, I huff a sardonic laugh. "Our companies are direct competitors. And our fathers hate each other. I thought that since Carter and Jay were friends, they'd moved past that, but I've never really kept up with the family business or any of that drama. But Jay works with his father. He'll take over their company. I get why he's more invested in this feud than I am. And as much as I want to see where things go with him, I refuse to beg for any man's attention."

Sophie purses her lips and watches me for another minute, and then she smiles. "Good. We'll go for drinks after work, and then you'll sleep over."

For a moment, I consider declining, yearning for another night in Jay's bed. Just one more night of wallowing. But instead, I straighten and force a smile. "Sounds good. Thanks."

"Now," Sophie says, holding up a red cashmere scarf and a green one, "tell me: which do you like better?"

I grab at them in excitement. "Oh, is this for the Christmas list?"

Sophie hums as she settles back in her seat.

"God, you are so lucky to be working on this. When I was in high school I would stalk this list every year! Are you loving testing all the products at home?"

Sophie shrugs. "Some of them."

Narrowing my eyes, I study her. She's acting strange. "What do you mean some of them?"

"I can't use a lot of this stuff, Cat," she says evenly, but she can't hide the undercurrent of hurt in her tone.

"What?" I ask, confused. "What else is on the list?"

Sophie points to her desk.

Shuffling closer, I peek at the printout full of items and the handful of samples scattered beside it. Makeup, fasting drinks, miracle teas, jewelry, belts, hair products—you name it, and the list has it. Or, as Sophie so aptly pointed out without actually using the words, you name it, and the magazine has it for white women. *Skinny* white women.

"What do you use for your hair?"

Sophie turns to me, a hand on one hip and her expression nonplussed. "Don't do that."

"Don't do what?" I ask, my forehead creasing.

"Think you can change things. We work at a fashion magazine, Cat. Not the Washington Post."

I huff out an annoyed laugh. "Just answer the damn question."

Sophie lists exactly what she uses, from shampoo to styling.

"And how long did it take you to find those products?"

She huffs. "I don't know. Are you writing a dissertation on this or what?"

I shrug. "Never mind. I'm not even working on this. It was just a thought."

Sophie softens. "Okay. Tell me what you're thinking."

"It's just…In high school, I was always dying to get my hands on Jolie magazine. This edition in particular. And look," I say, picking up the sample packet of Slim Quick tea. "This is what we're selling to teenagers. We're telling them that in order to be perfect, likable, desirable, they have to use stuff like this. It's just…" I look away, feeling foolish. I don't know what it's like to be like Sophie. To have almost no representation in the marketing world and very limited products tailored to her needs.

"We work at a fashion magazine, Cat," Sophie says again, this time her shoulders slump and her tone contains less bite.

"Right, but more women who *don't* look like her," I say, pointing to the beautiful woman on our September cover, "read our magazine than do. Shouldn't the list include items for every kind of woman?"

Sophie shrugs. "That's not what sells magazines."

I hum in agreement. "Maybe," I say as an idea forms in my head. "But can you do me a favor?"

Sophie smiles. "Sure."

"Can you make me a list of your favorite products, things you've tested yourself and use regularly? And also a list of things that have been a waste of money?"

"For Black girls, you mean?" Sophie asks.

I shrug. "Yeah. I can come up with a list of diets that don't work. And workouts and fad teas," I say, holding up the one in my hand. "But I don't have any experience with your hair or skin. Soph, what I know about all of this is limited to what I've read in magazines."

Her eyes soften. What's left unsaid is what is always left unsaid. My understanding, when it comes to so many things in life, is derived from what I've gleaned from resources like Jolie. Because I don't have a mother. Because I didn't have anyone to teach me what makeup to use or how to insert a tampon. The staff at my grandparents' home were kind and guided me when I needed help, but I'm sure they felt just as uncomfortable as Sophie does right now.

And if this were just about me, I'd drop it. But Sophie's right; this magazine caters to one distinct group of people. Yet it's consumed by so many. Wouldn't it be nice if others were reflected in its pages too?

"This is foolish, isn't it?"

Sophie smiles. "No, Cat, it's really not," she murmurs. Then, with renewed excitement, she says, "I'll make you a list. And in the meantime, we can test out some of this stuff."

KITTEN'S SONGS

Every night for the next week, we grab dinner, laugh, and talk for hours. Then her mother joins us for a glass of wine, and we fill her in on our days. Mia has stopped texting to ask when I'm coming home. I don't even know why I'm not talking to her. Maybe it's because I know she'll force me to talk about Jay, and I'm just not ready for that.

When I'm not at school or Jolie, I work on the plans for the masquerade ball. I have to coordinate with charities, review linens selections, flowers arrangements, and theme possibilities. I refuse to dwell on the lack of menu.

Jay promised we'd choose it together, but I'm not holding my breath. I haven't heard a word from him in five days, so I can't imagine any of his promises stand.

It's almost like the month of September was a dream. A crack in reality. A peek through a whirling vortex. The scene on the other side of what could have been, but never will be. I'm probably romanticizing our moments together because our connection was so forbidden. Were we not who we are, it probably would have been a two-week fling, if that. He would have tired of me quickly and moved on to his next hookup. It's better this way.

Or so I tell myself.

"Daddy asked if we wanted to go out tonight," Sophie says as she plops down beside me and hands me a coffee.

I roll my eyes. "You have to stop calling him that." Though I feign annoyance at the way she refers to Dexter, I can't help but break out in a fit of laughter.

Sophie joins in, and once we've calmed enough to speak coherently again, she says, "You can stay at my house tonight, but I'll probably end up at his. Do you mind?" Sophie is wearing red today, and she looks gorgeous. Dexter is going to be hard all day if he sees her before we go out.

"I'm good, Soph, I promise." I give her an encouraging smile. "Cynthia asked me to be in her office at ten. I'll see you later?"

"Bye, babe."

I hurry into the bathroom, smooth my skirt, and apply gloss to my lips. In the mirror, I study my reflection. My grandmother has always sworn I'm a carbon copy of my mother. I've seen pictures, and the resemblance really is striking. Cash and I look like her, whereas Carter is my father to a T, and Chase is…well, he's a mixture of both of his parents. But we don't talk about his mother. The affair happened after my mom died, and his has never been in the picture.

Growing up without a mother was hard on us all. But at least Carter had Mom until he was nine. I can recall snapshots of time with her. Her smell. Her laugh. But I don't know what she was like. Who she was. I wonder what she would think of my job. From the pictures I've seen, her beauty appeared effortless, and she was the epitome of fashion. I can't imagine she would condone the diets or the teas. From what little I do remember, she enjoyed lying in bed, snuggling with us kids. Dancing around the kitchen, laughs, smiles, comfort.

Before I can get misty-eyed, I halt that train of thought. I have a job to do and a boss to impress. After one last glance in the mirror, I pull my shoulders back and head to Cynthia's office.

Rose is perched in one of the guest chairs when I step inside. I give her a friendly smile as I drop carefully into the chair beside her and am met with a blank stare in return. Miraculously, I manage to hold in my eye roll. She's the stereotypical assistant to the editor at a fashion magazine. Straight down to the willowy frame and resting bitch face.

"Catherine, how has your week been?" Cynthia asks from across the desk.

Realizing I've been caught staring at Rose, I place my hands over my lap and fold my ankles like my grandmother taught me. "Great, good—I mean, everything has been fine."

She smiles. "Excellent. Mr. Hanson mentioned that the kitchen couldn't accommodate you last week, so he scheduled a tasting for today. They're expecting you at twelve."

I have to hold back a jolt at the mention of his name. "Wonderful. That will take care of all the big things for the masquerade, then."

"Yes, I'm impressed with how quickly you've moved through all the tasks. It's actually why I wanted to talk to you. Aside from the Hanson thing."

Hanson thing? Shit. Does she know about us? Did he say something? That bastard.

Out of the corner of my eye, I catch Rose inspecting me. She's likely ready to dance in excitement over the way I'm squirming.

I clear my throat and sit a little straighter. "Hanson thing?"

"Lunch," Cynthia replies, quirking a brow.

"Oh, right." God, I'm an idiot.

"Anyway. Every spring, I take two interns with me to Paris. We work from our office there through May. A few of those who have traveled with me have even been hired by Jolie Paris."

My toes dance in my pumps at the mere thought of Paris in the spring. Working there, exploring, even living there. More than anything, I long for a fresh start.

"That's amazing," I breathe out.

Rose frowns but doesn't join in on the conversation.

"Anyway, I've been watching you. I'm impressed, so keep up the good work."

"I've actually been working with Sophie Parsons on something as well," I say, pressing my lips together and scooting to the edge of my seat.

Cynthia raises her brow and leans forward, but Rose's frown only deepens.

"It has to do with the Christmas list," I explain.

Rose scoffs, "You're not to be working on that."

I turn to her. "You're right. It's something I've been toying with after hours," I explain, looking to Cynthia.

Without a word, she dips her chin, signaling me to proceed.

"It's just that, several interns have been tasked with testing products that, well"—I take a deep breath and get to the point—"they're geared toward white girls…and if I'm being completely honest, *skinny* white girls."

In my periphery, I swear Rose's eyes bulge, and she opens her mouth, likely to defend her boss.

But Cynthia merely twists her lips and nods. "You're not wrong. But what does your project have to do with that?" she challenges.

"We would like to add items that would be beneficial to a wider audience. Not just one subset of women." I swallow, afraid I've overstepped and sabotaged my chance at Paris.

Cynthia examines me for a few moments, and just as Rose opens her mouth to speak again, she finally nods. "Okay. Submit your list to me next week. If I'm impressed, I'll pass it along to the junior editors to vet."

Although my instinct is to stand and do a happy dance, I temper my excitement and simply smile. "Thank you so much. I'll work with Sophie on it this weekend."

She nods. "Enjoy lunch."

I stand at her dismissal and shoot Rose a winning smile.

Instead of responding in a similar manner, all she does is narrow her eyes.

"Have a good day, Rose," I say sweetly, then I stride out of the office.

28

CHASING PAVEMENTS BY ADELE

Cat

"**S**he really wants to see it?" Sophie asks again, shocked.

I dragged Sophie downstairs for a cup of coffee and a gossip session before I have to head to lunch with Jay. Thank God for the excitement over Cynthia's interest in our Christmas list. Otherwise, I'd be panicking about how the next couple of hours will go.

"Yes, Soph." I take a sip of the perfect pumpkin spice latte and sigh. "And she mentioned Paris. Paris! She takes two interns every spring," I whisper, because I'm not sure that's public knowledge.

Her eyes bulge. "I thought you were crazy when you suggested expanding the list. I figured Cynthia would shoot you down before you even finished the pitch. But maybe you're onto something. Can you imagine?"

I smile so big my nose scrunches. "Honestly, I'm more excited about this than the potential of being chosen for the Paris trip."

She hits me in the arm. "Shut up! Let's do both!"

I laugh. Yeah, let's shoot for the moon.

KITTEN'S SONGS

My anxiety finally spikes as I walk into the Beacon Hotel, prepared to meet Jay.

I give my name to the maître d', and he smiles as he leads me to the table. "Mr. Hanson should be here shortly," he tells me.

With a curt nod, I settle in to wait. It's Friday, so the lunch crowd is a little on the rambunctious side. Most people have drinks in hand, likely getting their weekends started early. Not me, though. I need all my faculties when it comes to Jay.

The waitress delivers an iced tea, and I bite back a smile. Asshole ordered for me already.

I squeeze the lemon and then take a sip, closing my eyes as I do. I'm taken back to the front porch of our house in Bristol. I was probably four, cuddled on my mom's lap, baby Cash was lying on her shoulder, and Carter was playing baseball with my grandfather in the yard.

My phone buzzes, and I wince.

> Jay: Running late. I ordered food. Enjoy.

I close my eyes and breathe. I'm not going to let him get to me. He doesn't want to have lunch with me, fine. I can eat alone.

The waitress arrives with a large tray. "Mr. Hanson ordered two of everything."

My eyes bulge at the assortment, and I'm not the only one taking in the sight. The women at the table beside me look on with pity in their eyes, likely thinking I've been stood up. And I suppose I have.

On second thought, I don't want to eat alone. And I don't have to. I pick up my phone and make a call. Then I shoot Jay a text.

> Thanks. My date and I will enjoy. Have a good day, Mr. Hanson.

29

BITTERSWEET SYMPHONY BY THE VERVE

Jay

The week has been unbearably long. Knowing Cat slept in my bed on Sunday night made it nearly impossible not to show up at the train station on Monday. But I couldn't. She asked me not to say goodbye; she asked me, instead, to walk away. And if I'd shown up, then I risked being forced to say it. A man can only walk away so many times.

I've gone in circles over our situation and the roadblocks that keep us apart. In the end, one thing remains clear: I can't go through with my father's revenge plan. Not if it means Cat could get hurt in the process. Even peripherally.

Her father and my mother made choices years ago, and we've paid for their actions. I lost my mother, and according to Cat, she has no relationship with her father. I have to believe some part of that had to do with his affairs. I refuse to make her pay for her father's actions any more than she already has.

And I'm done suffering for my mother's.

But convincing my father that the past should be left there won't be an easy task. And bringing Cat into my life—and giving him the opportunity to use her to hurt her family—isn't a risk I'm willing to take.

Which leaves me sitting at the bar, like a coward, watching her sit by herself. I wince at the sheer assortment of food that arrives. What was I thinking? Two of everything? She's going to be so pissed.

I glance at the text I sent her and wonder if she'll even reply. She smiles at the waitress and then picks up her phone.

Mine doesn't ring.

Her eyes light up, and she speaks into the phone briefly. Then she holds the phone in front of her, probably ending the call. Instead of putting the device on the table or back in her purse, she types something, her thumbs moving quickly over the keys.

When my phone buzzes in my hand, I freeze.

> Kitten: Thanks. My date and I will enjoy. Have a good day, Mr. Hanson.

She and her date will enjoy it? *That's* how she's going to respond? I have half a mind to walk over right now and demand to know who she's meeting. But then I might miss seeing the fucker show up.

I slap my hand against the bar, forcing myself to stay here, where she can't easily spot me.

At my outburst, the bartender looks up. "Mr. Hanson, need another drink?"

I run my thumb over my bottom lip as I watch her. "Yes, another iced tea, please."

What I need is whiskey. Something strong to take the edge off. But I want to be completely present. Alcohol will only blur my feelings and my emotional reaction.

This isn't her fault. She didn't do this.

Repeating that over and over doesn't minimize the desire to throw my glass at the wall, thinking about how someone else will get to admire her curves in that black skirt. Someone else will get to kiss those lips and hold her tight.

I wallow in my anger for a solid ten minutes before a woman approaches her table.

I study them as they talk and eat and laugh, dying to know whether this woman is truly a date or a friend but simultaneously dreading the answer to that question.

"Do you want to order something?" the bartender asks.

Fuck this. Why am I hiding in the corner? If she's moved on, then we can at least be friends. Anything is better than nothing at this point. It's only been a week, and not having her in my life period feels exponentially worse than watching her with someone else. I can sit with her and enjoy lunch.

Right, it's not at all about her date.

"I'm good, thanks. Just put this all on my tab, please."

The man nods, and I slide my chair back quickly. So quickly that I don't see the woman passing behind me with the tray.

"Shit!" the woman screams as all the drinks slide off the tray and right into my lap.

"Oh my God. Mr. Hanson, are you okay?" the bartender says, grabbing for a stack of towels behind the bar.

The cold liquid seeps into my pants, sodas and wine, mixed drinks and waters. I'm just lucky there weren't any fucking hot drinks.

"It's fine," I say, taking the towel from his outstretched hand and wiping at my pants. Looking back at Cat's table, I catch sight of her staring at me, her lips folded, as if she's trying to hold back a laugh. I shrug and drop my head, letting out a chuckle.

I'm soaking wet, my dick is shriveling from the ice-cold drinks, I've caused a scene, and I'm smiling because I made her laugh.

The fuck is wrong with me?

I look back up and meet her mischievous gaze. She loves this.

"Can I buy you a drink?" I shout like a lunatic.

She all-out guffaws, and even though she shakes her head, I make a beeline for her. When I reach her table, I slide out a vacant chair and sit. "Enjoy the show?" I grin, my hair falling into my eyes.

She takes a deep breath and schools her features. "You're late."

"And you replaced me rather quickly," I say, the double meaning clear.

She smiles wickedly as she grabs the hand of the girl seated beside her. "This is Sophie. *My Sophie.*"

The woman with dark skin, big honey brown eyes, and curly raven hair cocks a brow at Cat and mouths something I don't catch. "Yes, her Sophie," she enunciates, turning back to me with a harsh glimmer in her eye. "And you are?"

I hold out my hand. "Jay."

"Oh, don't be so modest, Mr. Hanson," Cat urges as Sophie grips my hand tightly. "This is Jonathan Hanson, the man, the myth, *and* the legend," she says with a bite. "He's the one who ordered all this food for us."

I cringe at the extravagant spread. It really is ridiculous. There isn't a spot of fabric to be found. Plates and bowls and platters cover every inch.

"It's good, I hope?"

Swiping at a lobster rangoon, Sophie chimes in. "It's delicious. You have to try one of these." The woman's hard eyes don't leave mine as she stuffs the whole thing in her mouth.

I grab one and hold it up like I'm toasting them with it, and Cat glowers at me. Then I slip it into my mouth and hum. "Delicious."

"Awfully chipper for a man with a cold dick," Cat quips, practically making me choke.

I reach for a glass of water on the table and clear my throat. "I've taken a lot of cold showers this week, knowing a certain someone was sleeping in my bed." I raise my brow.

With that comeback, she finally has the decency to blush.

"You slept in his bed?" Sophie snaps, her shrewd attention finally leaving me and darting to Cat.

196

Fuck, maybe they really are together.

Cat huffs. "It was a weak moment. We don't need your input, Mr. Hanson. I'm sure you're far too busy to pick out food with the likes of me. Wouldn't want you to be seen chatting with a member of the James family."

I scrutinize Sophie, waiting for her reaction to the truth behind Cat's identity. But she doesn't bat an eye. She more or less tips her head in my direction like she's ready to see what I'll volley back at the woman who clearly has her claws out.

"I'm here, aren't I?" I'm soaking wet, and she clearly doesn't want me anywhere near her, so I'm not sure why I'm fighting to share a meal with her. But I love to spar with her. So much.

She shrugs and turns to Sophie as if I'm invisible. "We should add that cocoa cream you love to the list," she says, her expression finally losing its edge.

Sophie grins. "Good idea." She pulls her phone from her purse and her thumbs fly across the screen. "What about that chocolate my mom mentioned last night? We could pick some up before we go out tonight."

"You're going out?" I ask.

Cat doesn't respond, and her focus never leaves the woman beside her.

I turn my attention to Sophie, staring until she squirms. "Um, yeah, with some friends." The second the words are out of her mouth, she jolts and squeaks. "Ow!" she says, leaning down and rubbing her leg. She glares at Cat, then she turns to me, and that glare turns into a smirk. "We're going to Rebel."

Cat folds her arms and sits back, glowering at us both.

"Aw, Kitten. Don't be so upset. Now I'll leave you and your date alone to enjoy lunch. I have to go get cleaned up and get some rest before our big night."

She shakes her head as I smile at her and stand.

"Sophie, it was lovely meeting you. Kitten, I'll see *you* later." I wink and turn before she can reply.

I've got my in. Now I just have to figure out what I'm going to do with it.

30

EVERLONG BY FOO FIGHTERS

Cat

Why, why, why, Sophie?

And why does Jay care where we're going, anyway? I don't hear from him for a week, then he summons me to a restaurant, only to stand me up. Except he actually was there. Just what, avoiding me? Watching me? Until he realized I wasn't alone. Then he plops down and butts into our conversation and freaking invites himself out with us tonight.

All while soaking wet, of course, which was the only bright spot of our interaction. When he pushed himself into the server and the sodas and wines toppled over in what felt like slow motion and landed spectacularly all over his pants, I felt nothing but pure joy.

It was perfect.

And so deserved.

"I swear, Soph. If he shows up with a date—or two, since that's clearly his MO—I'm going to murder you." I give the universal sign for slicing her throat.

The traitor just smiles serenely. "I thought he was rather charming."

"A snake can be charming as it slithers up to you, but it's still a snake." Glaring at her in the mirror, I apply my lipstick. Red. Not kissable.

"Why are you so mad at him, anyway?" she asks. "You were all 'oh, I understand where he's coming from' on Monday."

"That was before he stood me up at lunch. If he had been an adult and just shown up, or ya know, if he hadn't arranged the entire thing to begin with, I would understand. But this is a game. If he thinks he's going to get in my pants and then walk away, he has another thing coming. I was interested in him. Not his cock."

She arches a brow. "You sure about that?"

"Shut it." I storm to the couch to the tinkling sound of her laughter. "Come on, let's get this night over with."

KITTEN'S SONGS

Two hours later, after a ride in a cab that smelled like takeout, standing in line, and fighting for drinks at the bar, we're settled at a table in a corner of the room, sipping our cocktails and relaxing. Who am I kidding? Relaxation is a fantasy right now. Because Jay could show up at any minute.

Or worse, he could not show up at all.

It would have been better if he hadn't materialized at all today. But now he's got my mind all jumbled as to what it wants. As to what *I* want.

Sophie's eyes dance as she gives me a once-over for what's got to be the tenth time since we got here. "He's going to shit himself when he sees you."

Damn right. I paired a black skater skirt with a white T-shirt that exposes my stomach. I'm wearing black suspenders and a garter belt attached to black thigh-high stockings with a beautiful lace design at the top. A pair of killer knee-high black boots with the classic red sole complete the outfit. I feel like I could chew him up and spit him out. And I'm not going to lie, the idea of walking over him in these heels is far too tempting.

But none of it matters if he doesn't show up.

The cherry on top, though, is the blond wig Sophie had Dexter bring home from one of his photo shoots. It's giving me a bit of a Heather Locklear vibe, especially paired with this absurd outfit.

Eh, who am I kidding? I look fucking hot.

My phone lights up in my hand.

> Jay: Send me the name of the club. I tried the place Sophie mentioned, but I think she gave me the wrong name.

My chest tightens. Do I really want to see him tonight?

Before I can chicken out, I gulp down my drink, close my eyes, and send him a pin of my location.

Jay's response is immediate.

> Jay: You're really at Rebel? You're not just fucking with me?

I laugh uncomfortably and wave my phone in front of Sophie. "Why does he think I'm fucking with him?"

Sophie's legs are draped across Dexter's lap, and he has one arm around her as he speaks to the guy beside him. She shrugs and taps him on the shoulder, whispering something in his ear. When he responds, Sophie's entire body tenses. "Seriously?" she shouts so loud I can hear her over the music.

Dexter eyes me and then looks back at Sophie with a devilish grin before whispering in her ear again.

"What?" I finally shout, moving closer so I can find out what the actual fuck is going on.

Sophie sighs and glares at Dexter again. She hands me back my phone, and before she can fill me in, another text from Jay pops up.

Jay: Cat, are you seriously at a fucking sex club?

I frown in confusion, then burst out laughing. "Oh, this is too good!" I shout as I turn the phone to Sophie, still laughing. What an absolute idiot.

Sophie bites her lip. "Upstairs," she says, pointing to the open area above our heads. The entire space is bordered with balconies and windows.

"Upstairs, what?" I hiss, my nerves getting the best of me.

"People are"—she pauses, her eyes widening comically, and points up again—"up there."

"People are what up there, Soph? Use your words."

She chews on her lip and cringes.

"People are fornicating upstairs?" I ask in exasperation.

Dexter bursts out laughing. "Fornicating?"

"You, be quiet." Sophie smacks him.

He bites at her shoulder and grins wickedly before whispering in her ear again. This time, goose bumps pebble her arms.

I scrub my hand over my face. "I hate you both. You invited Jay. To a *sex club*. He probably thinks you did it for me. That I want to—" I bite my thumb as I scream into my hand. "Fuck!"

Another text comes through.

Jay: Cat, answer me!

Oh, screw him.

31

MR. BRIGHTSIDE BY THE KILLERS

Jay

I'm going to kill her. She is not seriously inside this place. Hands fisted at my sides, I glare at the entrance to the club. From out here on the sidewalk, the building blends in with the other brick structures surrounding it, but I know this place. I've *been* to this place. With the guys. I didn't recognize the name until I was standing out front.

There is no way in hell Cat's here. And if she is, like I said, I'm going to kill her.

I stare down at my phone with the pinged address and look back up at the building. I'm in the right place.

Fuck.

Passing a hundred to the bouncer, I skip the line. A few guys groan when I head for the door, but I don't spare them a glance. I'm on a mission. I have half a mind to text Carter and tell him where his sister is. But then I'd have to explain how I know her and why her presence here pisses me off so goddamn much.

It shouldn't piss me off so damn much. She shouldn't matter to me. I'm a fool if I think I'm only here trying to be her friend. We can't be fucking friends because no matter what I tell myself the feelings swirling through my body, the way my skin heats at the thought of her, the way my fists clench at the idea that someone else could touch her, none of that is fucking friendly. I've never felt this way about another person, and pretending the feelings aren't real isn't going to change the fact that I'm fucking gone for her.

She's the last person I should want and yet I can't stay away.

My eyes adjust to the dark space, and I scan the bar area for Cat's tall frame. When I don't spot her, I continue forward. The room is dimly lit with a haze of red. The bass thumps, and bodies mold together on the dance floor. Downstairs, it's like any other club. Upstairs? Well, I know what to expect.

Rooms with toys, ropes, curtains that hide nothing, and the sounds of pleasure echoing from every corner. It's seedy and the last place I want to imagine finding Cat.

I finally set my sights on a spot in the corner where her friend is curled up on a man's lap. The guy has to be in his forties. He's got mostly silver hair with a sprinkling of black finding its way through. His fingers are inching up under her skirt, and she's leaning back while he nibbles on her neck.

"Where's Cat?" I demand, hovering over them, my arms crossed over my chest to keep from pounding them on the table.

They both jolt to attention, and Sophie pulls her skirt down to hide her thick thighs. Her eyes are hazy from what I hope is only alcohol. "Huh?" she asks, pulling herself up straighter.

"*Where's Cat?*" I grit out, enunciating each word.

The man, who's still got an arm wrapped around her, interjects, "Who the hell are you?"

Sophie grabs his arm. "That's her Jay. Her *Mr. Hansonnn*," she says, drawing out my last name in mock awe.

Fuck, she's useless. Fortunately, my *don't fuck with me* face works on her friend, and he gives me the answer I'm looking for. "She went to explore," he says with a cheeky grin.

Or maybe not the answer I'm looking for at all.

Explore? Alone? Here? As in explore the sex club upstairs, or just explore the dance floor?

Once again, the guy reads my mind. "She was curious." He points upstairs.

Fuck. Covering my face with my hand, I let out a groan.

"Have fun," he says with a wink.

Yeah, if Cat is anywhere near as drunk as her friend, this is going to be the exact opposite of fun. I swear if anyone has laid a finger on her, I'll burn the entire building down.

Never in my life have I cared about another person in this way. Especially not a woman. She's not even mine, and I'm losing my mind over the thought of anyone touching her. Of anyone hurting her.

I close my eyes and pinch the bridge of my nose. Before I do anything, I need to calm the hell down. Getting caught in a sex club is bad enough for a board member. Getting caught beating the shit out of someone in a sex club would be significantly worse.

I pull my phone from my pocket.

> I'm here. Where are you?

Please be in the bathroom.

All I get back is a wink emoji.

"Fuck," I growl. What do I say to that?

Another text comes through.

> Kitten: Let's play a little game.

Another groan escapes as my dick decides it wants in on the fun. I adjust myself and text back.

> What kind of game?

> Kitten: A little game of cat and mouse.

Though I want nothing more than to find her and get us both out of here, I can't help but smile.

> You do realize you're the mouse in this game, right, Kitten?

> Kitten: We'll see about that.

With renewed purpose, I head to the elevator. The bouncer looks me up and down and frowns.

"My girlfriend is upstairs," I tell him. The words slipping from my lips too easily.

"You gonna get in a fight?" he asks.

I make a face. *Is that normal here?* "No. She told me to meet her up there. We're playing a little game," I add.

He nods like that makes total sense—and, of course, it does, because once again, we're in a sex club—and he motions for me to enter the elevator.

Moments later, the elevator doors open, and I'm met by hallways lit only by rope lights on the floor and the sounds of music mixed with moans. I slip my phone out of my pocket and call Cat. A phone rings down the hall when I do, so I stride toward the sound.

"You're cheating," she whispers.

I laugh with relief, knowing she's close. "You really want to hide from me up here?"

She hums into the phone. I can picture her biting her lip as she finally replies, "Yes, I think I do."

"Then you better be ready to run."

32

SECRET BY MAROON 5

Cat

I stare at the black screen of my phone. He hung up on me. I press myself against the wall, breathing deeply. Time to make a plan.

The low thrum of the music matches the pulse between my legs and the beating of my heart. It's exhilarating. With this wig, no one will recognize me, and I'm wandering the halls of a place I have no business being. My thighs clench in anticipation at the moans of ecstasy coming from a woman nearby. And when his heavy footsteps sound down the hall, I practically squeal in excitement.

Stopping at the first door I come to, I twist the knob and brace myself for what I might find. Fortunately, door number one leads to nothing but another hallway. At the quickening of his footsteps behind me, I sprint toward the end.

"Oh, Kitten," he purrs, his pace slow, like he has all the time in the world. Like he knows he'll eventually get what he wants.

I dip behind a nearby curtain in hopes of avoiding being caught so soon. As I spin around, a man growls "on your knees," and I practically faint.

Before I can react, a hand clamps around my mouth and pulls me backward. I bite and nip and attempt to kick.

"Shh, Kitten, I got you," he murmurs in my ear.

The man in front of me, I now realize, is talking to someone else. And she's now dropped to her knees. In front of her is another woman who's sitting on a throne—an actual *throne*—her legs spread wide.

I swear my eyes pop out of my head. *What. The. Fuck?*

"Now what?" the woman on her knees practically pants, her attention fixed dutifully on the man towering over her.

"Crawl to her," he directs.

The woman doesn't hesitate. She places her palms on the floor and inches forward, her hips swaying as she does. The woman on the throne has hair so dark it's almost black and supple red lips. Her smoky eyes are trained on the redhead crawling to her in light pink lace lingerie, her creamy white ass exposed for both of her partners to enjoy.

Without permission, a moan escapes from deep in my throat. At the sound, Jay pulls me back until we're hidden behind the curtain but with a view of the actions playing out on the other side.

"Is this what you want, Kitten? You want to watch?" he murmurs against my neck, nipping at my skin and making me whimper an involuntary yes.

When the woman reaches the throne, she turns back to look at the man. As she does, her eyes meet mine and light up in excitement. She wants an audience.

And I want to watch.

What the hell is wrong with me?

"She likes it too," Jay whispers.

I arch into him, desperate to know if he's as affected by the scene as I am.

He chuckles against my ear, knowing exactly what I'm doing, his fingers raking through the strands of the wig. "Blond? Really?"

I lean back so I can look at him. "That's what you like, isn't it?" I whisper, challenge in my tone.

He locks eyes with me, his expression hard, and shakes his head. "What I like is you. Blond, brunette, fucking panting over two women together, whatever you like, Kitten. However you are, that's what I want."

I bite my lip, and he pushes my chin so I'm facing the show again. "Eyes over there. I know what you like."

I want to protest, but when his hand skates down my chest, pausing at my nipple, where he squeezes until I buck against him, he's forced to clamp a hand over my mouth to silence me again. We both know exactly what I want.

The redhead is between the other woman's legs, her tongue drawing languid circles against her clit, causing her to throw her head back against the throne in ecstasy. And the man strokes himself as he watches, twisting his wrist with each upward stroke.

It's obscene.

"This is what you like," I say against Jay's hand. "Two women."

He slips a hand between my legs and slides his finger under my panties, making me hiss in surprise. His other hand presses harder against my lips. "Sweetheart, I'm not the only one enjoying the show. But I promise, this"—he bucks his hips against my ass so I feel every inch of his hard length—"is *all* because of you."

I whimper again as he presses his middle finger inside me, both of us groaning as he discovers just how wet I am. I crane my neck so I can look him in the eye as he pumps his finger in and out, driving me wild. He releases the hand covering my mouth and fixates on my lips, never slowing his movements.

"No man has ever touched me," I arch back and whisper against his mouth, knowing it will drive him to the brink.

It's driving me to the brink.

I have a feeling he's going to take all my firsts.

His eyes turn molten, and he slams his lips to mine, working his fingers inside me faster while his palm presses against my clit. Draping my arms over his shoulders behind me, I deepen the kiss and ride the wave of pleasure he's so expertly choreographing.

The sounds of the woman on the throne crying out mix with my own cries, and I don't even care. While he continues his assault between my legs, he slips his free hand under my shirt until he's cupping my breast through my bra and tweaking my nipple again. The move sends an explosion rocketing through my body, forcing a loud moan from my lips, despite his attempts to silence me with his mouth.

I come so hard I bite down on his lip, my body falling limp against his and my knees practically giving out.

"Care to join us?" one of the women calls.

I can't pull my attention away from Jay long enough to make sense of her question, let alone respond. He shakes his head at me, then pulls me back and murmurs an apology. Before we're out of view, I take one more peek at the throuple on the other side of the curtain. At that exact moment, the man slams into the girl in pink. She's still on her knees, with her head between the other woman's legs once more. The woman in black, the one poised so regally on the throne, bites her lip and grabs the redhead's long tresses, arching into her mouth as her head falls back and she screams through her release.

"Holy fuck," I whisper as Jay chuckles against my neck.

"Come on, Kitten. Game's over." He slips his hand into mine and leads me down the hall.

We make it three steps before I push him into the wall. For a moment, he just stares at me, but then a slow grin spreads across his face. He pushes the blond hair behind my ear and murmurs, "Hi, beautiful."

My breath hitches at his words. At the truth behind them. This isn't a *you look beautiful* moment. He truly believes I am. "Hi," I whisper back. "Are you really here?"

Angling closer, he kisses me without warning, his soft lips pressing against mine, his tongue licking at the seam until I let him in with a groan. One hand snakes its way up to my cheek, and he holds me as he pulls back and hits me with the warmest smile I think I've ever received. "I'm really here."

"Are you going to walk away from me again?" I ask, afraid of the answer but determined to be prepared.

Needing to be prepared.

Jay shakes his head. "No, Kitten. Your family will have to chase me away. I'm not giving you up for anything."

33

TWO PRINCES BY SPIN DOCTORS

Jay

It's sick and twisted of me to stride into my enemy's apartment with his daughter's hand in mine, with every intention of stealing another one of her firsts tonight. But I've never denied being a sick and twisted man.

Last time I was here, I couldn't wrap my head around the bomb Cat dropped on me. Now, I couldn't give a fuck what her last name is. I hate her father enough to want to destroy him in any way possible. In the past, I would have made this about him, taken everything I wanted and then some.

But now, all I see is her.

The girl I first laid eyes on in the coffee shop. The one I followed on the train just to get her to talk to me. The woman who shared a piece of herself that day at lunch, who misses her mother, who has insecurities that I'll never understand, and who gave me the first meaningful kiss of my life.

Others have come before her, but no one could ever come after.

Tonight is all about her.

She makes me want to be better. And so much worse. I want to give her everything. If that means a public act in a seedy club, then so be it. If it means giving her my blessing to experiment with other women, I'll make it work. Witnessing her pleasure is enough for me. I still have a rock-hard erection, and while I wouldn't turn her down if she wanted to address that, I'm so focused on tasting her, on watching her come again, I can't think straight.

My pleasure is derived from hers alone.

Cat moves around the kitchen, her heels echoing against the hardwood floors, while I settle on the couch, running my thumb against my lip, watching her.

"Here, you look like you could use this," Cat says as she hands me a glass of amber liquid.

"Whiskey?" I ask, clear amusement in my tone.

She nods, settling next to me, watching me, her eyes bright in anticipation. I bring the lowball to my lips and take a sip, grimacing when I recognize the James brand immediately and cough obnoxiously.

"Jerk," she mumbles through a laugh, pushing against my arm.

"It's terrible," I say, smirking back at her.

Cat rolls her eyes and takes a sip of her water. She sets her glass on the side table and unzips one of her knee-high boots, then the other.

"You didn't want to have a glass of terrible whiskey like me?" I ask in mock horror.

She laughs, tossing a boot to the floor. "I don't drink whiskey."

With my free hand on my heart, I fall back against the couch. "You wound me, Catherine Bouvier. Wound me!"

The smile that lights up her face is worth millions.

"You'd change your mind if you tried my whiskey," I tell her, hauling myself up and setting the whiskey on the table. I don't need the buzz, anyway. Not when I have her by my side.

Cat moves so she's sitting on her knees and leans back against the couch. "I prefer vodka."

"And how do you like it, Kitten?"

She bites on her plump red lower lip. "Extra dirty," she purrs.

DIRTY TRUTHS

At the innuendo in her voice, I haul her onto my lap so she's straddling me, her skater skirt riding up and the fucking suspenders over her white T-shirt straining against her tits. Fuck, she's perfect.

"After tonight's little performance, I don't doubt that," I tease as my hands find her bare ass beneath her skirt. I groan at the contact. She's smooth and soft and all fucking mine.

Without hesitating, she cants forward and presses her red lips against mine. Automatically, I open for her, ravenous and dying to taste her again. I knead her ass with both hands, rubbing her against me until she moans into my mouth. I want to eat up all her little sounds. Hear her scream my name. Make her come again and again. I want everything with her.

Cat arches back, her hands on her thighs as she watches me, a coy smile playing on her lips. If only I could read her mind. Instead, I settle for rubbing my thumb against my bottom lip and holding her stare, waiting to see what she'll do.

"Let's go swimming!" she cheers.

I cock a brow in surprise. "Swimming?"

She bounces in excitement, the friction and the way her tits shake making me go impossibly harder. "Please?"

And damn if I can say no to her when she looks this happy. It's official. I'll do anything to keep that smile on her face.

"Okay, Kitten, let's go swimming."

Cat lifts herself off me and offers me her hand. When she pulls me to my feet, I immediately find the smooth skin of her waist and let her lead me to the roof. "Don't we need towels?"

I take it bathing suits aren't an issue.

"They're up by the pool," she replies.

"And it's heated?" I ask stupidly. It's a pool on the top of the James building. Of course it's heated.

She turns back and gives me a fuck off look in answer.

As she opens the door to the deck, the cool air hits me, making me second-guess the wisdom of our plan.

"We could take a shower if you want to get wet, Kitten," I murmur as I brush the hair off her shoulder and kiss her neck. She leans back into me and moans. Sneaking my hands below her suspenders, I squeeze her tits, eliciting another one of those sexy-as-fuck moans of hers. Her sounds drive me crazy. Every one spurs me on until I'm searching her body for other places that will give me hits like the ones I've experienced so far.

I drop another kiss to her neck, and she rolls her hips against me. Inhaling deep, I get lost in everything that is Catherine Bouvier. She's intoxicating.

She takes my momentary stillness as an opportunity to push away from me, spinning, a glint of mischief in her eye. "I wanna swim," she whispers into the dark sky, gripping her suspenders and pulling on them.

I lick my lips.

She snaps one of the suspenders, and it drops to her hip.

My eyes narrow.

Her fingers move to the second one, and I focus intently on her movements. Snap. The other one goes down.

She rubs her fingers slowly across the hem of her skirt, teasing me.

"Don't you want to watch me swim, Jay?" she says in a breathy voice.

My cock jumps.

I lick my lips again and nod.

Ever so slowly, she slides the skirt down her hips, her eyes never leaving mine. With her heels, she kicks the skirt away and stands before me in a black lace thong, a fucking garter belt, knee-high lace stockings, and her white T-shirt.

My cock has never been so hard in my life. It takes a Herculean effort not to pull it out and stroke myself while I watch her undress. I bite my fist as I commit every inch of her to memory. "Fuck, Kitten. I'm—I'm losing my goddamn mind right now."

She smiles as she toys with the hem of her shirt, then pulls it off over her head, exposing what no man's seen before.

DIRTY TRUTHS

The woman is a goddess. Smooth golden skin, large breasts that spill out of her black bra, curves I ache to touch.

Fuck. This.

"I need to touch you," I beg, making my way toward her.

She unclips her bra, drops her panties and her stockings to the ground, and jumps into the pool before I have a second to enjoy her gloriously naked body. All I see are long lines cutting through the water as she floats below the surface, lit by the underwater lights. I rush to the edge, undressing as I go. When she surfaces and turns to me with the biggest smile, her body mostly hidden below the surface, I groan.

Glistening and grinning, Cat stands, and finally I get my first glimpse of her perfect nipples. They're pebbled and dark, her breasts round and buoyant above the water.

I dive in and don't surface until I'm upon her. When I come up for air, we stare at one another for a long silent moment.

"I really need to touch you," I rasp, my desperation almost painful.

"Then touch me," she says, wrapping her arms around my neck and pulling her naked body against mine. Without thinking, I've got my hands on her ass, and I'm hauling her up so her legs are wrapped around me. The water is warm, but even if the pool wasn't heated, I don't think I'd notice. Because her breasts are pressed against me and her pussy is bare against my pelvis, her heat soaking into me everywhere we're connected.

"This is dangerous," I growl.

In response, she simply shrugs and squeezes me tighter. "I never took you for the type to be afraid of a little pussy cat," she teases, rubbing herself against me and groaning when she realizes how hard my cock is.

I throw my head back and guffaw into the star-filled sky. This girl.

"Make me come," she pants as she writhes against me.

I squeeze her to me to hold her in place. "I'm not fucking you in this pool."

"Why?" she almost whines.

I let out a short laugh. "For one, you're a virgin."

She pouts at this declaration.

"And we don't have protection."

She smiles. "Aww, you care about me."

I bring my forehead to hers and rub circles across her back. "More than I've ever cared about anyone or anything. Now go grab towels so I can make you come."

She bites her lip and leans in for a kiss. Roughly, I take her mouth, my tongue tangling with hers, the hint of chlorine mixing with her sweet flavor. I move to the edge of the pool and spin before breaking our kiss, and then I lift her onto the edge. She scurries away quickly, her ass jiggling in the hottest fucking way as she beelines for the towel bin. When she returns, wrapped in plush white terrycloth and hiding that gorgeous body of hers, she waits for me to get out.

I have other plans, though. I pat the cement in front of me. "Ass here and spread your legs."

Cat's eyes go wide. "What?"

"You heard me, Kitten. I've waited long enough to have that pussy. Now sit your ass down and let me eat."

She bites her lip, eyeing me warily. But then she does as I say. She tosses the folded towel she brought for me to the spot I've designated and sighs as she drops to the ground, her knees folding in on themselves.

"Nuh-huh," I say as I pull her legs apart and kiss her ankle before sliding it over my shoulder and wrapping my arms around her ass to pull her to the edge. She leans into my touch as I pull her to me.

She giggles. "What are you doing?"

"What does it look like I'm doing?" I eye her wickedly between her parted thighs. "I'm bringing my food closer." I kiss her stomach and throw her other leg on my opposite shoulder. My hair falls against my forehead, and I flip my head up so that I can see her more clearly.

Cat's soft fingers brush the hair out of my face, and she studies me, her lip caught between her teeth, her skin still damp, and oh so fucking soft. "Can I make you come, beautiful? Can I make you scream my name tonight?"

She swallows, her focus never wavering.

"Is Mia the only other one?" I ask.

She nods almost imperceptibly.

I kiss her pelvis, eliciting a groan from her. "And what did she do to you?"

Cat grasps my head almost subconsciously, her fingers running softly against my scalp as she pulls me to where she really wants me. I don't waste a moment in my position. Tongue out, I run it between her lips, watching her reaction.

She drops her head back and bucks in surprise. "Oh God," she murmurs.

"Not God, Kitten. Just me. You'll say my name next time, hear me?"

She laughs, and I lick her again. This time stopping when I reach her clit and sucking it into my mouth.

She groans. "I can't," she pants. "Jay," she rasps. "Fuck, baby. That feels so good."

She's never come up with a pet name for me, and I fucking love it.

"Tell me what she did, Kitten. Tell me what you liked."

She flings her arms out wide, dropping them to the cement, palms down, as she offers more of her pussy to me. "She—she, uh." She pants as I run circles against her lips, dipping inside every few seconds and making her squirm. I can't help but suck on her clit again, relishing in her sweet taste, while I wait for her to speak. "She, uh—she liked to use the vibrator on herself while she got me off."

I close my eyes and bring the image to mind. And fuck, I don't want to think about anyone but Cat right now, but the idea is now permanently plastered inside my brain. "She'd fuck herself while she sucked you off?" I ask, my warm breath sending a shiver through her body.

Erratic breathing and pebbled nipples are the only reaction I get.

She lifts her head up off the rough ground, her amber eyes molten, a fire dancing within them as she stares down at me. "Jay, I'm gonna come. Just your words, that mouth, oh my." She stops herself. "Jay, fuck."

I don't stop. I pull her closer and feast, sucking and licking, and then I bring a hand between her legs and sink my middle finger into her hot, throbbing pussy. She screams at the intrusion, and I wince, remembering she's a virgin.

But then she says the word that unleashes me. "*More.*"

Gauging her reaction, I push another finger in as I massage her clit with my thumb.

"More, Jay. Give me more. Give me everything," she pants, her chest heaving.

At her command, I bring my mouth back to her clit and suck as I slide in and out of her body, fingering her until she cries for me again. "Yes, Jay, right there. Oh fuck. Yes, I'm coming. I'm coming." Without stopping, I study her, watching as her mouth falls open and her eyes shut in pure ecstasy, her pussy gripping me tightly as she catapults over the edge.

It's the most beautiful thing I've ever seen. *She's* the most beautiful thing I've ever seen. Naked, panting, legs spread, pussy pink and glistening with her pleasure. I kiss the inside of her thigh and lean into the soft flesh. I've never enjoyed eating a woman out. I rarely do it, instead letting the women take care of each other. But I want her for breakfast, lunch, and dinner.

And, fuck it, I always get what I want.

"Come on, Kitten. Let's go to bed," I say, finally pushing out from between her legs and lifting myself out of the pool.

34

SUNDAY MORNING BY MAROON 5

Cat

Despite his assurances, I'm nervous. It's obvious that Jay is far more experienced than me. There's no doubt he's been with many women who are far more experienced than me too. Most of the time, I do a good job of hiding my insecurities. And right now, I want to be sure of myself. Confident. I want to swing my hips and know that I'm enough.

But I have to own what I don't know. That unknown being penises. How to make him feel good, or whether I'll gag if I give him head. Because I got a peek of his cock for two whole seconds before he jumped into the pool, and I felt its girth when I rubbed up against him. The veins pulsing against me. The way he rubbed against my clit made my eyes want to roll back into my head. If a teasing touch affected me like that, I can't imagine the ecstasy of him moving inside me.

I clench my legs at the thoughts and crawl into bed. Jay follows behind me, naked and clean from our shower.

"C'mere," he murmurs, pulling my ass against his heated skin as he spoons me. Immediately, he squeezes my breasts, exploring every inch, ramping up my desire again. Nuzzling into the crook of my neck, he inhales deeply, then kisses my ear. "Thank you, Kitten."

I hum to myself. "For what?"

"Forgiving me. Giving me a second chance to make this right. I promise it's you and me from here on out."

I close my eyes at the delicious thought and attempt to maneuver myself onto my back so I can grip his length. I want to take care of him.

"What are you doing?" he rasps.

"I want to make you come," I say, trying to turn again.

He holds me in place with an arm banded around my waist. "Not tonight. I'm okay, I promise."

"But—"

"Sleep, baby. We've got plenty of time for lessons."

I let out a breathy giggle. "Lessons?"

Cocky bastard.

He rubs against my ass. "Yeah, lessons. You have a lot to learn, and I'm going to have a fucking ball teaching you."

"And what was my lesson tonight?" I tease.

"How to scream my name," he quips, biting my shoulder.

"Got it right on the second try."

"I have a feeling you're going to be an excellent student."

I smile as I shake my head and nestle in closer to him. "Good night, Jay."

KITTEN'S SONGS

I wake up moaning, my body heated and on the brink of an orgasm.

Needing release more than I probably ever have, I snake a hand down my abdomen to the juncture of my thighs, but instead of finding bare skin, my hand lands on hair, and I grip it when I realize Jay is between my legs and eating me out like I'm his damn breakfast.

"Finally, you're awake," he says before licking me again.

I moan nonsensically, not awake enough to form words and too damn turned on to try.

"You are so fucking pretty in the morning," he growls, swiping his tongue against my clit and watching me. "I want to see just how beautiful you are riding my tongue first thing in the morning. Will you come for me?"

My eyes roll back, and my thighs clench reflexively around Jay's head at the way he works my clit.

When the phone rings on the bedside table, I groan and reach over to silence it, quickly bringing my hand back to Jay's hair, pulling on it and pushing his face deeper into my body. He moans against me, murmuring something like, "Yes, ride my face."

The phone rings again. "Fuck," I mutter, "it's my brother."

Jay doesn't stop his licking.

"I should get this. What if he's here?"

That's unlikely, since no one knows I'm here. But the thought takes me from my brink of an orgasm to practically dead.

Jay presses a finger inside me and rests his chin against my leg, wearing a wicked smirk. "Answer it."

I narrow my eyes. "You want me to answer my phone while your finger is inside me?"

"You can answer it, or I will, and we both know what that would mean."

I roll my eyes. "You so wouldn't."

He lifts up quickly, like he just might go for my phone.

The action makes me nervous enough to grab for it first, and I squeak out a "hello" before I've had time to even take a calming breath.

"Hey, are you coming to brunch?" Carter asks.

"Uh, yeah," I reply, pulling the phone away from my face to check the time. Fuck, it's already nine thirty.

"Put him on speaker," Jay mouths.

I shake my head, and he presses two fingers inside me. Despite my best efforts, the move forces a whimper from my lips.

"You okay?" Carter asks.

I glare at Jay as I put the phone on speaker. "Yup, just, uh, stubbed my toe."

Ignoring my response, he asks, "Can you get a table for five? I'm running late."

I laugh. When is Carter not running late? "Sure, is Cash picking up Chase?"

"No, he's not coming. Jay's meeting us."

I regard the man between my thighs in confusion, and in return, he gives me a frustratingly relaxed smile and lazily pumps his fingers in and out of my body. I squeeze my lips shut to keep myself from reacting.

"Oh, is he?"

"Yeah, he texted earlier. Wanted to grab breakfast since we never see each other anymore. Since we already had plans, I figured I'd invite him along. I can't believe you two have never met."

I manage to squeak out a "yeah, me neither" as Jay's tongue flattens against me.

"So you'll call the restaurant?" Carter asks again.

"Uh-huh," I assent, a desperate pant almost escaping.

"Okay, see you there," he says, finally ending the call.

I click off the phone and toss it. "Oh my God. You are such an ass," I shout, but as I get to the last word, he presses his fingers upward, making my legs quake. "Oh fuck," I mutter, knowing I've lost complete control over my body.

"Say my name, baby. Come for me and say my fucking name."

My body explodes at his command, and I pulse around his fingers. "Fuck, Jay, yes." I ramble through a litany of moans.

He sucks so hard, refusing to let up, that I swear I could pass out. When I've come back to earth, I finally take him in. His eyes are shut, and he's still licking. He's enjoying this. Eating me out is as much for him as it is for me.

The way he looks right now—the desire etched into every line of his face; the way his eyes are shut like he's savoring the way I taste—makes me crazy with lust. It makes me want to pleasure him the same way. To know whether I'll feel the same pleasure just watching him get off.

"I need you," I plead, dropping my arms to his shoulders and trying to pull him up.

He shakes his head as he continues his torturous licks. "I need one more," he says, thrusting his fingers back inside me.

And really, who am I to deny the man?

35

FALLING FOR YOU BY COLBIE CAILLAT

Jay

C at is adorable when she squirms. Normally, she's so put together. She's snarky, beautiful, and in control almost all the time.

But not today.

And watching her squirm is almost as satisfying as witnessing those rare glimpses of her vulnerability. Every hint of it makes me fall a little more. Makes me want to fix things for her, to be better for her, to just be *there* for her.

Feelings I've never experienced before.

But when she's uncomfortable like she is now, when I know she's okay, that nothing will hurt her, it's fun to poke at her. To watch her come undone just a little. To see beneath her finely tuned mask.

And Catherine Bouvier is currently coming undone.

"Hi, guys," she says as she settles into the booth, taking the only seat left, right next to me. I got here before her, leaving while she was still showering, so I could meet up with Carter first. "You're never here on time," she says to her older brother, ignoring me still.

I smirk at the way her brothers study her. They all see what I see. Her posture—how she's perched on the edge of the booth as far from me as possible, her back ramrod straight. Her blatant disregard for my presence. I take a sip of my coffee to hide my amusement.

"Uh, Cat, aren't you going to say hello to Jay?" Carter asks, his eyes darting from her to me. "Jay, this is my sister, Cat. And we weren't on time; you're just exceptionally late," he says, scrutinizing her.

Cash and Frank are watching her too. With every set of eyes on her, she turns to face me, her cheeks going pink and then crimson. "Oh, h-hi," she stutters, thrusting her hand toward me awkwardly.

Seeing her like this leaves me licking my lips. I put my coffee cup down and take her hand in mine, squeezing it when she tries to pull away. "Pleasure's all mine," I say with a wink.

Carter scoffs, "You don't have to work your charm on her, Jay."

Cat pulls her hand back and picks up her menu, failing at affecting the nonchalant tone she's going for. "How was everyone's weekend?"

Cash replies first. "Good. We won our game. Pretty sure we'll be going to state."

She beams at him. "Promise I'll be at next weekend's game."

"Don't you have to work?" Carter asks, quirking his brow.

Her eyes bounce toward me and then she scans her menu before replying. "I, uh, I actually quit," she says.

Carter straightens. "You need money?"

She scoffs and finally looks his way. "No."

Her brother props his elbows on the table and leans forward. "Why did you quit?"

I bring my coffee to my lips again, enjoying the show.

"My boss was an ass—wouldn't take no for an answer," she replies without breaking a sweat.

I cough into my cup and spit out my coffee.

"Jesus—" Carter says, focusing on me for half a second before looking at her again. "What's the cocksucker's name? Jay and I will pay him a visit."

236

I clear my throat, trying to catch my breath. So much for her being uncomfortable. Fucking minx is cool as a cucumber over there.

"Oh stop. All I mean is that he wouldn't take no for an answer when I said I couldn't work Sundays and during the week. I have more responsibilities with the magazine now, so I'm up here more often." She hands me a napkin and gives me a demure smile. "You okay?"

I wipe my mouth with the proffered cloth and then stretch my arm out along the top of the seat so my hand rests just above her shoulder and my body is angled toward hers when I reply. "I'm fine, sweetheart. Thank you. Which magazine do you work for?"

She nibbles her lip, a tell that she's nervous.

I bite back a smile at her reaction. Back on solid ground.

"Jolie," she murmurs before turning back to her brothers.

"How's that going?" Cash asks before I can respond to her. Before I can mention the shared project. Bring up the excuse we have to get to know one another. Fucking A.

Cat brightens. It's clear she and Cash are close. "It's going really well. I was asked to work on a ball they're throwing at the end of the month," she says, keeping her attention trained on Cash and ignoring my pointed stare.

Dammit.

A waitress approaches to take our order, and while the guys are focusing on the pretty brunette, my eyes skirt to my obsession beside me. With my hand on her shoulder, I inch her closer. "Kitten," I murmur.

She twists her lips, trying hard to ignore me.

Now that she's within reach, though, I drop my hand from behind her and place it right next to her hip, rubbing my pinky against her outer thigh.

She shoots me a look, and I respond with a smirk.

"And what would you like?" the waitress asks Cat.

She orders a coffee and fruit with egg whites.

Grimacing, I place my hand on her thigh and squeeze.

The waitress turns to me next. "And what can I get for you?"

"I'll take eggs, bacon, and hash browns. And a waffle with powdered sugar and whipped cream on the side."

I smile at the way Cat licks her lips at the mention of her favorite breakfast food. That is exactly what I was going for. Subtly, I slide my fingers into the space between Cat's legs. She's wearing a skirt similar to the one from the day before, and her soft skin beneath my fingers makes me hard as a rock.

"And a mimosa. Anyone else want to have a drink with me? Little Sunday funday?" I say with a teasing glint cast in Cat's direction.

Cash and Frank shrug since they aren't old enough, and Carter sighs. "I mean, YOLO, right? Make that three mimosas," he says as he nods in Cat's direction. "You could use one. You seem stressed. Sure you're okay?"

The waitress takes that as her cue to exit, and Cat shrugs. "I'm fine."

Deftly, I skate my pinky up between her thighs to the spot where my head was buried only two hours ago. I lick my lips at the memory. She wants to react—to tell me to stop, or maybe to tell me to move a certain way—but she takes a deep breath and keeps herself steady. A fucking goddess under pressure. I love it. When I brush against her panties, she hisses a breath, but I cover it with conversation.

"What's new at James Liquors?" I ask Cash since we all know Carter has no idea.

Cash rattles off information about their newest malt, the pride he has in his family's business evident even at the ripe old age of eighteen. It's too bad Carter doesn't show as much interest. Cash will likely be the easy choice when it's time to hand over the reins of the company. I can't imagine letting the opportunity slip away. I have two older brothers, and I don't give a fuck how old they are. Hanson Liquors will be mine. I've spent years watching every move my father makes, carrying out every one of his directives. There's no way I'd let one of them run it.

Why doesn't Carter have the same fire?

Not that I honestly care right now. Skirting Cat's panty line, I watch her reaction from my periphery, then sink into her warmth. As suspected, she's soaking wet. And I'm so close to giving away what I'm doing when the waitress returns with our mimosas. I can't keep my hand where it is when she holds out my drink to me, so I regretfully slip out of her warmth to accept the glass.

But I can't help but tease my girl a bit more. My eyes locked on Cat, I dip my pinky into the drink and swirl it before sucking it into my mouth. "That's delicious," I say, then tap my drink to hers.

Cheeks flaming, she hides behind her glass and mouths, "Deviant."

I raise my eyebrows to hers in acknowledgment. "And you love it," I mutter.

"Love what?" Carter says.

"Mimosas. What's not to love?" Cat quips.

Carter takes a sip and nods. "Sure, tastes like orange juice but makes my meeting with Pa this afternoon less stressful."

"Meeting with your grandfather today?" I ask.

His lips form a flat line and his eyes dull. "Yup, he wants to talk about my future."

The conversation turns as Carter really has no interest in discussing business, and soon, plates are being set in front of us. I don't miss how Cat gazes longingly at my waffles.

"I think I ordered too much," I say, leaning back in the booth. With my arm, I nudge the plate the waffle is on toward Cat. "I'll need a nap if I eat this all myself. Help yourself."

The soft smile she gives me in return is one I pocket. I'm stealing so many things from this girl—firsts, moments, smiles—and I don't intend to give any of them back.

When we're all just picking at the remnants of our breakfasts, I pull out my phone and shoot a text to Cat.

Me: Spend the afternoon with me.

When her phone lights up beside her, she turns it over and looks at it. Biting her lip, she taps out a reply.

"What do you have going on this afternoon, Cat?" Cash asks after the server drops off our checks.

"Um, not much. I probably need to head back to Providence. I haven't been home in a while."

"Everything all right with Mia?" he asks.

My ears perk up at his question. The way he asks is like he knows. But Cat said no one knows the real her. No one but me. I love the notion of holding her secrets.

She looks in my direction and then back toward her brother. "Everything's fine. *I promise*," she emphasizes. "You know how Mia is," she adds.

I narrow my eyes. Does he?

"You'll really be at the game next Saturday?" he asks, his previous question all but forgotten.

I check my phone while they continue talking.

Kitten: What do you have in mind?

I quickly type back,

Another lesson.

A shiver of excitement only I would recognize passes across Cat's chest and shoulders as she reads the text.

Kitten: Penthouse?

I shake my head.

I'll text you the address.

> Kitten: I really need to go back to my apartment to get more clothes for this week.

Her reply is laced with hesitation. She doesn't want to go back there. She wants to stay with me, but she doesn't know how to do both. Good thing she's dating a billionaire. Not that she isn't one as well. Honestly, part of me wants to knock Carter in the head for allowing her to do everything herself. The other part of me loves that she doesn't allow them to push her around. That she doesn't rely on the family name.

> Let me take care of everything. I know you don't normally let go, but please, Kitten, just let go for today.

She bites her lip, and then after a moment's hesitation, she simply nods.

"Who are you texting?" Frank asks quietly beside her. While her brothers seem happy to take Cat at her word, nothing seems to get past Frank. I couldn't help but notice the way he was watching me before. As if he knew precisely where my hand had been. The kid makes me nervous.

"Just a friend," Cat replies, unbothered by his inquisition. They must be close too. More ties to unravel. More layers of Cat to uncover.

"Seeing anyone?" he asks, his voice still low. Carter and Cash are focused on their conversation relating to seeing their grandfather this afternoon. Cash is obviously bothered about not being invited, and Carter is all too happy to switch places.

Cat gives him a coy half grin. "It's new."

And now I smile. Because she's not hiding it. We may not be out in the open, but she isn't hiding her relationship status. Pride fills me, knowing I'm the one who put that look on her face.

"Whoever it is, they better be good to you," Frank says, his expression stoic. I don't miss how he doesn't say he. So Cash isn't the only one who knows about Mia.

Interesting.

Cat's reply pulls my attention right back to her, though. "*He*'s very good to me."

36

ONLY WANNA BE WITH YOU BY HOOTIE AND THE BLOWFISH

Jay

I stand outside the brick building and watch as the tall brunette with a cautious smile walks toward me. She wears an adorably confused expression, and her cheeks are tinged a rosy red. Maybe from the mimosas. Maybe from the cold.

The sick bastard in me hopes maybe I have something to do with it too. That just seeing me makes her cheeks heat. If I weren't better at hiding my emotions, I'd be just as fucking flushed as the girl who makes my heart trip over itself.

"What are we doing at the library?" she asks, gaping at the mammoth building behind us rather than looking me in the eye.

Grabbing her by the hip, I pull her to my chest and sink my lips into her neck. I had to hold back for two whole hours in front of her family; my restraint is gone.

"Time to find out what you like, Kitten," I murmur into her ear as I nip at the lobe and then suck it into my mouth, my cock jumping as a groan slips from her throat.

She pushes against me, craving me as much as I crave her. Wrapping her arms around my neck, she arches back and looks up at me. "What I like?"

"Libraries are for learning, Kitten." I tug her hips closer to mine. "It's time for another lesson."

She sucks in a breath, her eyes dancing with mirth. "What *kind* of lesson, though?"

"The kind where we figure out what you like."

"What I like." She tests the words out on her tongue. "And why do you care what I like?"

"I should know the kinds of things my girlfriend likes so I can be sure to please her," I say, holding her steady, my eyes locked with hers, hoping she sees how serious I am.

"Girlfriend?" she squeaks.

I nod. "I did just have breakfast with the family, didn't I?"

With a chuckle, she says, "You had brunch with my brothers as Jay, my brother's best friend. Not as Jay my boyfriend."

"Semantics," I scoff. "We've gone through the family thing, so now it's all about things you like. I think they approve of me, don't you?"

She rolls her eyes. "You haven't 'gone through the family thing' until you've met my grandparents."

"I got it in the bag, Kitten." I shrug and plant a kiss on her forehead. "Grandparents *love* me."

With a swat to my chest, she huffs a laugh. "No, they don't. And mine definitely won't."

I smirk, unfazed. "Yeah. grandparents really don't love me."

With that, I wrap my arm around her shoulder and walk into the library. "But I don't care, beautiful. Because with or without their approval, you're mine."

She pauses and pops up onto her toes, pressing a kiss to my cheek. "Fine, I'll be your girlfriend."

My heart squeezes at her admission, but outwardly, I remain aloof. "It's cute that you thought that was a question."

KITTEN'S SONGS

Hidden in a corner between shelves of the second floor of the Boston Public Library, Cat is settled in my lap. With a book in her hand and my arms wrapped around her, we take turns reading lines from a romance novel of her choosing. This is the fourth book she's picked up. There was a shirtless man with long hair on the cover and a woman looking at him longingly. That was the only clue we needed when gauging the story's steam level.

She giggles as I deepen my voice for my line. "I want you to swallow every drop. Be the dirty whore I know you are and suck me off."

With every word I speak, I draw circles against her smooth thigh, noting the way her knees shift open each time I stroke upward.

"Does my dirty girl want to play?" I whisper, watching goosebumps erupt across her skin.

When I lick them away, she moans.

Cat tosses the book to the side, surprising me, and flips around so she's hovering above me, her knees on the ground, her hands on either side of my hips, and her eyes blazing with lust. With the way her skater skirt fans out and how her tight T-shirt hugs every curve, she looks like a fucking prep-school girl and every one of my teenage dreams. "I'm ready for my next lesson, professor."

My mind goes blank at the display, but my cock practically rips through the seam of my pants at her words.

"What are you doing, Kitten?" I ask, fisting my hands to stave off the need to touch her.

The smell of old books mixes with her vanilla perfume as she presses closer to me. "Say it again."

"Say what again?" I ask, truly confused.

"Tell me to suck your cock," she says as she sits up on her knees and reaches for my belt.

I grip her wrists to stop her, and she practically hisses at me like a fucking cat. Releasing her, I fall back against the shelf and prop myself up on my elbows, letting her take control.

"Say it," she demands.

I shake my head, speechless and lost at the sight of her on her knees before me in the library aisle. When my cock springs free of my boxers, looking angry and ready, she licks her lips like it's the greatest thing she's ever seen.

"You're going to need to talk me through this," she says, bringing her attention up to my face, her brow furrowed seriously, as if she's studying to take a test.

My blood has all traveled to one area, as is obvious from the swollen head already leaking for her attention, so my thoughts are jumbled.

"Kitten, be more direct. What do you need?" I grit out, lifting slightly while she slides my pants all the way down. When she's forced them past my knees, I drop back down, my bare ass touching the rough carpet.

"Tell me how to make you come. Tell me what you like. *Teach me*," she says, her eyes locked with mine and holding a vulnerability that brings me back to the present.

I take my hand and grip myself like I like, stroking up and down, never looking away from her. "Hold me like this and then move with some pressure."

Her intense focus turning to my cock, she wraps her soft, slender fingers around mine. For a moment, I don't move my hand, savoring the sensation of her over me. Then she makes eye contact again, her brown irises liquifying as she melts for me.

"Like this?" she asks softly. Her tongue darts out, and she swipes it across her bottom lip as she drags her attention from my face to my dick and back again.

I release myself, only to envelop her hand, guiding her. "Yeah, like that," I say. I close my eyes for a second, relishing the way her smooth fingers tug so gently.

"Can I—" she says, but clamps her mouth shut, her cheeks going pink. I grab her chin so she's forced to look me in the eye. "Can you what?"

"Can I taste you?" she asks, her voice barely a whisper.

Fuck.

"Kitten, you can do whatever the fuck you want to me. But yeah," I say with a dry laugh, "you can fucking taste me. Please. Wrap those gorgeous lips around my cock and suck me like the good little slut you are."

She squirms, rubbing her legs together as she tips at the waist.

"Just the idea of sucking me off in public has you dripping right now, doesn't it?"

The fucking noises that come from her throat as she peeks up at me. Goddamn. But they don't compare to the sound she makes when she finally lowers herself and licks along my shaft. She moans like she's just had a taste of the best fucking piece of chocolate.

She swirls her tongue over my tip, licking up the precum. Evidence of just how fucking much her presence alone excites me—memories of eating her out yesterday and today spurring me on. Pent-up desire after a month of no company except my own because she's the only woman I can even think about, let alone touch. And then she circles my cock with her mouth and slides down, attempting ever so gallantly to take me all the way in before she gags and coughs, and fuck if that doesn't make my ego swell.

I tug her hair gently to pull her back and dip my chin to gain her attention. "Go slow and breathe through your nose. And use your hand. You don't have to take me all the way down your throat just yet. You'll get there, but for now, it's okay to cheat a little."

She nods, her cheeks flushing, and then she dips back down and takes me in her warm, wet mouth again. It takes an insane amount of restraint not to thrust, wanting nothing more than to fuck her perfect lips. To come down her throat. To watch her eyes tear as I pull on her hair and fuck her until she's begging me to make her come.

But I don't. I let her set the pace. Because even this slow, it's the best blow job I've ever had. Knowing it's her first time, that I'm the first one to have my dick in her mouth, has me so fucking hard.

She swirls her tongue as she sucks, and I can't help but groan a little too loudly for such a public place. She whimpers, and with her legs straddling my knee, she rubs herself against me.

"That's it, baby. Use me," I encourage as she works me up and down, all while getting herself off. "Fuck, you look gorgeous on your knees." My praise only spurs her on, her grinding turning frantic, saliva dripping from her mouth as she takes me deeper.

Less controlled. *Desperate.*

On the edge of losing it, I wrap a fistful of hair around my hand, pushing her down and swelling as she gags. Her eyes meet mine, full of unshed tears but alight with desire, her hips rolling against my knees more persistently.

"You're close, aren't you? Come for me, baby. Come all over me, and then I'll clean you up. I'm going to lick you so hard you come again."

She whimpers around my cock as her legs tremble, ecstasy overtaking her and sending me following after.

"Kitten, I'm going to come."

She nods around me, and I spill down her throat. Her eyes go wide at the first jolt of my cock, but I talk her through it. "Just swallow, baby. You got it. Such a good girl. Look at you, *fuck.*"

"I think the book is in Aisle twelve," a feminine voice echoes.

With a jerk, I pull Cat up and press her against my chest, panting as heavily as she is.

"Shit," she mutters, her face flushed.

She scrambles to stand, and I grab for my pants, which are down at my knees. I pull them on and jump up just as two older women round the corner.

"Um, I think the book is over there," Cat says, pointing to the book she threw before we got caught up in the moment. "Yup, right here!" she cries.

The woman wearing a beige cardigan eyes her like she's crazy.

I laugh. "Library voice, Kitten."

Blushing, she ducks her head and snatches the book up off the floor.

The women turn to me, giving me matching awe-filled looks. "Oh, how sweet. Are you on a date at the library?"

I wrap my arm around Cat, pressing her to my front so the ladies can't see my unbuttoned pants. "Only the best for my girlfriend," I say proudly, shooting them a wink.

"Earl never took me to the library," the woman wearing cat-eye glasses mutters.

Her friend retorts, "Earl couldn't read."

Pushing her glasses up the bridge of her nose, the woman looks back at me. "She's not wrong. Man was dumb as a doorknob." She elbows her friend. "But he was good in the sack."

Cat bursts out laughing, and I follow suit.

Both of our new friends just shrug. "You laugh now, but at least he's pretty. He can get away with being lousy in the sack. Earl, not so much."

Turning to Cat, who's slapped a hand over her mouth to hide her laughter, I say in a louder than library voice, "You're supposed to tell them I'm excellent in the sack."

She bends at the waist, still covering her mouth. "Can't," she says, her voice muffled. She shrugs at the women. "Virgin here. Sorry, ladies." She takes a step away from me, but I grab her hips and pull her close.

"If you make another move," I whisper, holding her in place, "these women are going to know just how *not* virginal you are, you little minx."

She laughs, the sound vibrating against my hand. "Ladies, if you don't mind, my boyfriend and I just…um, we need a minute," she says, nibbling her bottom lip.

They eye her, both squinting, and then it's like they finally get it. They turn to one another, their mouths forming identical *O*s, before turning to me again.

"Of course. Oh, to be young again," beige cardigan says. "We'll be in the next aisle. Take your time." They turn around and scurry off, snickering as they do. But I don't miss the way they gawk at us as they round the corner, probably trying to get one last peek.

"*Fuck*," I rasp, finally zipping my pants and adjusting myself. Talk about a one-eighty. One minute, I'm coming down Cat's throat, and the next, I'm chatting with senior citizens about my future sex life. And let's not forget about poor Earl.

Cat spins to me, her eyes as big as saucers. Then we're both laughing. I wrap my arm around her and pull her against my chest. "No more public lessons," I say and press a kiss to her forehead.

She nuzzles against my chest, then pulls back and grins. "At least you got off this time."

With a look that I hope conveys my sincerity, I caress her cheek and pull her to me again. "You were perfect."

"Got it right on the first try?" she asks proudly.

I chuckle. "Yeah, A-plus student."

"Yesss," she hisses in excitement.

"Now kiss me," I say before pressing my lips to hers.

37

I GOT YOU BY JACK JOHNSON

Cat

With the cool air nipping at my nose, I don't even attempt to hide my smile. I've never been the kind of person who dreads Mondays. Especially since starting at Jolie. I love the anticipation of jumping into the projects I've been assigned and catching up with Sophie. But this buoyant feeling eclipses every bit of excitement I've felt over the last few weeks.

After the library, Jay took me shopping for clothes for the week. Normally, I'd never allow a person to spend money on me. In my experience, when money is bestowed upon me, it comes with strings. My compliance, my diet, my independence. But Jay doesn't try to control me or make me conform to any ideals he may have. He lets me be me.

So when he dragged me down Newbury Street and into one boutique after another, I smiled and let the stylists work their magic. Then we had dinner at his apartment, listened to music, played a few rounds of gin rummy, and made out until we fell asleep. It was perfect.

For the next few weeks, my sole focus needs to be on making every detail of the ball perfect. And when I have time, I'll work on ideas for the Christmas list. I'm just opening the door to the building, ready to greet the security guard on duty, when a familiar voice echoes through the space. "Cat, wait!"

I turn, brow furrowed and head tilted, to my handsome and very out of breath boyfriend.

"Miss me already, baby?" I purr, closing the door and giving Jay a thorough once-over.

He's in a navy blue suit with a light blue shirt that is the exact shade of his eyes. A hum escapes my throat at the sight of him.

At the sound, the smirk he normally sports falls into place. "Always, Kitten. I always miss you."

My hair flies in my face as a gust of wind whooshes past us. With one finger, Jay slides it back into place, then drags his thumb down my cheek, landing at my jaw as he inspects me. "God, you're gorgeous."

"Not here, Jay," I mutter, biting back a smile.

"I know," he whispers, pulling his hand back.

We haven't exactly discussed the parameters of our relationship, but I think we both know it can't be public yet. Not if we stand a shot of making this work. He's my brother's best friend, and my brothers are nothing if not dramatic. We might as well settle into this and see where it leads before we dive into that disaster. He hands me the coffee I hadn't even noticed he had. "Your coffee. Pumpkin spice, just the way you like it." He says, reaching into his pocket and pulling out a silver device. "And your iPod."

"Thank you," I say, bringing the paper cup to my lips. He's right. It's exactly how I like it. "You didn't have to do this."

He smiles as if he can't even hold it back. Wide and easy. "I know, but I wanted to. Have a good day, Kitten."

The urge to grab a hold of his suit jacket and pull him in for a kiss, or even just a hug, is intense. He walks by me instead and grabs the hand closest to him where it hangs at my side, squeezing as he looks me in the eye, and then he's gone.

I sigh, momentarily floating in a love-drunk haze.

Renewed and energized by the delicious coffee and affection, I head to the door for the second time. This time, the security guard opens it for me. "Good morning, Ms. Bouvier."

"Thanks, Tim. How was your weekend?"

He smiles as he follows me to the check-in desk, and I slide my card across the reader. "It was great. How about yours?"

Flashes of my time with Jay cycle through my head. The sex club, Jay's hands, the pool, the library, brunch, shopping, his smiles. "It was epic."

He arches a brow and puts his hands on his hips. "Epic, eh?"

I smile. "Epic. Have a good one."

I slip my headphones into my ears and press Play on the iPod, knowing that Jay won't disappoint with today's choice. Sure enough, I step into the elevator, laughing as Mariah Carey's "We Belong Together" blasts into my ears.

KITTEN'S SONGS

"You didn't come back this weekend. Does that mean things went well with Jay?" Sophie asks, brows waggling, when I prop myself up against her desk.

"It was great. How was your weekend?" I grin behind my coffee cup. The last time I saw her, she was staring at Dexter like she wanted to fuck him in public.

She takes a sip of her coffee and smiles. "Dexter wants to take me away next weekend."

"Things are getting serious, then?"

She spins to face me fully. "He wants to meet my parents," she whisper-shouts. "My dad is gonna flip!"

I laugh. "Because he's closer in age to him, or because he's a photographer for a fashion magazine?"

Sophie hides her face in her hands. "Both." She groans and drags her hands down her face. "*Shit*. I didn't even think about the career thing. My dad keeps his mouth shut about my choice of careers, but I know he wishes I'd gone to medical school like him. So dating a magazine photographer? This is so not what he'll want. And the age thing…" She drifts off as she stares, unseeing, at her computer monitor. Then she turns back to me, clasping her hands in her lap. "But I really like him. And not just because he's hot and the sex is hot and everything is just so fucking hot."

We both laugh.

"Like, I really like him, Cat. Am I crazy?"

I shrug. "If you are, then so am I." I straighten and tug on the hem of my top to smooth it out. "But right now, we have a project to work on. Let's get that list together."

For the next few hours, Sophie and I sift through products and reviews. We order lunch and laugh while we devour sushi at our desks and get looks from the modelesque figures around us. We definitely don't fit the mold in this office, and I couldn't care less. It's freeing to stop worrying about what others think.

"You coming home with me tonight?" Sophie asks as we head toward the elevator at the end of the day.

I shrug. I haven't heard from Jay all day, and I didn't expect to. It's been a hectic day for me, and I'm just an intern. I imagine his was even busier since he's got a real job.

At Hanson Liquors.

I groan at the reminder. That fact will definitely take some getting used. Not only does he work for my family's competitor, but one day, he'll be the CEO. Once in the elevator, I spin to face the doors and slip my phone out of my purse, ready to catch up on any communication I may have missed throughout the day. I blink at the sheer number of notifications.

The first is from Mia.

And the second. And the third.

I ignore them and go straight to Cash's text.

> Cash: Frank thinks there's something going on between you and Hanson. Have anything to tell me?

I throw my head back and groan. "Fucking Frank." The guy misses nothing.

"Who's Frank?" Sophie asks, one brow cocked wickedly. "Sounds hot."

I laugh. "So not your type."

"Why's that?" she asks, turning to face me, one hand on her hip.

"He's about twenty years off your typical type."

"Oh my gosh, a real daddy?"

I laugh. "No, he's my younger brother's age. Eighteen."

She makes a face. "Yeah, so not my type."

"Told you!" I laugh again.

"So what did the baby do to you?" she says in a mocking, childlike tone.

I contemplate the text, working out a response. I *hate* lying to Cash. But with his love for the company and his loyalty to everything James, he'll be more opposed to a relationship between Jay and me than anyone. I blow out a breath. "He's my brother's best friend. And he misses nothing. It's annoying."

"And what didn't he miss?" she prompts, rolling her hand for me to go on.

"Uh, that something is going on with Jay. We went to brunch yesterday and acted like we'd never met. But, uh—" I blush, embarrassed to admit what Jay did while my brothers were sitting right across from me at the table. And how much I enjoyed it. I palm my face. "Jay tried to finger me under the table."

Sophie bursts out laughing. "Oh my God. Sweet little virginal Cat's not such a virgin anymore," she sings.

I glare at her. "Still a virgin," I mumble as the elevator doors open and more people step on.

"What are you going to say?" she asks, pushing closer to me to make room for our companions.

"What can I say? I can't very well admit that, yes, my family company's mortal enemy had his finger in my pants while they sat across from me!" I hiss.

Two men in suits in front of us turn, one with a brow cocked, and the other one giving me a once-over. Shit. Didn't use my library voice. Or elevator voice, in this case. My face and neck heat, and from the looks of my hazy reflection in the stainless wall beside me, I'm the shade of a tomato. I sink back and stare at the ceiling.

Sophie slaps a hand to her mouth. "Smooth," she whispers between giggles.

"Shut it," I snap.

I jump and almost drop my phone when it rings in my hand.

Sophie snatches it from me and ends the call. "Calm down." She holds the device out to me. "Your brother's not going to come through the phone and force you to tell the truth."

I sigh and hold my phone to my chest. He could. If he asked enough questions, I would cave. Or he'd know I was lying and call me out on it. Then I'd cave. Either way, talking to him right now is a bad idea. I need a plan.

As the elevator dings our arrival on the ground floor and the doors open, my heart rate kicks up. My phone rings again, but I haven't had more than two seconds to even think about a plan. But the name on the screen isn't my brother's. It's Jay's. I click Accept and bring my phone to my ear just as I spot him leaning against the glass wall near the door, his legs crossed, his blond hair falling across his forehead, and those azure eyes lighting up as they track my arrival.

"Hello, beautiful," he murmurs, not taking his eyes off me.

My thighs squeeze together, and I practically trip over my feet. "Hi."

"Come to dinner with me," he says.

It's not a question. I do love his confidence.

I grab Sophie by the arm and come to a halt in the middle of the lobby. If we head to the doors now, we'll pass right by Jay, and I don't want anyone else to know we're together yet. "I'll see you tomorrow," I say to her, nodding in Jay's direction.

Her eyes light up as she looks from him back to me. "Have fun," she whispers before waving goodbye and strutting to the exit.

"Tell me where to meet you," I tell Jay.

He shakes his head as he pushes off the wall and stalks toward me. He pulls his phone away from his ear and pockets it before he reaches me. "Ms. Bouvier, it's so good to see you again," he says with a sly grin.

"Uh, you as well, Mr. Hanson," I enunciate a little too loudly. I almost giggle at how bad we are at this undercover stuff.

"I was just coming to see if you were available to discuss a few details for the masquerade ball."

"Oh, were you?" I tease, easing into the ruse a bit.

He nods and swipes at his bottom lip with his thumb as he takes me in from head to toe. He's undressing me as we speak. It's exhilarating. Images of him naked in the pool filter through my mind. I wouldn't mind a repeat. Of anything we've done so far.

"Would you be available to discuss it this evening?" he asks, pressing closer.

"It *is* your event." I shrug. "And it's my job to make myself available."

Jay's lip ticks up. "That's true. You are working under me for this event, aren't you?"

I nibble at my bottom lip and smile. "For the time being, yes. Although I think you'd enjoy me on top too."

The laugh that escapes Jay's mouth and the bursts of joy it sends through my body are like sparklers on the Fourth of July, shooting off in every direction.

I love laid-back Jay. Teasing Jay. *Smiling Jay.* If I'm not careful, soon I'll be *in love* with Jay.

He holds out his arm, palm open. "Shall we?" When I lead the way to the door, he presses his other hand to the small of my back, and just that little touch, the warmth of his hand, has me squirming.

The feeling is short-lived, though, because my phone vibrates in my hand again, and this time, it is Cash's name blowing up my screen.

"You going to get that?" Jay asks, tipping his head toward the device.

I slide my gaze to his. "Haven't decided what I'm going to say."

We step outside, and before I can even comment on the rain, a man appears with an umbrella and ushers me into a black sedan. Jay's hand never leaves my back, though. Not until I'm fully inside the car. Once he's settled next to me, he takes my hand and brings my knuckles to his mouth, his full lips touching my skin in the most cherishing way. "Missed you today," he says with an ease that feels natural.

How is it that we've only just begun? I'm more comfortable with this man than I am with anyone, including Cash. He understands me, respects me, and shows me nothing but adoration. The grin that stretches across my face is so big, I probably look like a maniac. "Where are we going?"

Jay sways closer and kisses me. At first, it's just a press of his lips against mine, but then it's like he can't *not* make it more. He palms my hips, pulling me onto his lap as his kisses grow needy. When his hands start to roam beneath my skirt, I laugh breathlessly and push him back. "We aren't alone, buddy. Slow down," I whisper against his lips.

With a groan, he drops his forehead to mine and cradles my cheek with a warm palm. "Sorry, Kitten. I just…fuck, I can't get enough of you." He frowns like he's in pain. Like he can't believe he's admitting that little secret.

"Oh yeah?" I can't help but smile.

He shakes his head, his forehead rubbing against mine. "Yeah." He pulls back but keeps a firm hold on my waist. "Since we can't take things further, why don't you tell me why you're ignoring your brother's calls?"

I huff. "Do I have to?"

Brows furrowed, he watches me. "What's the problem?"

"Nothing." I let out a long breath. "It's just…" I turn my attention to the scenery outside the window, searching for the right words. But there's no way to sugarcoat the truth, so I just tell him. "I think Frank saw you touching me the other day."

Jay arches back and scrubs his hand over his face. "Fuck. That was reckless, wasn't it?" He smirks, but there's no amusement in the expression.

In a voice barely above a whisper, I agree. "You tried to finger me in a restaurant while my brothers sat across from us. It wasn't our proudest moment."

He laughs. "Speak for yourself. I, for one, am extremely proud. And if I remember correctly, you didn't hate it."

I let out a huff of a laugh. "Obviously, we're both deviants who are oddly turned on by this stuff. Now let's figure out how to deal with it."

Jay grabs my hand and presses it to his lips while he thinks. When he opens his mouth and gnaws on my knuckles, I laugh.

"Is that helping you think?"

He smirks and then lets out a breath. "Okay. Just deny it. I doubt he saw anything. I barely touched you. And they're fucking eighteen. What the fuck do they know?"

His suggestion shouldn't bother me. Does an idealistic part of me want him to say "fuck it; let's tell the truth"? Sure. But in reality, am I ready for that drama? No way. And if I'm not ready for the ramifications, then how can I expect him to be?

I can rationalize it all I want, but his answer plants a seed of doubt in my mind that I know will sprout and grow the longer I keep quiet.

I attempt to wiggle off Jay's lap, but he wraps his arm around my waist and holds me in place. "You're not happy with that answer," he says, reading me like a book.

"Cash is my best friend," I say, admitting at least a half-truth.

He blows out a breath. "Didn't realize you were so close with your family."

"Just Cash," I defend. And there lies one more thing I'm uncomfortable with. Carter and I have never been overly close, but he's my brother, and I love him. And he's Jay's best friend. Why do I feel like he wants me to distance myself from them? Or is it just the James name in general?

The chasm widening during this single conversation makes me wonder how we could ever have a future together. Yet I don't voice my thoughts. Too afraid to hear his answers.

"What do you want to tell him?" Jay brushes a piece of hair from my face, his thumb stroking back and forth reverently.

I get lost in the depths of his glacier eyes. They're brimming with warmth, a genuine affection reflected only for me, and suddenly, the cracks I was concerned with moments earlier dissipate. Shrinking and contracting until they're barely noticeable. This isn't an easy situation, but he's trying.

With a half-smile, I place a hand on his cheek. "I want to tell him how I'm falling for the most incredible man. How happy I am. How good it all feels. I want to share all of this with him because I have never felt like this before, and Cash would be thrilled about that."

Jay's eyes warm, and his smirk transforms into a beautiful smile. "You make me happier than I've ever been too."

I sigh. Why does he have to be a Hanson? How could something so easy, so simple, so natural, be so difficult? I grab my phone and type out a quick message.

No idea what Frank is talking about. Sorry, grabbing drinks with Sophie. I'll call you later and see you Saturday. Love you.

DIRTY TRUTHS

Tossing my phone to the seat without waiting for a response, I press my lips against my boyfriend's. His last name is a problem for another day.

38

THE WARMTH BY INCUBUS

Jay

With my father out of the country for the last week, I've been breathing easy. I spent time with Cat without having to look over my shoulder. And I was given the responsibility of day-to-day operations in the Boston office with little oversight.

But as I look out my office window, scanning the cityscape, I can't help but ruminate over my father's plan for the James family. What the fuck am I going to do?

My mind turns to the morning that set all of this in motion. Over a decade ago. I woke early, excited about my school project. My mom made breakfast.

Pancakes.

I haven't eaten them since.

"Don't think too hard. You might hurt yourself," Kevin says from the door of my office.

I turn around and smile. It's forced. Nothing like the easy way it comes when I'm with Cat. But she wouldn't smile at me so openly, with so much trust and affection in her eyes, if she knew what my father was up to. What I've been up to. She's close with her brothers. She may not care for her father, but he's not the only one who will be hurt by this plan.

What the hell *is* the fucking plan? I need to figure it out so I can prepare for the fallout.

"Drink?" I ask my friend. Kevin started as an intern at Hanson Liquors along with me. It's nice to work side by side with someone I trust. Even if he's Carter's friend too. He doesn't spend all that much time with Carter. When my father's accomplished his mission, he'll choose me...maybe.

I glare at the bottle of whiskey as I pour us each a finger without waiting for his response. Then he's beside me and picking up his glass and clinking it against mine, grinning. "Where are we headed tonight?" he asks.

Cat texted an hour ago to say she was going clubbing tonight. Mia has been calling and texting her like crazy. Last night, she said she was coming to Boston and wouldn't take no for an answer. While I don't love the idea of Mia and Cat hanging out, I trust Cat, and that's all that matters.

Before all of this, Mia was my friend too. I still feel for her. Yeah, she's a mess, but who isn't?

"I'm exhausted," I admit. And it's the truth.

It's been a long week. After long days at the office, I go home and have dinner with Cat. Her enthusiasm over her projects at Jolie feeds into every conversation we have. She wants this Paris internship with Cynthia more than anything. The idea of being apart for months doesn't sit well with me, but the look on her face when she gushes about it keeps me from voicing my concern. And I'll do anything to make it happen for her.

Except I want to be with her when she experiences Paris for the first time. I want to experience everything life has to offer with her.

And when we aren't talking about Paris, or work, or any of the random thoughts that pop into her head, I'm staying up late making her come over and over again. I can't get enough of her. Even without sex. We're taking things slower than she'd like, but I want to make her first time special. And the plan I have for that is epic.

Kevin eyes me. "You're twenty-four, not fifty. Have a fucking red bull and let's go."

DIRTY TRUTHS

I laugh. He's right. "Feel like going clubbing?"

39

GET YOUR NUMBER BY MARIAH CAREY AND NELLY

Cat

I make one last sweep of the penthouse before the chaos begins. The candles are lit, and the smell of pumpkin spice fills the air. Mariah Carey's *Emancipation of Mimi* album is playing, and I can't help but shimmy a little to the music.

Sophie is the first to arrive. She steps out of the elevator decked out in a silver sequin dress that leaves absolutely nothing to the imagination. "Holy shit!" Her mouth drops open. "You said your family was rich, but this is just…fuck, Cat, I don't have words. I'm literally speechless!" She shuffles closer, still scanning the open area. "Why would you stay at my house when you could stay here? Can I stay here? We should move in. It would be amazing. Have you *seen* the elevator? I could live in there." She points a thumb over her shoulder toward the stainless-steel doors. "It's bigger than my old dorm room, and I did just fine there. And the security guards downstairs? Hot. Like not Daddy-level hot, but I wouldn't kick any of them out of bed for eating crackers. I mean, shit, Cat. Look at how you *live*!"

I press my lips together to keep from laughing. "Are you done?"

She shakes her head, sashaying to the windows. She's silent and oddly still for several heartbeats. Then she spins on me, hands on her hips and a smile on her face. "Cat, seriously, what *is* this place?"

I make my way and lift the champagne bottle from where it's nestled in a bucket of ice. "It is pretty nice, huh?" I admit, pouring us each a glass of bubbly.

Sophie saunters over and takes the glass from my outstretched hand, then clinks it against mine. "To roommates?" she says, her eyes soft and sparkling with hope.

Sipping my champagne, I scan the room. "We can't live here." I laugh.

Sophie pouts and goes back to her perusal of the place. "But it's so pretty." She runs her fingers along the back of the leather couch. "And empty. It's such a waste," she whines.

My lips twist. "It's fun to use, I know. But living here comes with strings I'm just not ready for."

Sophie tilts her head and studies me. "Does your family know you're here?"

My grandfather misses nothing, and he only works a few floors down. But he's not like my grandmother. *He's* not the one who's always tried to control me.

The boys? Knowing Cash and how close he is with my grandfather, he probably does. But he hasn't mentioned it. In fact, we haven't spoken or even texted since that panic-inducing exchange on Monday.

We don't talk every day, but I am not foolish enough to believe that was the end of the conversation. But for the time being, I'll take the reprieve.

I shrug and take another sip of my champagne. "No idea." I let out a breath and move to where Sophie's inspecting a sculpture in its built-in alcove. "Okay, enough of the serious talk. Tonight we're celebrating!"

Sophie and I presented the first few ideas for the Christmas list to Cynthia, and she loved them. She said she'd pass them off to the junior editors to get their feedback. In the meantime, I've come up with an idea for a Facebook account where we review products that people recommend and determine whether they work for real. I grab my phone and hold it up in front of us. "Smile, bitch," I say just as we clink our glasses together and smile for a perfect picture. "I'll post this later," I promise.

At the telltale sound of the elevator, I suck in a breath to prepare myself for the next few hours. I came to a conclusion this week. I need to be honest about who I am. If I don't accept that I'm a James and Jay is a Hanson, then I can't expect others to accept it either.

Which starts with opening up about my connection to the James family. And even though Mia and I have been spending less time together, she is still one of my closest friends. Outside of our crash-and-burn relationship, we were inseparable for years. On my loneliest days, the days I would have done anything to have my mother back, Mia would sit with me in bed and watch movies. Or read. Or take my mind off my woes and force me to dance around our bedroom to No Doubt or scream our lungs out to Alanis Morissette.

She was my best friend, yet I've hidden this version of myself from her for years. That ends tonight.

If being with Jay has taught me anything, it's that I shouldn't shrink or hide who I am. Not a single part of me.

Needing a hit of his joy before the elevator dings, I shoot off a quick text with the link to a song.

> Incubus, "I Miss You."

It only takes a moment for him to reply.

> Jay: Pitbull, "I know you want me."

I laugh out loud and drop a Katy Perry song into the text chain just as the elevator opens and Mia walks into the penthouse with a tall brunette and shorter blonde by her side.

> Katy Perry, "I kissed a girl."

No more than five seconds later, the phone rings in my hand. I laugh as I pick it up. "Hello, Mr. Hanson. To what do I owe the pleasure?"

"Fucking knock it off, Kitten," he growls.

I grin…and maybe squeeze my thighs together at the rough tenor of his voice. I turn, realizing then that all the women in the room are staring at me, wearing confused smiles. "I'm teasing. Listen, I can't chat; the girls just got here."

He sighs heavily, the air escaping his lungs crackling down the line.

"It was a joke," I murmur, turning away from my audience.

"But it's not really," he replies softly.

"You," I say with genuine affection. "Only you."

I can picture him standing in his office, facing the Boston skyline, holding the phone up to his ear. Looking serious and rubbing his thumb along his bottom lip roughly. And then breaking into a small smile as he responds, "Only you, Kitten. Have a good night."

I click off and hold the phone to my heart, a warmth filling my chest. I'm falling for him. Hard.

"Hey," Mia says softly. When I turn, she's headed my way with her arms outstretched.

"Hi, sorry about that." I lean into her for a hug. "It was just…"

She eyes me. "Jay," she says. Like I'd be an idiot to think she didn't know already.

I can't hold back my smile. "Yeah."

"Let me guess," she cocks a hip, "he's not thrilled about you going out with me."

Tilting my head, I study her expression. There's a glimmer of hurt hidden below the teasing. She's wearing a pair of black leather pants, like every other girl in the room, with a low-cut bright red top that highlights her perky breasts. Dark eyeshadow, glossy lips, and light blush finish off her look but do nothing to hide her true emotions.

I pull her in for another hug. "I missed you," I say, surprised by how true the statement is. Seeing her again, after taking time apart to wrap my head around the change in our relationship now that we're older and living in the same area again, brings so many good memories and positive emotions to the forefront of my mind.

"What is this place?" Mia whispers as she turns a slow circle.

"My family's penthouse," I admit.

Mia narrows her eyes at me, but before we have time to discuss it further, her friend interrupts. "This place is amazing. I'm Vanessa, by the way," she says with a small wave.

"I'm Cat," I say to the pretty brunette. "You guys want champagne?"

The blonde who arrived with Vanessa and Mia smiles. "Yes, please. I'm Nikki, by the way."

I pour three more glasses while Sophie introduces herself.

"Where are we going tonight?" Vanessa asks.

I look at Sophie and smirk. "Anywhere but Rebel."

KITTEN'S SONGS

Shots line the bar, and the tattooed bartender with a killer jawline and muscles I'm pretty sure could never fit in a suit raises his eyes to mine in challenge.

I throw back the shot, and when it tastes exactly like apple pie, I try my darndest to hide my surprise. He points to me. "I told you!"

I can't help but laugh. He so did. I don't do shots. That's what I said when Mia forced us to the bar and ordered a round. Sure I'd get away with passing on the liquor, I told her that unless it tasted like chocolate cake or apple pie, I wasn't having one. Who makes shots that taste like freaking apple pie?

This dude. That's who.

I swipe my tongue through the dollop of whipped cream sprinkled with cinnamon in a second shot glass. Freaking delicious. When I look up from all but making out with the glass, two sets of eyes are homed in on me. Mia and the bartender.

"Okay, okay. It's good," I admit.

He folds his arms over his chest proudly. "What are the chances you'll agree to go out with me tomorrow night?"

Mia moves in too close and wraps her arm around my waist. Immediately, I take a step to the side. "Sorry, I have a boyfriend," I reply, lifting one shoulder and emphasizing the boyfriend part while I glare at Mia.

She rolls her eyes. "Does he know that?"

The bartender waves at me when I hold my card out to him. "That one is on the house. Can I get you anything else?"

"She'll take a martini. Extra dirty. Blue cheese olives if you have them." Then, glancing back in my direction, Mia repeats her earlier question. "Does Jay know he's your boyfriend? Because last I checked, that man is not the boyfriend type."

"For her I am," a deep voice rumbles as an arm loops around my waist and I'm pulled back into a strong embrace.

I tip my head back so I'm looking straight up at Jay's chin. "What are you doing here?"

He spins me and grabs my face with both hands, but before responding, he looks at the man to his left. "Kevin, this is Carter's little sister. If you want to keep your job, you'll forget what you see next." Then, without waiting for his friend's response, he seals his lips with mine.

I pull back. This was so not part of our plan. "What are you doing?" I whisper, a smile sneaking through, even though I'm freaking out right now.

"I fucking missed you, Kitten," he says, refusing to release me, his thumb playing with my bottom lip like he so often does with his own.

I shake my head, speechless. "What is happening here?" I ask in a whisper.

He grins. "Hell if I know, but I'm pretty sure this is what they call falling in love."

My eyes go wide, and I suck in a breath. I study his ocean-blue eyes, finding nothing but sincerity in their depths. No nervousness. No doubt.

And along with the candor sparkling in them, there is a heavy dose of determination. The man is determined to steal my heart.

Before I can formulate a response that could even touch the way he makes me feel, he presses his lips against mine again. "Dance with me," he whispers when he pulls back. Then he's tugging me toward the dance floor. Over his shoulder, he shouts, "Drinks are on me, Kev."

KITTEN'S SONGS

It's after two when we finally leave the bar, voices raspy, hair tangled messes and perma-smiles plastered to our faces. "Shit, we need to call a cab," I say to Sophie, who's drunk and focused on one thing and one thing only.

"Pizza. Get me pizza, *now*," she cries, staring at her phone as if the pizza will magically appear.

Kevin has his arm wrapped around Nikki's waist. They made out no less than six times on the dance floor. When Mia and Vanessa file out of the club behind us, Mia grabs for me. "Let's go back to your place and dance!"

With a huff, I let out a groan. "I'm exhausted and I have to be up early for Cash's game tomorrow. Let's get a cab back to the penthouse, and then I'll get everyone set up in beds. You're all staying, right?"

Mia nods. "Definitely missed the last train back to Providence."

Jay nuzzles my neck. "I'll have my driver take you back."

I shoot him a look. "You just want to come back to my place and snuggle, don't you?"

He laughs. "Busted. Besides," he says, shooting a look in Kevin's direction, "I can't touch you tomorrow at the game. I need to get my fill tonight." He traces the waistband of my pants, his fingers dipping below and sending shivers through my body.

I spin to face him. "You're coming to the game?"

He looks at me like I'm nuts. "It's Saturday."

"And?" I say, humor entering my tone.

"And I have to go all week without seeing you during the day. I have to share you on Sunday mornings. There's no way I'm losing an entire Saturday too."

My grin expands. "You really like me," I tease.

"Yeah, Kitten," he says as he presses a kiss to my cheek. "I *really* like you."

40

I KISSED A GIRL BY KATY PERRY

Jay

"Holy shit, is that a hot tub?" Nikki shouts as we step out onto the roof.

Kevin nudges me. "This place is fucking sick. How come Carter's never brought us here?"

I shrug. "If you mention a word of this to him—"

He cuts me off, throwing both hands up. "It's your death warrant."

Pulling in a deep breath, I watch Cat while she takes in the view of Boston at night. She's in sweats, her shoulder peeking out of the slouched shirt as the wind blows her hair around her wildly. "Worth it," I say without taking my eyes off her. Though she's been in my arms all night, I itch for her touch, so I ditch Kevin and beeline for her. With an arm circling her waist, I pull her until her back is flush with my chest and press a kiss to that exposed shoulder. "Tired?"

She nods. "If not for the guests, I'd be curled up in bed with you right now."

I hum. "Fuck 'em. Let's go."

She laughs softly, and like a bolt of lightning, the tinkling sound hits me right in the chest. Fuck, I'm crazy about this girl. She spins and loops her arms around my neck. But her eyes don't find mine. Instead of meeting my gaze, she cranes her neck to the side and mutters, "Holy shit."

Without letting her go, I turn, and suddenly her outburst makes perfect sense. Kevin is stark naked and heading for the hot tub. Nikki is already slipping below the water, not a stitch of clothing on. "Fucking A," I mutter. "I'm sorry. I'll tell him he can't…"

I lose my words as Cat steps back and saunters in their direction, her hands on the hem of her top. She turns back at the last minute, hitting me with a mischievous smirk. "Last one in the hot tub buys coffee for the week."

I growl and rush across the rooftop, trying to get to her before the sweatshirt slips over her head, but it's too late. She's topless, her full breasts on display. She turns to face me, walking backward. "You chicken, Hanson? I thought this was your thing." She tips her head to the hot tub. "Two women, your friend…isn't this how your nights normally end?"

My jaw tics, and I shake my head. What the fuck is she doing? She slips her fingers below the waistband of her sweatpants and shimmies them down as she continues backward.

I holler to Kevin, "Eyes shut, asshole."

He laughs as he covers them. God dammit. Yeah, we've been in similar situations before. But this is *Cat.* I should be the only one with this view of her.

Cat kicks her pants in my direction. "Come on, tight-ass, I know you don't want me in the hot tub without you."

I yank on my tie, working it back and forth as I stalk toward her. "You're dead, woman."

She smiles. "Worth it." She slips into the water, and I fumble with the buttons of my shirt, watching Kevin, who keeps his eyes closed until Cat is fully submerged in the water and only her shoulders and head are visible.

"Can I open my eyes yet?" Kev asks just as I've kicked my boxers off.

I huff and step to the edge of the hot tub. "Yeah." I slide into the water beside Cat and pull her close. "But touch her, and you're dead." I glare at

Nikki as well. She's friends with Mia. I wouldn't put it past any of these fuckers tonight. Then I tug on Cat's hip and press my face into her neck. "You trying to give me a heart attack?"

She pulls herself onto my lap and straddles me. With her breasts in my face, her ass in my hands, and her pussy warm against my rock-hard cock, I mutter, "What are you doing?"

She wiggles on top of me and giggles. Then twists at the waist and quips, "Can someone tell him to calm down?"

Kevin smirks as he meets my eyes. "Your girl has a point. Relax."

Snuggled up next to him, Nikki smiles, but she's mostly silent. It takes me only a minute to realize she's jerking Kevin off while he sits there with a smug, calm look on his face.

I shake my head with a laugh. "Fucker."

Cat rubs against me again.

Turning my attention back to her and gripping her hips, I say, "Let's go to bed."

Her lips find mine. Her skin is damp and heated, and her cheeks are rosy. "I thought this was what you liked," she whispers.

"Cat," I say seriously. "I'm not sharing you."

"Who said anything about sharing? I just want you to touch me." With deft fingers, she grabs my hand and places it on her breast. When I squeeze, she moans and rubs herself over me again. Fuck, she feels good.

I slide my thumb against her nipple, and she arches back, seeking more friction between us. Giving her the attention she wants, I lean down and take her nipple in my mouth.

"Yes," she hisses.

"My girl likes the audience, huh?" I ask, peering up at her.

She bites her lip and nods, her eyes flashing hot.

"You want to give them a show, Kitten?" I ask darkly. Once we do this, there is no going back. And yet the shiver of excitement that rolls through her seals the deal. Over her shoulder, I grit out, "This isn't a fucking invitation; you can look, but that's it."

Kevin smirks. I've never been so fucking crazy in my life. He moves Nikki onto his lap, her back to his chest and his hand between her legs, but his attention remains focused on us. He knows the real prize is in my arms right now.

Cat is the unattainable. The girl a guy would do any fucking thing to keep.

I snatch a towel from the stack next to the hot tub and lay it on the edge, then lift Cat onto it. Her eyes go wide from the shock of the cool air against her heated skin. She's nibbling that bottom lip and scanning our faces. It's obvious she's nervous, but she doesn't cover herself either.

Naked and fucking gorgeous, she settles her gaze on me like she's waiting for direction. "Spread your legs for them, Kitten," I murmur, sinking lower in the water and nudging her legs apart with my head.

Pressing my palms against her legs, I hold her still as I kiss up her thigh. Behind me, Nikki moans, but my focus is entirely on the mouth-watering vision before me. I slide my middle finger between her warm lips, relishing in just how aroused she is being on display like this. "Look at this perfect pussy. So pretty and weeping for me. You want my mouth, Kitten?"

With her lip caught between her teeth and her eyes darting between me and the voyeurs, she moans. It's high-pitched, and I'm not even sure she's aware of it.

Kevin's rasp breaks through the silence. "She's gorgeous, isn't she?" The splashing of the water tells me he's working her over good.

She groans. "So gorgeous."

"She's even prettier when she comes," I say, teasing her lips with my finger. "Should we show them, Kitten? Will you show them how beautiful you are?" Dipping closer, I slide my tongue against her soft lips.

"Oh, so good," she murmurs, head thrashing and hands grasping fistfuls of my hair, guiding me to exactly where she wants me. The world

284

falls away as I lick and suck, her moans the only sounds I hear, her taste my only interest, and her pleasure my sole focus. But as much as this is for her, I get off on it too. When I peer up at her to gauge her reaction, she's staring at the scene behind me.

I press a kiss to her thigh and turn around, making Cat whimper at the loss of me.

Kevin stares right back, waiting to see what I'll do. I have no fucking clue. But I know what Cat wants. She wants Nikki. She can say only me, and I truly believe I'm all she wants on an emotional level, but watching Nikki get off is making her hot.

"Come here, honey," I say, motioning for Cat to join me in the water. Her concerned eyes find mine.

"It's okay, I'm going to get you there," I promise.

Nikki scrutinizes me, and then she turns her head and looks back at Kevin. Before Cat can move, she's swimming over to me. "Let me."

Cat lets out a crying sigh and turns her wide eyes to me.

"It's okay. If you want this…it's okay with me."

Kevin is behind Nikki, his hand on her ass as she settles on the underwater bench, her lips skating across Cat's other thigh. I squeeze my girl's knee in what I hope is a reassuring gesture.

She watches Nikki, her brow furrowed, then she drags her attention back to me. "Kiss me," she begs.

I push to my knees and do her bidding, my lips meeting hers languidly. "If you're nervous, baby, you don't have to do this."

"I just want you," she whispers, her breath skating across my skin.

With that declaration, Kevin pulls Nikki back onto his lap, and I grab another towel from the pile.

Wrapping the terrycloth around Cat, I promise her, "You've got me, baby. Let's go inside."

With a towel wrapped around my hips, I snag her around the waist. "I'll come back for our clothes, okay?"

Her focus drifts back to Nikki and Kevin. She's straddling him now, moving straight to fucking. So much for protection. "I'm sorry," she murmurs softly.

I don't waste another minute out here. I lead her inside, tiptoeing through the house until we reach her bedroom. Everyone else is passed out—thank fuck—and I bring her right to the bathroom, set her down on the toilet seat, and start the shower. Once the water is warm enough, I drag her inside with me.

"Look at me," I say, pulling on her chin so she's forced to meet my eyes. "Do I look like I'm upset?"

She frowns, vulnerability painted across every inch of her face, as if she's disappointed in herself. "It's just…I wanted to; I did…" She studies a spot somewhere along my throat and swallows thickly. "And I also didn't," she rushes out.

I pull her in close, one arm banded around her and the other pressed to her face, guiding her head to my chest. I brush my lips against the crown of her head. "You are the only person I want. Not a threesome, not a fucking show, not anyone but you. *Only* you."

"But normally—" she starts, trying to pull back.

"Fuck normally," I grit, holding her in place tight against me. "Nothing is fucking normal about us. We're extraordinary, Cat. This is special," I tell her, rubbing circles on her back. "You're special. If you want others, I'll let you have them. But if all you want is me? Fuck, I hope that's the case. Because all I want is you."

She loops her arms around my neck and kisses me with a desperation I've never experienced. Our teeth clash, our tongues circle, our bodies fuse, and she whimpers against me.

"I need you inside me," she begs.

I shake my head, blowing out a harsh breath. "No."

"Please," she begs.

"Cat, you…" I press my lips together and take her in, my hands cupping her cheeks. "You deserve special. Not a quickie in the shower because we're horny. I'm going to take you to fucking Paris—to the fucking Eiffel tower. I'm going to wine and dine you, take you shopping, kiss your fucking feet, and then I'm going to make love to you."

Her eyes shine with fresh tears. "Now I want to fuck you more."

I chuckle and kiss her again. "Baby, I'm going to take that virginity. It's mine. Swear it."

She nods. "All yours."

"But right now," I say, slipping my hand between us and running it along her throbbing, swollen lips. "Right now I'm going to get you off, because like I said before, you are so fucking pretty when you come."

She melts against me as I sink my fingers deep, working her over until her legs are shaking and she's screaming my name. And then, just as I think I've entered heaven, she drops to her knees and begs me to fuck her mouth while she fingers herself.

But the best part of the night comes once we're in bed—her head on my chest, her heart pounding against mine, our legs tangled together, as we fall asleep.

41

UMBRELLA BY RIHANNA AND JAY-Z

Jay

The sound of a trumpet echoes through the air, pulling my attention to the field we're approaching. I stuff my hands in my pockets and hunch into my jacket as best as I can. It's fucking cold. Feels like winter is coming early to New England, and I'm not thrilled about it. The grass crunches below our feet as we make our way to the stands. All the while, I search for the tall brunette who forced me out of her bed this morning so she could get her mind ready for battle today.

She's adorable when she's flustered, and I'm already looking forward to the little ways I plan to tease her since Frank won't be in the stands to watch us. Fortunately, the fucker plays with Cash, and unless he has eyes in the back of his head and is more concerned about us than the game, we should be fine.

"I can't believe you came. You had nothing better to do today?" Carter asks as puffs of cold air dance out of his mouth. He brings his gloved hands up to his lips and blows on them.

Kevin cocks a brow in my direction, deferring to me.

"We never get to see you anymore. Besides, who doesn't love high school football?"

Me. I don't love high school football. Didn't love it when I was in high school either. I was a bit of a loner. Until college, when I was given strict instructions to get chummy with Carter, I never saw the benefit of friends.

He cocks a brow in my direction and shrugs. "If you say so." Bouncing on the balls of his feet, he rubs his hands together. "All right, boys. Let's watch some football. Tonight, we're going out."

Kevin eyes me again, his lips folding over as he tries and fails to hide his smirk. The last fucking thing I want is more time away from Cat, and the only other option is to invite her out with us. Which means *more* hiding from her brother. But ditching Carter won't work either, since he's staying in Boston tonight. And if he doesn't hang out with me, he'll likely want to make plans with her. It also means he's going to want to stay at my place.

Motherfucker.

"Sounds like a plan," I relent.

Carter's phone dings, and he smiles when he holds it up to read the incoming text. Then he points toward the fence. "Cat's over by the players. I'm going to say hi. You guys want to get seats?"

No, I want to see my fucking girlfriend. I don't want to sit on cold-ass bleachers and watch her from a distance like a creepy motherfucker. "Sure. Would you like me to get you a pretzel too?" I bite back.

Carter smirks. "Yeah. And a beer."

"They don't serve beer at high school football games," I mutter, walking away.

"Oh, this is going to be such a good fucking day," Kevin teases beside me.

I round on him and poke him in the chest. "This is your reminder. You were sitting in the hot tub last night with *his* naked sister. I wouldn't laugh so hard if I were you."

"And what a pretty view that was," Kevin says, goading me.

"Fucking A," I mutter under my breath as I take off again, the asshole trailing behind me. This is going to be a long day.

KITTEN'S SONGS

"With all the brains in this damn country, how has no one come up with a better seating arrangement at high school football games? Metal fucking bleachers? Seriously? My ass is frozen," I grit out.

Cat folds her lips in on themselves, her eyes dancing with mirth, and Carter lets out a whoop of a laugh when the man sitting with what looks like his wife and two young kids shoots me a glare.

I throw my arms up in defense and roll my eyes. "Are you not cold?"

Kevin thought he would be cute by slipping in behind Cat like he was going to plant himself between us. When he turned to smirk at me, I clenched my jaw so hard I think he felt it. He shuffled back out to the stairs to let me in awfully quick. Now Carter bookends our row, with Cat beside him, then me, then Kevin. Cat brought a blanket and offered to share across the row, but I grabbed it and placed it on the seat and then pointed for her to sit while Carter was down talking to Frank. Turns out, the guy isn't playing today, and I'm starting to get the sense that he actually does have eyes in the back of his head. And they've been firmly planted on me this entire damn game. I thought maybe I could sneak my hands beneath Cat's blanket once I wrapped her up in it, but no such fucking luck.

The game's that way, motherfucker, I want to shout every time the red headed eighteen-year-old turns his beady green eyes on me.

"Take some blanket," Cat says softly.

"Yeah, take some blanket, Jay. We wouldn't want your ass to get too cold," Carter laughs.

Just for that, I'm going to make his sister come while he's in the next room tonight.

Cat eyes me as she holds up the blanket. "I won't bite, I promise," she teases.

I pull her leg to me and snuggle in. "But I might," I mouth to her, evoking the smallest of smiles from her. Below the blanket, I squeeze her leg but keep things PG. There are families around, after all. I'm not a monster.

Beside me, Kevin whines, "Hey, I'm cold too. Want to share your blanket with me?"

The icy glare he's met with only leaves him laughing.

"Sorry, blanket is too small," I say as I slide my hand between Cat's thighs and soak in her warmth. Now *this* is how you watch a high school football game.

KITTEN'S SONGS

As it turns out, Cat and Carter weren't the only Jameses in the stands. As we're waiting for Cash to change, still freezing our asses off, Cat hisses under her breath. When I turn, her grandparents are shuffling toward us. I've seen pictures of them before, but I've never seen them in person.

"Looks like I finally get to meet the grandparents," I whisper.

She's gone stiff, though, and I don't miss how she's moved a fraction of an inch over, creating more space between us.

"Sunshine," her grandfather says, making a beeline for his granddaughter while ignoring the rest of us. The smile that warms her face at his greeting melts any ill will I may have had toward the man. If he makes her smile like that, there's no possible way I could hate him. It's just…fuck, I'm crazy about her.

Cat steps forward and hugs her grandfather tight, their verbal exchange indiscernible from where I force myself to remain standing. Theodore James is a tall man. He's got a full head of silver hair, blue eyes like

Carter, and broad shoulders. He squares them in my direction when he releases Cat.

Beside him is Cat's grandmother, who's just as formidable as the man beside her. She's tall like Cat, her hair doesn't have a lick of gray, and her face holds far fewer wrinkles than is natural for a woman who's got to be in her mid to late sixties.

They're both in warm wool jackets and gloves.

"And you must be Jonathan Hanson," her grandfather says as he holds out his hand to greet me.

Swallowing thickly, I steel myself. I have imagined this day for years. But beside me, Cat has gone rigid as her grandmother comments on her weight gain.

What. The. Fuck?

"I've been busy, Grandmother. I haven't had time to get to the gym. But I'll get back to it," she says quietly, her chin tucked and her eyes downcast.

I close my eyes and suck in a deep breath, grasping for a sliver of control.

But I lose that battle pitifully quick. "I think you're beautiful."

Cat's eyes shoot to mine. As does every other set in our vicinity.

"Uh—" Cat gapes, her jaw hanging open. "Thank you," she murmurs, wringing her gloved hands.

I simply nod and turn back to her grandfather. He appraises me with those keen cobalt eyes, and his lips twitch with what could maybe be a smile. "I happen to agree, Sunshine. I think you're perfect."

Pink paints Cat's cheeks, and she ducks her head.

Her grandmother sighs loudly. "I wasn't saying she's not perfect. I was just saying that she should take time for herself." The crone turns back to her granddaughter. "Are you still going back and forth between Providence and Boston? You know you have a place to stay here. No need to run yourself ragged commuting every day."

Her grandfather chuckles as he meets my eye. "She's been staying in the penthouse. Haven't you, Sunshine?"

The tone is unmistakable, and the way he grips my hand, the one he's yet to let go of since our first exchange, sends me a clear message. He knows we're together.

Cat trips over her words. "I—uh—yes. Sometimes—is that okay?"

Her grandfather finally releases me, but not before raising his brows and giving me a smirk. "Of course it's okay. Use it as often as you like."

Before we wind up involved in another interrogation—by her bitch of a grandmother or Theodore—Cash and Frank saunter out of the gym, and all attention turns to them.

It's clear Cash is a favorite. His grandmother fawns over him the second he appears at her side, and Theodore beams proudly, reminding him of his five touchdowns during the game.

The team was good. I'll give them that.

Cat grins just as proudly, swooping in for a hug. Taking a small step back, I take in the interaction, tightness growing in my chest. This family is close. Really close. How will I fit into this world?

But the much bigger question? How could I ever walk away from it? How could I ever walk away from *her?*

The answer's easy. I can't. I won't. Somehow, I have to accept that the woman I've fallen for is the daughter of the man I despise. The man who destroyed my family. And hope that her family makes up for the inevitable loss of mine when the truth comes out.

42

LIPS ON YOU BY MAROON 5

Cat

After a very strange dinner with my brothers, my grandparents, Jay, Frank, and Kevin, wherein my grandfather sat next to Jay and asked him question after question about his family business and talked shop regarding the whiskey business in general, we finally relax at the bar.

Carter wandered off to the dance floor with a random blonde, and for the moment, I have freedom to unabashedly check Jay out. His blond hair falls lazily across his head—a far cry from the way it was swept back from his face all day as he ran his hands through it anxiously. His blue eyes glitter as he looks at me over his whiskey. "C'mere," he murmurs, smacking his knee lightly.

I scan the dance floor, but Carter is nowhere to be found, and I really do need to touch this man. Even if just for a moment. I settle on his lap while Kevin looks the other way, shaking his head with a laugh.

"I'll go keep an eye on Carter and give you guys a few minutes," he says, gaze fixed on the drink he's spinning on the bar top. With a slight frown, he turns to Jay. "But don't be stupid. You have, like, five minutes, tops."

Jay smirks, then with his hands on either side of my neck, his thumbs brushing my jaw, he pulls me in, planting his mouth on mine. "Then I better make the most of them, eh?" he whispers against my lips. Our kiss is lust-filled and frantic, but also sensual. He takes his time, despite our time constraint, but I feel his impatience as he tugs me closer and holds me in place with a firm grip. "Fuck, I missed you," he mutters, still holding my face and kissing me again.

I laugh as I pull away. "You've spent the last twenty-four hours with me."

"Kitten, you seem to forget that I've yet to be inside you. I fucking need you," he says, his voice smooth, hitting me right in the chest like the first sip of a strong drink.

I need him too.

All of him.

Peering at him through my lashes, I admit, "I want that too."

"Can you sneak away with me to Paris next week?" he rasps, his hold on me possessive.

I press my thumbs against his cheek, massaging, trying to calm him. "I can't do anything until after the ball."

He closes his eyes, accepting defeat.

"But I don't need Paris, Jay. I just need you."

He shakes his head. "I want it to be special. I want to take you shopping at the Champs Élysée. I want to see your response when you see the Mona Lisa and realize just how hideous and small it is."

I laugh. This man. Serious and desperate one second and teasing in the next.

"I want to sip champagne with you with a view of the Eiffel tower. I want to feed you crepes," he says as he squeezes my hip. "And I want to make love to you. Slow. In our own world. I want everything for you, Cat. It's what you deserve."

My smile is wide. The idea he paints, the memories I know we'll make, they're beautiful. "Someday I want all of those things too. But I'm not waiting, Jay. Figure out a way to make it special here, because I can't wait for a special trip to fuck you."

He groans and presses his forehead to mine. "You can't talk to me like that, Kitten, or I'm going to find a corner and make a meal out of you right now."

I drag my hand down his chest and slip my fingers between the buttons of his shirt. We both hiss at the connection. "Do it," I murmur. "I dare you."

Before I know what's happening, he's lifting me in one quick movement. Then he lowers me, making sure I feel every inch of his body on the way down. Once my feet are planted on the floor, he presses me forward and whispers in my ear. "You're going to pay for that mouth, Kitten. I'm going to fuck the sass right out of it."

Of their own accord, my thighs clench, and a rush of warmth spreads through my body. "Yes," I rasp.

We descend the stairs that lead from the bar area to the main floor, and a voice calls from behind. "Where you guys going?"

I groan as I turn to find my brother and Kevin ambling toward us. "This place sucks. Want to go somewhere else?" Carter asks, his hands in his pockets like he's bored.

"Fucking cock block," Jay mutters under his breath, covering his mouth with his hand so that only I can hear his words.

I press my lips together to keep my laugh from escaping. "What happened to your friend?" I ask Carter.

He shrugs. "Wasn't feeling it."

Kevin smirks and shakes his head. "No. Turns out Cindy wasn't thrilled when she realized Carter didn't recognize her. He fucked her a few weeks ago, and she thought he remembered."

Jay chuckles beside me, and I find myself wishing he would pull me against his chest so I could feel the way his deep laughter rumbles through him.

Carter throws up his hands. "It was a year ago, asshole. I'd remember her if it was only a few weeks."

I groan. "You're disgusting."

Carter lets out a heavy sigh. "Don't let these two fool you. One of you probably fucked her after me. Maybe together." With a brow cocked, he scrutinizes Jay and Kevin.

I close my eyes, trying to unhear that comment. The last thing I want to think about is my brother and Jay fucking the same girl. Or Jay fucking anyone but me.

Jay grips my hip and mouths "never," as if he knows precisely where my thoughts have gone.

I take a deep breath.

"Stop hitting on my sister," Carter says, although there's no real heat behind his words. He waves a hand and heads for the exit. "Let's get out of here."

Jay presses behind me as we follow him. In my ear, his steady voice grounds me. "He should be a hell of a lot more worried about me spanking you, don't you think?"

I laugh out loud as we step out into the cool night.

43

CRAZY IN LOVE BEYONCE & JAY Z

Jay

Carter did find a girl he hadn't hooked up with and forgotten, so not long after we ordered drinks at our second stop of the night, he disappeared. Kevin called Nikki and went to her place, probably realizing I wasn't going to let him follow us home. So I brought my girlfriend back to my apartment, where I made good on my promise to fuck the sass out of her mouth. Her ass was red from the spanking I gave her, but she was drenched when I finally settled between her thighs and made her come repeatedly until neither of us could keep our eyes open.

Unfortunately, I can't spend today in bed with her like I want. Cat has brunch with her family, and I've been summoned by my father.

I press my thumb to her bottom lip as she stands at the door, ready to leave. "Dinner?" I ask, nibbling on her lip before slipping my tongue in her mouth. I fucking can't get enough.

She hums as she kisses me back, and I snake my hands around her waist, pulling her closer. My other hand runs through her hair. Fuck, I need her.

She pushes me away. "Can't. I need to focus on this idea that Sophie and I are working on for Jolie. I really want this internship in Paris."

Cradling her face, I give her a half smile, then press another kiss to her lips. "And I want it for you. Come over when you're done with Sophie, then? Please, Kitten. I need you in my bed at night."

She smiles softly and puts her hand on the doorknob. "So needy, Mr. Hanson."

"For you. I'm *everything* for you."

And I don't even try to hide it.

KITTEN'S SONGS

My father is dressed in a suit when I arrive for lunch. He takes one look at my jeans and grimaces. "What the hell are you wearing?"

It gives me sick pleasure watching him twitch over a pair of jeans. Holding my arms out wide, I look down at my outfit like I don't understand the issue.

My father growls. "You're late, so this will have to do."

"Is someone joining us?" I ask, knowing it'll just be us.

He glares at me but doesn't respond as he walks to the dining room.

The table is set for two, his plate at the head and mine at the other end. The other four spots remain vacant. What's with the formality? I haven't really thought about it before, but watching Cat with her family has made me realize that the relationship my father and I have isn't normal. Why we don't sit side by side, or at the kitchen island. But even when my mother was around, we had dinner in the dining room every night. Formal dinner. Never mac and cheese or pizza or takeout.

It's been steak and potatoes, mahi-mahi with jasmine rice, escargot, and caviar since I was a child.

And it's only now, when I'd rather have a waffle out of a to-go box while lying in bed with my girlfriend, that I even question the life I've lived for the past twenty-four years.

DIRTY TRUTHS

"Have you cleared everything out of Carter's apartment yet?" my father asks as Sienna places our food on the table and blushes when she makes eye contact with me.

She's stunning. Poor thing will be fired if she doesn't look at my father the same way.

Every woman on staff in his home is gorgeous. And young. When they hit twenty-eight, he lets them go. Then he starts again.

And he fucks every single one of them.

My skin crawls because, until recently, his actions didn't even bother me.

I see the world through a different lens now.

The only constant in my life outside of my father is Wendy. She helped raise him, so she's older, and she runs the house perfectly. She's not soft in any sense of the word. No one could be soft and survive my father.

But she has a soft spot for the both of us.

Sienna, on the other hand, clearly prefers me over him.

I avoid her gaze, knowing that giving me too much attention will cost her this job, and because, as beautiful as she is, she doesn't hold a candle to Catherine.

"Not yet. I haven't had the chance," I reply.

My father cuts into his steak and holds his fork aloft. "Get it done soon. Dean is going to put the plan in motion next week, and you don't want to be anywhere near that apartment when that happens. There can be no trace of our family's involvement in this."

My heart rate skyrockets, and I put my hands on my knees to keep my father from seeing the way they tremble. "What is the plan?"

He shakes his head as he chews. "It's better that you don't know. Since you were his roommate, we need to keep you as far removed from this as possible so there's no inkling of your involvement."

I grip my knife and saw through my steak, avoiding his gaze. "The point is to go after his father," I remind him.

"I know what the fucking point is!" His shout startles me, and I drop my knife to my plate with a clang. "I don't need the reminder!"

"I just want to make sure innocent people aren't hurt," I say, keeping my voice even. "His father is the one who should pay."

He laughs. "Not a single James is innocent, and you'll do well to remember that."

"Dad, by that logic, I'm guilty of your sins."

"You are," he says, wiping his face with his napkin, his eyes never leaving mine. "You're as entangled as I am. We're in this together."

My conscience screams at me to beg him to stop. To do anything but sit here and let him destroy the family of the woman I love. But I keep my mouth shut. To him, my silence is acquiescence, so he places his napkin on his lap and takes a sip of his whiskey. "I'm thinking London for Christmas to see your brothers."

44

SWEET DISPOSITION BY THE TEMPER TRAP

Cat

Cynthia studies the computer screen, her eyes roving over the proposal for what feels like hours. I peek at Sophie, and she gives me a shrug, just as anxious for our boss's opinion as I am.

The air is filled with possibility. Like it has been for the last two months. Ever since I moved back to New England. Jay, this job, school. There is so much potential on the horizon. I've woken up in Jay's arms every day for the last two weeks. The ball is in two days. And I think I have everything covered.

We've gone over every detail ad nauseum every night over dinner. He's unperturbed by my constant chatter about it and my nervousness. He's patiently gone over it all with me. The drinks, the linens, where the photographers will stand, the lighting, the flowers, the candles, the food.

Over the weekend, he surprised me with a trip to New York, where we shopped for my dress for the ball and matching masquerade masks. My dress is a deep royal blue with black lace on the bodice. I wasn't sold on the idea of matching attire until he convinced me that since we're running the event together, we should coordinate. Although it makes sense, a small part of me worries that it'll lead to questions. But mostly, I'm happy. Jay is happy. And everything else fades to the back.

"Hmm." Cynthia snaps her fingers, and Rose moves from her spot in the corner to peer over Cynthia's shoulder. "This. I like this," she says.

Which one?

Rose takes notes on her pad and brings her attention back to the screen. "And this. I like this. *A lot.*"

"Yes, it's amazing," Rose parrots. She glances in our direction, her normal smugness transformed. For the first time, I see…admiration, I think…in her eyes. "Really amazing," she remarks, her focus solely on me.

My heart flutters, and I squeeze Sophie's hand.

"And what is your plan with this?" Cynthia asks as she sets her glasses on the desk in front of her and grants us her full attention.

I look to Sophie, but she motions for me to speak.

"Well," I clear my throat, "we've noticed that Facebook has really taken off for college-age people, and it's becoming more and more popular all the time. In my opinion, it's the future of advertising. Jolie needs to be there. We would post content. *For everyone,*" I emphasize, and Sophie bobs her head beside me. "Since there will be a face—or two," I say, smiling to Sophie, "behind the account, people our age may trust it more. Essentially, the content will be similar to what's printed in the monthly issues, but it'll be promoted daily on this page in an organic way."

Cynthia shakes her head. "It's…" she hesitates, breaking into a wide smile, "brilliant. I think you're right. This is the future. *You* are our future," she says.

My body tingles as my chest expands with pride. Magic. Possibility. "Once the ball is over, I want your full attention on this project. We'll start testing it quietly, and when we go to Paris this winter, we'll present it to the board."

I bite my lip. *Paris.*

"Paris?" Sophie squeaks.

Cynthia settles back into her chair. "Yes, girls. Congratulations, the internships are yours."

KITTEN'S SONGS

I practically sprint to Jay's office after a celebratory lunch with Sophie. I'm a teensy bit buzzed from the champagne we splurged on. "Paris!" she screamed as we walked out of Cynthia's office. "We're going to fucking live in Paris!"

Jay's secretary tells me he's expecting me and to go on back. I barely make it through the door before he's dragging me in, shutting his door, and pressing me against his wall, his hand traveling up my skirt and his mouth on mine. "I'm so fucking proud of you, Kitten."

It's not lost on me that the man hasn't once voiced concern over this trip or tried to talk me out of my desire to take an internship thousands of miles away.

He encourages me. Listens to me. Supports me. All things I've rarely experienced in my life. Someone in my corner for the simple reason of just *being* in my corner.

"Thank you," I say, searching his eyes for any hint of hesitation on his part. But they sparkle with nothing but pride. His lips curve into the most genuine smile, and with his body pressed against mine, our heartbeats sync.

"So, Paris in the winter," he murmurs as he pushes the fabric of my panties aside with his fingers and presses inside me. We moan in unison.

"Paris in the winter," I repeat as I drop my head to the wall behind me and Jay's fingers slide in and out of me, bringing me to the edge quickly. I've only been in his office for two minutes, and I'm about to come. "Fuck, Jay," I pant.

He smirks and presses a kiss to my neck. "Such a good student you are, Kitten. Coming with my name on your lips, riding my finger like you're going to ride my cock this weekend. Show me, Kitten. Show me how you're going to squeeze me."

My walls clench around him, and before I can make too much noise, he takes my mouth in his, kissing me hard. When he pulls back, a smirk he's more than earned in place, my knees go weak. He removes his fingers, slips them into his mouth, and closes his eyes as he cleans them of my orgasm. Then he hums in appreciation, and with his hand on the small of my back, guides me to the chair in front of his desk.

I sit, and he takes the seat next to me rather than on the other side of his desk. With a smile, he reaches for my ankle and rubs circles on it with his thumb. "I'm so fucking proud of you," he says again.

"I'm so proud too. This is…shit. I'm at a loss for words. I'm going to Paris."

"Yes, baby. You're going to Paris."

"Are you nervous?" I ask.

He tilts his head and hums. "Why?"

Before I have time to broach the subject of where he sees things going, if he wants to do long distance, if his lack of nerves is because he doesn't plan on it…because when the time comes, he'll want to let me go, the buzzer on his phone sounds.

"Mr. Hanson, Mr. James is here to see you."

I dart a glance at Jay, who's already standing and picking up his phone. "Which Mr. James?" he asks, his tone all business. Then his shoulders drop in relief. "That's fine. Send him in."

"Are you fucking nuts?" I say, jumping to my feet. "Your hand was just down my pants, and you're going to let one of my family members in here?"

He huffs and settles in his chair. "Relax," he says, running his hand through his hair. "Sit down." He points to my chair. "It's just Carter."

"And how exactly will we explain my presence?" I ask, quirking a brow in his direction.

The door opens before he can reply, but he mouths, "And my hand was up your skirt, Kitten, not down your pants." Then, without missing a beat, he smiles broadly at Carter. "Look what we have here. Visits from two Jameses on the same day. How did I get so lucky?"

Carter's smile falls as his attention lands on me. "The fuck?" he curses, halting at the door. "What are you doing here?"

I huff out a laugh. "Nice to see you too, brother."

He shakes his head. "It's not. Sorry." Finally, he steps into the office and leans down to kiss me on the cheek before settling in the seat beside me. "I just didn't expect to see you here."

"She's handling the ball for Jolie magazine, and my company is partnering with them, so Cat and I have been working on it together," Jay says easily, leaning back in his chair. It's not exactly a lie, though it's not the reason I'm here right now.

"Oh," Carter says, turning to me, then studying his best friend. "So you've been seeing each other to work on this?"

Jay nods, his lips quirked in a smirk and his eyes alight as he considers me. "Yes, she's been coming every night."

I press my lips together and focus on my clasped hands.

"This is great," Carter says, slapping the armrests of his chair with unexpected excitement.

"It is?" I ask, chancing a glance in his direction.

He smiles. "Yeah, now we can go to lunch together. My sister and my best friend are friends. Perfect."

I nod. "Yeah, great. But I can't join you for lunch."

Carter scoffs. "And why the fuck not? You too good for us?"

I laugh. "No, you idiot. I already had lunch. You realize it's already two, right?"

"So early dinner, then," Carter says with a smile, his eyes on Jay.

Jay shrugs.

"I have an appointment," I say, getting to my feet and smoothing my skirt. "But enjoy lunch."

"What kind of appointment?" my needy brother asks. Seriously, does the guy have *any* boundaries?

"None of your business," I scoff.

He scowls at me.

"I'm going to the doctor," I huff.

"Why do you need to go to the doctor? You look perfectly healthy to me."

"It's none of your business." I roll my eyes.

"Fucking A. I know I'm not your precious Cash, but I'm still your brother, and I deserve to know if something is wrong."

Jay smirks from behind his desk and steeples his fingers in front of him. He knows exactly why I'm going to the doctor. I turn back to Carter with a hand on my hip and sigh. Normally, I'd ignore his outburst, but there's a glimmer of genuine concern under the mask of outrage he's hiding behind. Health isn't something we take lightly. Not after losing our mother so young.

"Fine. If you must know, I'm going to the gynecologist."

He scrunches his nose and frowns, but I continue. He asked for it.

"To get birth control."

He covers his face. "Why the fuck would you say that to me? And in front of Jay! What the fuck?"

I snicker. "You asked." I turn to Jay and smile as he holds back his own laughter. "Have a good lunch, boys."

As I step into the hall, Jay teases Carter. "What? I happen to find the topic fascinating."

"Don't you fucking…" The end of Carter's sentence is lost when the door closes, and I huff out another laugh.

45

IT HAD TO BE YOU BY RAY CHARLES

Cat

Makeup artists and hair stylists arrive at the penthouse early on Saturday. Sophie and I crank Mariah Carey and Katy Perry up loud while we primp and sip champagne all afternoon. Dexter and Jay arrive around the same time, and I can't help but feel like everything we've ever wanted is laid out before us, ripe for the taking. Not only our career dreams, but the men who have taken us completely by surprise.

"Are you making it official tonight?" I ask Sophie as she applies her last coat of lipstick before we leave.

Her eyes meet mine in the mirror as she blots. "I'd say your night will be more monumental than mine."

I dip my chin and blush at what she's referring to.

"But yes. With me going to Paris, it probably makes more sense to pull back. We'll be long distance…but," she spins to face me and shrugs, "he says he wants to try."

I smile. "Of course he does. Who would want to risk losing you? It's only six months. In the grand scheme of things, what could really change in six months?"

In reality, the pep talk is more for my benefit than hers. Jay and I still haven't talked about what those six months mean for us. Last night, he was out late with Carter, and when he came to bed, I was more focused on returning the favor he'd given me in his office than broaching that terrifying subject. This morning, I woke up with him between my legs, and then he had to rush off for a meeting.

But tonight…tonight will change everything. Jay reserved a room for us at the Beacon Hotel for after the ball, and then I'll finally experience what it's like to have him sinking inside me. But I'm not naïve enough to believe that, in his eyes, having sex automatically means we're serious. That he's interested in trying the long-distance thing.

But I do trust in the way he looks at me, the way he's cared for me. The way he insists on spending our evenings and nights together and how he begs to hold me every morning. Though I won't assume to know his thoughts on the matter, I don't think either of us believes that Paris will be the end of us. We'll figure it out.

"You nervous?" Sophie asks.

"About the ball? God, yes. I think Jay and I have thought of everything, but this is freaking Jolie magazine! *Everyone* who's anyone will be there."

Sophie squeezes my hand. "The event will go great. I mean are you nervous for tonight?"

I bite my lip as I study Jay. He's talking to Dexter by the window with a whiskey in his hand. Perhaps feeling my gaze, he turns to me, stops talking, and breathes deeply before mouthing, "Gorgeous."

I smile and look back at Sophie. "No. I'm not nervous. Jay will take care of me."

She laughs. "Yeah, I'm pretty sure he will."

I smack her, the warmth of the moment drowned out by her teasing. "Let's get going." I stride toward the door, but after a few steps, when she hasn't moved from the spot, I sigh. "Are you coming?"

"Yup, and so are you tonight," she says with a laugh and does a mock drum tap.

KITTEN'S SONGS

The images I conjured of this event in my head don't do it justice. Black organza fabric sparkles above us as it hangs from the chandelier and drapes across to the windows, giving an elegant, otherworldly feel to the room. Each table is adorned with onyx candelabras of different sizes and vases filled with burgundy roses with the tips painted black.

The entire space glows lavishly from nothing but flickering candlelight. The masks we've all donned for the ball hide our identities from all but those who know us well, which brings a freedom to my movements beside Jay.

Yes, Cynthia is here, but she's busy working the room.

And outside of her, Sophie, and Dexter, no one has any idea who we are. Or, more accurately, they don't know who I am. Everyone knows Jonathan Hanson. And that's who he is tonight. Working the room with me at his side, Jay is every bit the future CEO of Hanson Liquors.

"Dance with me," he murmurs in my ear as a masked man consults him about the fires that are affecting the grains this year. "I'm sorry, Carl," he says, interrupting the old man's rantings. "My date has been patient all night, but I promised her a dance."

The older man turns to me and shakes his head. "Of course. Enjoy yourselves."

With a warm hand on my lower back, Jay pushes me a little too eagerly toward the dance floor.

I stifle a giggle at his enthusiasm. "I'm fine if you want to continue the conversation," I tease.

"Shut it, you," he says as he pulls me into his arms and sways. "I'm not going to lie, Kitten. You in that fucking mask? Damn. I can't stop fantasizing about you sucking my cock while you wear it."

"So romantic," I say, putting my hand to my chest in mock offense.

He laughs. "Please. You've already thought of seven different ways you want me to fuck you tonight, haven't you?"

I burrow into him and hum with a smile. "If we're bringing toys into the room, those strap-on dildo things look fun."

Jay pushes back and considers me like he's gauging my sincerity, and I can't help but giggle. "No fucking way," he says as a shudder runs through him.

I laugh harder.

"I'm serious, Catherine."

"Oh, pulling out the full name. I'm in trouble now, *Jonathan*."

"I'd prefer you to call me sir," he muses, pulling me close as we continue to sway.

"When I'm on my knees?" I tease.

"Fuck, are you trying to get me hard while we dance in a room full of people?"

I so badly want to kiss him. I love getting him riled up. He absolutely loses it. "How much longer?" I whisper.

He scans the room and then looks back at me. "We *should* stay for another few hours, but fuck it. I'm over it."

I laugh. "Don't you have a speech or something to give?"

"Someone else can give the damn speech," he says in frustration. "I just want my girlfriend—"

A man clears his throat behind Jay. "Jonathan."

Jay's hold on me tightens, and his back goes ramrod straight. "I'm sorry, Kitten. Just go with it," he whispers before turning us to face the intruder. "Father," he says, holding out his hand to the man.

The other Mr. Hanson does not wear a mask. He has furry eyebrows that take up the majority of his forehead, a Jay Leno chin, and he's wearing a scowl. "Why don't you introduce me to your *girlfriend*?" He enunciates the last word, as if it's foreign or troubling to him.

Jay keeps his arm firmly looped around my waist. "This is Catherine Bouvier. Catherine, my father, Warner Hanson."

The whiskey magnate holds out his hand, examining me with keen awareness.

I slip my hand in his and give it a firm shake. "It's a pleasure to meet you, Mr. Hanson."

"Pleasure is all mine. I had no idea my son had a girlfriend. This is…a pleasant surprise," he says in a tone that indicates that it's anything but.

"Yes, well, we would love to chat, but Catherine isn't feeling well, so I'm going to make my rounds and say goodbye. Then we're heading out," Jay says as he tugs me away from his father by the hip.

"What about the speech?"

Jay looks back, regarding his father. "Now that you're here, you can handle it. They'd much rather hear from the CEO anyway. It is *such* a surprise seeing you," Jay says, the bite in his words evident. He doesn't talk about his father, so I don't know what their relationship is like, but right now, it's obvious that he doesn't want the man to know who I really am.

I offer a wave and a warm smile. "It was nice meeting you."

Jay practically drags me from the ballroom, only allowing me to stop and check with the event staff to make sure everything is handled before we're dashing to the elevators.

As soon as we step in, Jay breathes a sigh of relief.

"Are you okay?" I ask, pressing my hand to his shoulder as I study him.

He slides the mask off his face and then removes mine as well, sliding it up into my hair. "Ah, fuck, you're beautiful. I just needed to see your eyes."

His are wild, the tension creating deep lines on his face.

"What's wrong? Talk to me." I press my hands to his face, trying to smooth the lines around his eyes with my thumbs.

"I need you," he murmurs, pressing me against the wall of the elevator, his lips taking mine in a rough kiss.

I push back gently. "And you'll have me, but not like this. Not when it's not about us…talk to me."

His face falls, and he presses his forehead to mine, letting out a sigh. "Fuck, Cat. I'm sorry." He blows out a breath. "Tonight is supposed to be special. He just…" Jay pushes away from me and slams his palm against the stainless-steel wall of the elevator car, making me jump. "I don't want him around you. I don't want him to know you."

"You didn't want me to meet your father?" I ask, hating the insecurity that thunders through my veins.

The elevator door opens, and he grabs my hand and pulls me down the quiet hallway. "I'm doing this all wrong," he mutters, coming to a halt outside our room and eyeing me. He closes his eyes, takes a deep breath, and tries again. "He's not a good person, Cat. And he *hates* your family."

"It's business," I reply flippantly, hating that the night has turned into this.

Jay shakes his head, his jaw tight. "It will never be just business."

"And us?" I ask, my nerves taking over.

With his palms pressed to my cheeks, he dips his head and catches my gaze, his sky-blue eyes more genuine than I've ever seen them. "Us… we're…separate from that. Or at least I'm trying to keep it that way. God, Cat, you have no idea what you do to me. How I feel about you. I'm insane right now, and nothing's coming out right."

I place a hand over one of his. "Just tell me what you feel, then. Talk to me. It doesn't have to be pretty or perfect; it just needs to be true."

He licks his lips and presses them together as he studies me. And then, in the hallway of a hotel in Boston, Jay sweeps me off my feet.

"I'm in love with you. Irrevocably. Completely. Head over *fucking* heels in love with you. I want to shout it to anyone who will listen. But I also want to hide us away from the world because I'm afraid, Cat. I'm so goddamn scared that the minute our families find out, I'll lose you. And I just…" He stops and sweeps a thumb across my cheek. "I can't lose you. That's the truth. I'm in love with you, and I'm scared."

Swallowing thickly, I allow Jay's words to seep into my skin, to race through my veins, to shock my heart. Each and every one of us should hear *I love you* millions of times throughout our lives, the syllables the most vital in the English language. And while friends and maybe even my brothers have uttered that phrase to me over the years, no one has spoken them to me so earnestly since my mother took her last breath.

"I've never heard something so beautiful, Jay," I whisper with a smile, leaning into his touch. "I love *you*. Irrevocably. Completely…*I'm* head over fucking heels in love with you."

The tension in his face finally relaxes, replaced with the most brilliant smile. "You stole my line."

"You stole my heart," I reply easily, my smile soft, my face warm.

His breath whooshes out quickly. "You really love me?"

I lean into him. "So needy," I tease. "But yes, I really love you. And I intend to show you how much tonight. Now, can you please take me into that room and take my virginity?"

Jay laughs against my lips. "I think that can be arranged."

46

PRECIOUS LOVE BY JAMES MORRISON

Cat

"**D**on't," I say, placing a hand on Jay's forearm as he reaches for the light switch. It takes me a moment for my eyes to adjust to the moonlit space, but it's clear we're in a suite. Or maybe something even larger. There's a couch and a living area. Likely a big-screen television and a full bar hidden in the shadows. But none of it interests me. Not when there's a bed and privacy. And Jay.

"I want to see you," he rasps as he tugs at his tie. "I can't see you in the dark, Kitten. I can't watch the way your lips pout when I drive my cock inside you for the first time. Or the way your eyes light up when I shove it down your throat."

I whimper, desire sparking in my core, my need for him animalistic.

"But if you want darkness, I'll give it to you." He tugs at my lip and drags his teeth along it. "Because you're all the light I need."

His mouth crashing against mine in a frenzy, he pushes me against the wall, his hands roaming my body. Studying every inch like the contact is brand new. Like he's never touched me before and he's memorizing the way I feel beneath his fingers.

"I need three minutes," he says into my mouth.

I laugh. "Only three? Geez, I thought you'd last a little longer than that."

He runs his hands down my hips and squeezes my ass roughly. "Smart-ass. I need three minutes to get things set up. We're a little early, so the staff hasn't been up to do it for me like I planned."

An unbidden smile breaks out on my face. "Go on." I tilt my head and survey him. "I won't turn into a pumpkin on you."

He laughs as he presses a kiss to my cheek. "Fuck, I love you."

When his back is turned, I silently scream into my hands. He *loves* me. Jonathan Hanson loves *me*.

And we're finally going to have sex.

I rush into the bathroom, relieved to have a few minutes to wrap my head around his admission and to try to keep myself cool, calm, and collected.

Beneath my dress is a navy blue mesh corset Sophie helped me pick out on Newbury Street. Jay is going to lose his fucking mind when I walk out of the bathroom in heels, with the mask back in place, and my breasts spilling out of this corset.

I fix my hair, gargle with the travel-sized mouthwash I find on the counter and take a deep breath.

Jay isn't in the living room when I make my way back out there, so I head straight to the bedroom. As I push open the door, I'm met with the most beautiful sight. Candles glow on both bedside tables and the bureau. And there are more vases of red roses scattered around the room.

His voice startles me. "You're beautiful," he rasps, like the words are hard to get out.

I turn to him and smile softly. He's still in his pants and button-down, but it's undone at the top. His jacket is gone, and his tie is missing.

"I love when you say that," I admit.

He stalks toward me until he's clasping my hips and his mouth is brushing against mine. "Say what?"

"You don't say I *look* beautiful; you say I *am* beautiful. There's a difference."

He nods. "I'm aware. And you are." He presses his lips to mine, bringing one hand to my cheek while his other holds me steady. "I could get lost staring at you, Kitten. I love all of your looks. The suits and dresses you wear to work, the fucking skirt you wore to the club with the suspenders, tonight's dress, this—" he pauses and gulps as he angles back and takes in the corset—"fucking get-up." Blue flames flashing in his eyes, he brings his focus back to my face. "But at all times, you're beautiful. The most beautiful woman in the room, if you ask me."

"You're the only one I care to ask so…" I shrug.

His eyes soften. "Good." He presses another kiss to my lips. "Only you, Kitten," he reminds me of our promise.

"Only you," I whisper back. The candles flicker around the room, and heat crackles between us. "I'm nervous," I murmur, unable to hide a single thought from him.

Softly, he brushes a thumb against my lip. "Don't be. We'll go slow."

The tension in my body wanes with his every word as lust coils tightly in my core. I blow out a breath and then bite at his lip.

He smiles as he pulls back. "Let me really see you, sweetheart."

With three strides backward, his legs hit the edge of the mattress, and he plops down on the bed, his eyes never leaving mine.

I nibble my lip nervously. "What do you want me to do?"

With a hand in the air, he twirls his finger. "Spin for me."

I giggle but do as he says. When I turn back to face him, he's got a fist pressed to his mouth and he's sinking his teeth into the flesh. "I don't know how I got so damn lucky…"

I roll my eyes, though behind my mask, the gesture is lost.

He summons me with the crook of his finger. "C'mere, Kitten."

I prowl toward him and eat up the way his eyes track my every movement. He reaches for my hand, pulling me between his legs and dropping his head to my stomach.

Taking in a calming breath, I rub my hands through his hair and watch him.

With a sigh, he tips his chin and rests it on my abdomen, studying me. "I really need to see you tonight. Take off the mask and let me make love to you. *Please*."

When I pull at the string behind my head and tug, the mask falls to the floor beside me.

He tips back, his hands gripping my hips roughly so I'm forced to move with him. Once I'm straddling him on top of the mattress, his lips move to mine, and we kiss for what feels like hours. Soft, warm, needy kisses that say everything we've been building toward for the last few months.

"I love you," he whispers between kisses.

"Irrevocably, completely, head over fucking heels," I reply.

He smiles and flips me onto my back, caging me in with his arms as he props himself above me. "Thief," he taunts.

I quirk a brow and smirk. "What are you going to do about it?"

His smile practically hurts, it's so beautiful. The joy, the happiness, the abandonment of all worry is so evident. "I suppose it's deserved, Kitten. I've been stealing all your firsts."

Pressing up on my elbows, I kiss that smile like I can somehow figure out a way to keep it. "It's not considered stealing when those firsts are willingly given."

"And what are you giving me now?" he asks, his blue eyes almost silver in the candlelight, shadows dancing across his gorgeous face.

"Everything, Jay. I'm giving you everything. My heart, my body, my future…it's all yours."

He closes his eyes like he's really soaking that in. As if the promise of the future may mean more than the rest. It does for me. Giving him my heart? That could be a temporary offering. My body? People do that all the time. But my future? Only one person can have that. And it's him. I can't imagine a world where I love anyone but this man. A time where I wouldn't move heaven and earth to be with him for eternity.

An eternity wrapped up in his warmth, surrounded by his promises. The idea makes it feel like time stands still. Like it's forever and too quick. It makes breathing easier and harder at the same time. Because there is no greater feeling. But the thought that it could end is debilitating.

So I promise him my future. Because I don't want to steal his breath; I want to give it back to him.

With no words left to say, I work the buttons of his shirt and slip it down his shoulders. He slides down my body and shucks his pants, then turns to my garter belt and removes it with deft fingers. He lifts one ankle and kisses it softly before sliding his tongue up my calf, to my thigh, and then between my legs. With a provocative groan, he runs his tongue straight up my seam, sucking, licking, and teasing me until I'm panting and begging for more.

I watch every brutal minute of it. Every circle of his tongue and every needy growl makes my heart pound faster. When he slides a finger inside me and fucks me slowly with his hand, focused on my face, gauging my reaction, I come apart at the seams, moaning his name.

"Good girl," he says, pressing a kiss to my thigh and nudging it back with his head when I try to close my legs. "You said my name like you promised, and now you'll be rewarded."

"Jay, up here. I need you now."

He shakes his head. "Another one. Give me one more, Kitten, and then I'll give you my cock."

I squirm and grab at his shoulders, but he holds me in place. He's in no rush. This is for him. This is his time, and the knowledge of that makes me want him more. He takes me to the edge again and then sucks on my clit until I'm exploding in his mouth, and only when my legs have lost all semblance of fight does he finally kneel on the bed, peering down at me with pride.

"Corset off," he says gruffly as he grabs for a condom he must have stashed on the bedside table.

I hiss a breath as he strokes himself slowly. I've had my mouth on him plenty, felt him swell in my hand, but the idea of him finally sliding between my legs and piercing me makes me rub my legs together in anticipation.

"I need your help," I say, turning around so he can untie me.

Jay chuckles, his warm breath tickling the back of my neck. "My fucking pleasure," he says and nips at my shoulder blade while working the strings at the back of the corset.

As each loop loosens, I breathe a little easier, but the swipes of his fingers against my skin and the nips he steals on my neck leave me panting.

"Fuck, I can't tell you how badly I want to slide my cock inside you right now. Just like this. Watch your ass while I fuck your pussy. Spank it until it turns red."

Whimpering, I clench in response to his confession.

Without warning, he grabs my arm and pushes so I roll to my back. His hands find my breasts as he kneels between my legs. "But I need to see your eyes when I slide inside you. I want your greedy sounds against my mouth. I want to watch you when I take what I've earned. When I ruin you for everyone else. When you become mine."

Chills cascade down my body. Little pinpricks of lust dust my chest, and my nipples harden to the point of pain. I need him so badly; I'm ready to snap.

Using one hand, Jay lines his cock up at my entrance. He taps me with it once, twice, three times, and runs it through my wetness. "Fuck," he groans, "I can feel you through the condom, Kitten. I can't wait until your birth control is all set. Then I'm gonna fuck you bare."

I whimper. "Yes, please."

His eyes darken, and he props himself up on one hand so his face is inches from mine. "You want that, don't you? Just for a minute. Just you and me?"

I nod, my heart racing, my chest heaving. *"Please,"* I beg.

Popping back up on his knees, he slides the condom off and throws it to the floor. Then his cock is against me again, the feel of his skin against mine burning me from the inside out. The air shifts, and everything falls away. His gaze locked with mine, Jay nudges into me. "I love you, Catherine."

My body warms as he presses in slowly, and I cry out as I reply, "I love you too." And fuck, that hurts, the pressure, the stretching. His fingers, the toys, nothing prepared me. Propped on his elbows so our foreheads are touching, he takes my mouth with his, kissing me as I moan in a pleasured pain.

"Ahh," I cry, squeezing my eyes shut.

"Baby," he whispers, concern dulling the blue of his irises. He angles back like he's going to pull out, but I grab at his ass and hold him in place, then push him in farther.

As he stretches me further, I scream, "Fuck," and pant out another breath. "It's okay, it's okay," I chant, willing it to be true. But the burn is making it difficult to speak.

Jay settles between my legs, but he holds his upper body up, as if afraid to give me his weight. He's squeezing his eyes shut like maybe I'm doing something wrong.

"Does it hurt you?" I ask, my body finally getting used to the feel of him, finally accepting him.

Through gritted teeth, he says, "You're so fucking tight, Kitten. It feels so good I'm trying hard to control myself."

I smile and lift my hand to his face. "Open your eyes, Jay. Look at me."

Jay's eyes fly open, wild with lust. "Fuck," he curses as he shifts again. "Baby, seeing your tits…I'm sorry. Nothing I'm saying is romantic or right. You just feel and look and…fuck," he says as he moves again.

A breathy laugh escapes my chest. "Fuck me, Jay."

He groans and starts up a slow rhythm. I watch in fascination as his thick cock slides inside my body, the veins that run along it angry, just like the ones on his arms as he holds himself above me.

"Look at us, Kitten. Look at how well we fit together. This is how it was always meant to be. You and me. *Just* you and me," he growls.

"Only you," I rasp. With each press in, the pain lessens and the pleasure compounds. Wanting him closer, I loop my arms around his neck and bring my lips to his, kissing him languidly as he fucks me into oblivion.

We pant our *I love yous* and make a million promises. There's no one I trust more in this world. And there is nothing I believe more than exactly what Jay said. We are meant for one another. Nothing else matters.

When we're lying together in the darkness, the candles blown out, our bodies tangled together, sleep trying to steal what little of the night we have left, I smile against his chest.

"Who meets their soulmate at twenty-one?" I ask, genuinely shocked that we could be so lucky.

He laughs. "I don't know; I didn't."

I push against him, and he grabs my hands, waffling our fingers together before pulling them above my head. He stares down at me. "I met mine at twenty-four."

47

BUBBLY COLBIE CAILLAT

Jay

Soft feet pad into the bedroom as light filters through the open door. I crack one eye open to find Cat in a white waffle-knit robe, her long hair in a messy bun, pushing what appears to be a cart of food. The cart creaks as she rolls it over the rug, and I blink a few times, trying to jostle myself awake so I don't miss a minute. We were up far too late, but when I glance at the clock, I see it's almost noon.

"Morning," I rasp.

Cat's face lights up with a smile as she realizes I'm awake. "Thought I'd have to wake you up with a blowie," she teases.

My hands fall behind my head quickly, and I close my eyes. "Don't let me ruin your plans."

Her loud laughter draws them open again. I selfishly want to witness every moment of her happiness. It's easily become my favorite view. Her smiles. Her joy. *Her.*

She moves to the windows and draws the curtains back, bathing the room in a golden light. "Rise and shine, Mr. Hanson. The entire world is awake."

"I don't give two fucks about the entire world, Kitten. *You* are the only thing that matters." I pat the space beside me on the bed.

"Well, I'm awake too. And I'm starving. Someone had me up late into the night."

"And you loved every minute of it."

Cat settles beside me in bed, her gaze eating up my naked body, which is tangled in the sheets. Her hand goes to my heart, and those brown eyes find mine. "I did. And I love you," she says softly, her lips tilting up.

"Fuck," I whisper. "Say it again."

"I love you, Jay. *Only you.*"

She doesn't know it, but no one has ever said those words to me. My father doesn't deal in emotions. If something doesn't make him money, he gives it no thought.

And my mother? I'm not sure if she never used those words because we lived in such a cold house, or if she was like him too.

So many of my memories of her are tinged with betrayal, so it's hard to know if I've colored her that way, or if she really was always without light.

Cat's bathed my world in yellow. Brightness and joy I never even considered, let alone hoped for.

Leaning down, I press my lips to hers, and she meets me with a hungry kiss. I grasp her hips and tug, lining her up precisely where I want her.

But she smiles as she shakes her head. "I'm starving, Jay."

Smirking, I thrust upward, giving her a taste of what I have to offer. "As am I."

She smacks me lightly. "For food, you goober."

Chuckling, I slide my hands up and down her bare legs. "Goober? Really?"

Her head hits my chest as she laughs, and the sound fucking does things to me. *She* does things to me.

My heart is in fucking knots, and it's all because of this woman.

She presses her lips to my chest and then slides off me too quickly for me to stop her.

Begrudgingly, I sit up. "What'd you order?"

Shimmying her shoulders, she croons, "Everything. Waffles, pancakes, bacon, eggs, croissants, yogurt. You name it; I got it."

It's the pancakes that I zero in on. "Haven't had them since my mom died," I whisper.

Cat's eyes find mine and she gazes back at the platter, like she's trying to ascertain what I'm referring to.

"The pancakes," I say, my tone rough gravel. I clear my throat, not wanting to ruin the moment. "Sorry, it's not a big deal."

Cat shakes her head and covers the offending dish. "It absolutely is," she whispers, sliding back over me again.

"Eat, beautiful," I tell her, but there's no bark to it.

She kisses my jaw. "No."

I sit straighter, bringing her with me, and grab a piece of bacon, forcing it to her lips. She nips at it, and I smile. "Good girl."

Her eyes light up as she chews.

"You like when I praise you, huh, baby?"

She smiles with a shy lift of her shoulders. "Maybe."

I reach over and rip off a piece of waffle, then dip it in the syrup before brushing it across her lips. She waits, knowing exactly what I'm going to do. The girl can read me like no one else. She edges closer, and I bite the waffle, then lick across her lips. "Delicious," I say around a mouthful.

She laughs. "I like this."

"What?" I ask, reaching for another waffle piece and feeding her.

"Lazy Sunday mornings with you." She lets out a happy sigh. "Just being with you in general. Tell me about her, baby," she whispers.

My mom.

I tilt back, but Cat pulls at my hand, keeping me close. Then she reaches for a piece of bacon and tears it apart, offering me a bite before she takes her own.

"I don't have beautiful memories of my mother like you do, Cat. I'm not even sure my mother cared for me."

"I find that impossible to believe," she whispers.

"Why?" The question is practically a plea. I can't hide the broken desperation that seeps through.

"Because I love you so deeply, and I tried so hard not to. You're easy to love, Jay. Incredibly easy to love."

She rubs the pad of her thumb along my cheek, wiping at a dampness I hadn't realized was there. Embarrassed that I've let a tear escape, I duck my head.

She doesn't allow it, though, pulling me back to look at her. "I think…" She pauses and holds my gaze. "I think it's impossible to know what our mothers were really like. But Jay, I know for a fact that if she took the time to get to know you, she loved you. Even if she struggled to say it."

I get lost in her eyes, the way the sun makes them sparkle and how a kaleidoscope of colors appears. "Thank you," I whisper.

She smiles. "For what?"

"Before you, my life had very little meaning. I was frozen. My heart, I…" I struggle to put into words what she's done for me. The way she's brought me back to life. "Just know, Catherine, that every day in this life, I will choose you. Don't ever doubt that. Only you."

48

JUST GOT STARTED LOVING YOU BY JAMES OTTO

Cat

As much as I want to spend the entire day in bed with Jay, there's somewhere I have to be tonight, and he can't come. Since I can remember, my grandparents took my brothers and me out for hibachi for our birthday. It's our thing.

I'm not sure when precisely it started, but it was sometime after my mother's death. Carter's was the first birthday we spent there. He took her death incredibly hard. He was nine when he watched her get sick, watched her deteriorate. Memories like that don't leave a person. I vividly remember my mother's laugh—soft. And her scent—sugar and cinnamon with a hint of lemon. Why I have no idea. And dance parties in the kitchen when it was just the four of us, Carter by my side, Cash in my mother's arms, and my mom spinning me in circles like I was a ballerina.

But I don't remember losing her. Maybe my brain blocked it out. Or maybe she hid how sick she was from me, and Carter just saw more of it.

Without her, Carter barely spoke, and a birthday party was the last thing he wanted. So our grandparents took us out for hibachi, and when the chef took out the water bottle that looks like a man peeing and aimed it at Carter's face, he burst out laughing. It was the first time I remember hearing his laughter after her death.

After that, our grandparents took us there for each of our birthdays. It's a tradition we've kept up to this day.

So I'm not surprised when I walk into the restaurant at the agreed-upon time and spot all of my brothers at the table with my grandparents. Frank is with Cash, of course, because he's his shadow, but the unexpected additional guest has my mouth falling open.

"Happy birthday, Kit Cat," Cash says, standing and wrapping me in a hug before I can react to my boyfriend's presence at my birthday dinner. Suspiciously, the seat between him and Frank is unoccupied.

I offer hugs and kisses to everyone and am treated to more birthday wishes before settling in the chosen seat. "Hey," I say, my gaze turning to Jay.

He smirks. "Happy birthday, Kitten," he mouths.

Squirming under his gaze, I scan the table to make sure no one's watching. But, as usual, Cash is delighting them all with a story, so I have nothing to worry about. "Surprised to see you here," I murmur.

. "It's Jay's birthday too," Carter says, hearing my comment despite my attempt at discretion, "and since he didn't have plans, I told him to join us." He studies us, as if he's on to us. Or maybe that's just my imagination. My guilt. This is his best friend.

"It-it's your birthday?" I ask as my brain catches up to my mouth.

Jay laughs casually. "Yup, twenty-five today. Although, I'm pretty sure nothing will top twenty-four," he says smoothly before picking up his drink and taking a sip, his eyes dancing with humor.

Carter laughs. "Am I ever going to meet the girl that has you smiling like a virgin?"

Jay sprays the table in front of him with his drink, and I snort in laughter.

Carter passes him a napkin, grinning, and I have to turn away, trying to avoid Jay's eyes.

"You okay over there?" Cash asks, drawing the attention of my grandparents.

DIRTY TRUTHS

Jay elbows Carter, who only laughs harder, and mumbles, "Sorry."

Carter's smug as he extends his arm behind Jay's chair. "I was just telling Jay that I never see him anymore. My hunch is that he's met a girl." He eyes his best friend and smirks. "When are we going to meet her?"

If I could sink below the table and disappear, I'd do it in a heartbeat.

"The only woman I've been spending time with is your sister," Jay says casually, as if he didn't just drop a bomb. The entire table goes silent.

"Because of the ball," I rush out.

Jay's eyes light up. He loves to make me squirm, but we both know he's not any more ready to expose us than I am. I drop a hand to his thigh and bite back a smile when he stiffens beneath it.

"Leslie said it was the best event she's ever attended," my grandmother says, surprising us all.

My hand stills, and Jay rests his on top of it, giving it a squeeze. "Catherine did an incredible job. I've had multiple calls asking for information about who planned the event. Her ideas and designs were inventive and beautifully executed. According to Cynthia Caldwell, at least."

Pride surges through my veins and warms my cheeks.

"I've heard the same thing," my grandmother says, a rare warmth emanating from her. "Wish we'd been there," she adds, that warmth cooling drastically and a tightness to her tone.

My shoulders fold in on themselves, but Jay doesn't allow it. He squeezes my hand again. "My apologies. That was an oversight on my part. I'll make sure you get a personal invitation next year."

My grandmother nods, and fortunately, the waitress arrives to take our orders. For the next ninety minutes, we're entertained. We laugh and tease, and it feels oddly perfect having Jay by my side. He fits in with my brothers so well, and I can't help but envision a future where we're doing this out in the open.

"I still can't believe we have the same birthday," I mutter when no one else is looking. "How did I not know this?"

The flame from the hibachi reflects in Jay's eyes when he smirks at me. "You going to get me a present?"

I roll my eyes as I focus back on the show in front of us. "Pretty sure I did last night."

Not missing a beat, he stabs the shrimp on his plate and brings it to his mouth. "And twice this morning."

The waitress arrives with the fried ice cream and two candles and my family sings to the both of us. When Cash tells us to make a wish, Jay and I lean in.

"Every wish I've ever made came true last night, Kitten," Jay rumbles quietly. "So this one's yours."

I close my eyes and wish that I get to spend every birthday for the rest of my life with this man by my side.

49

YOU WERE MEANT FOR ME BY JEWEL

Jay

The first few weeks of November are a blur. They're nights wrapped in Cat's arms, mornings between her thighs, stealing her away from work for lunches. Sunday afternoons at the farmers' market, brunch with her brothers, dirty martinis on the rooftop of the penthouse in the hot tub. It's everything my girl likes. And I fall harder for her with every passing day, every kiss, every whispered *I love you*.

My father has been unusually quiet. He's gearing up for a trip to London and dealing with his ex-wife, my brothers' mother, which always takes a lot out of him, so I chalk the unusual behavior up to that.

He hasn't said a word about Catherine Bouvier, and I'm cautiously optimistic that it's because his worries lie elsewhere.

As far as I can tell from my conversations with Dean, the plan my father put in place has not been set into motion yet, which means I still have time to figure out what it is and to make sure that Cat remains unscathed.

The door to my office flies open, and before she even sets foot inside, I know it's her. My secretary is under strict instruction to let her come back at any time. In the beginning, Cat insisted on waiting for approval before just walking in, but she's beginning to find the joy in surprising me. And because I love nothing more than seeing her excited or on her knees, I still pretend that I'm shocked every time.

"Kitten, I wasn't expecting you. Come over here." I pat my lap.

She stalks over to me and settles between my thighs, dropping a kiss to my lips, her hands on my cheek and her eyes sparkling.

"I missed you," she says simply.

I give her a lazy smile. "I always miss you."

Our movements are quick, deliberate. My pants are down, her skirt is up, and I'm inside her in under a minute, pounding her against my desk, loving on her, kissing her, tweaking her nipples, and making her cry out my name. I muffle her sounds with my hand, which she takes as an opportunity to bite and then lick and then bite again. And then we both come hard. In less than ten minutes, she's completely unraveled me.

"What the fuck was that?" I laugh, falling to her chest.

"That's what we kids call a quickie, Mr. Hanson," she teases.

I bite my lip, but the smile slips through. "Oh, you teaching me some lessons now, Kitten?"

I pull myself off her and reach for a tissue so she can clean herself up. As I buckle my pants and settle back into my chair, my eyes don't leave her. She settles herself on my desk and crosses her legs.

"Pizza tonight?" I ask, already aching to get out of this office and take her home.

She frowns. "Can't. I have plans."

"You're gonna fuck me and not even feed me?" I joke.

"What can I say? I was horny and needed my fill."

Chuckling, I pull her onto my lap and run my hands through her hair. "What are these plans you have?"

She winces, and the easy feelings are replaced with anxiety.

"I told Mia I'd meet her for dinner."

It's been over a month since I've seen or spoken to Mia. Not since that night at the club. I don't know whether Cat regularly keeps in contact with her, but to be honest, it would surprise me if she did.

"You've been talking to her?" I ask, a bolt of jealousy coursing through me.

Cat shakes her head. "Not really. That's why she wants to grab dinner. We haven't seen each other in over a month."

Not sure why they need to now, but I keep that to myself. I school my expression and calm my jealousy. "Right. Well, tell her I said hi. Will you be over after?"

Cat rakes her fingers through my hair and brushes a thumb against my cheek. "Don't do that."

"Do what?" I feign indifference.

"You know I will be. We haven't spent a night apart in over a month."

I sigh in resignation. I can't hide myself from her like I can with everyone else. And I hate that I even tried. She doesn't deserve that. "I'm sorry."

Angling close, she presses her lips to mine softly. "Don't apologize," she murmurs, pulling back and settling on my desk again. "I get it. If it makes you feel any better, if you were going to dinner with an ex, I would lose my mind with jealousy."

I smirk. "Oh yeah?"

Huffing a laugh, she swats at my chest. "Yeah. But there's no reason for me to be jealous, right?"

I roll my eyes. "For you? No. Women who aren't you don't exist to me."

She licks her lips. "You really don't even have to work to come up with those lines, do you? They just slip out."

I shrug. "They're the truth. I can't lie to you, Cat. I'm in love with you. It's that simple."

"I love you too," she says softly. "And no one exists for me in the way you do. Completely. Irrevocably. Head over heels." She presses her hand to my heart.

"Completely. Irrevocably. Head over heels," I repeat.

50

WARNING SIGN BY COLDPLAY

Jay

One more afternoon spent doing the opposite of what I'd like to be doing—Cat. I leave for the dreaded Christmas trip to London next month, and then she's heading to Paris for her internship the first week of January. How is it that I already miss her, and I woke up beside her this morning? Hell, I woke up inside her mouth this morning. Not a fucking horrible way to start the day. Yet she's not here, so it's gone downhill quickly.

The buzzer on my phone summons me from my delicious memories.

"Yes?" I reply, waiting for my secretary to speak.

"A Ms. Alves is here to see you," she says, her tone dripping with disapproval.

Mia? Here?

"Send her in," I say with a sigh. Cat got home late last night, and then we got lost in one another and didn't talk about her dinner with Mia. An uneasy feeling settles in my stomach, though, when Mia walks in with her chin jutted petulantly and her nose turned up.

She throws a thank-you to my secretary as she crosses the threshold, but her eyes remain on me, as if I'm somehow going to slither away when she's not looking.

I don't slither for anyone.

"Mia, to what do I owe the pleasure?" I ask, pointing at the guest chairs.

Still on her feet in front of my desk, she narrows her eyes as she purses her lips, clearly thinking she has the upper hand. And maybe she does, because I don't have a clue what the issue is. Cat and I have been together for almost two months—longer if you count the inordinate amount of time it took to win her over. The last conversation that Mia and I had about Cat was before we made things official, and that feels like a lifetime ago if I'm being honest.

Life can be categorized into three parts for me. Before my mother's affair, the time in which I sought revenge for a decade and subsisted on nothing but that, and the time since meeting Cat. I wouldn't return to either of the previous chapters for anything.

"She's fucking Catherine James," she says, as if the information should shock me.

I steeple my fingers in front of me and wait for her to go on.

"Is this all a game to you?" she shouts. "Make her fall for you so you can take her down with the rest of them? I can't believe I actually thought you cared about her." She scoffs.

I shoot to my feet, sending my chair knocking into the wall behind me. "Wait a fucking minute. I do care about Cat."

"More than your revenge?" she asks, her eyes wide.

I take a deep breath and blow it out slowly. Mia doesn't recognize the change in me, and that's my fault, not hers. For years, I cursed the James family. She knew my plans. She knew why I made friends with Carter. She helped me when necessary.

But she didn't know her best friend was a James then.

"Yes," I breathe, letting my shoulders drop. "Cat means more to me than revenge."

Mia finally drops to the chair like her legs can no longer hold her, her face etched with confusion. "Does she know?"

I shake my head. It's the one secret I've kept. Maybe it's more than

352

one secret, but they're all twisted in a malignant knot.

"She knows I hate her father. And that my relationship with Carter is complicated by that."

Mia scoffs. "So she doesn't know you used Carter to exact your revenge. How do you think she'll take it when everything goes down? Do you even know what your father has planned?"

Her questions eat at my soul. Day in and day out, I work to anticipate my father's next move. I dig for information. But truthfully, I can't prepare. If Cat learns the truth, that I've been working on setting her family up for the last five years, and why I hated her father so much, would she ever forgive me?

The answer is likely no.

And that's not a risk I'm willing to take.

I scrub at my head and huff. With my father heading to London, all I can do is hope that his plan is on hold until after he returns. By then, Cat will be headed to Paris. While she's gone, I can work to unravel the plan or at least minimize the fallout. With her overseas, I can only hope to keep her from suffering the consequences of it all.

But now that Mia knows, that plan may be nothing more than a wish whispered into the wind. She'll never let me keep her.

"This will break Cat's heart," I say to Mia, pleading with her.

Her eyes are wild. "You think I don't know that? It's the *only* reason I didn't say anything last night. How could you be so selfish? You can't claim to love someone and then trick them like that."

"That's rich coming from you," I counter.

She reddens. "I stepped back. You asked me to give you a chance to make her happy. I stepped back because I care about her." Her eyes well with tears. "I care about her, Jay, and this is going to break her heart."

Standing, I tug on the cuffs of my sleeves, then round my desk. Kneeling beside her, my hands on the arms of the chair, I plead my case. "That's why she can't know. We need to fix this. I'm trying to stop my father's plan, but I need more information to do that. I need to get that damn tracker they had me place in Carter's room. I slipped it into his computer. It's an SD chip. I have no idea what's on it or what intel my father's looking for, but we should start there."

"We?" she scoffs.

Falling back on my ass, I sigh and fold my arms over my knees. "I can't do it, Mia. It's too risky."

"Why?" she demands.

"Because I'll have no reasonable explanation if I get caught."

"And what if I get caught?"

I give her a look, and her mouth drops open. Then she crosses her arms and glares.

"Don't look at me like that," I argue. "You flirt with everyone. If you get caught, just bat your lashes at him. He'll think nothing of it. Carter thinks with his dick around women…and you'll be protecting Cat," I add for good measure, suddenly realizing the brilliance of this plan. We can get the chip back, and once I have it analyzed, hopefully I'll know what my father is planning. Then I can protect Cat from the fallout and make sure it doesn't touch anyone but her father.

Because knowing my father, the goal is to take down the whole family.

"When?" Mia asks.

"I'll call Carter today and ask if he wants to come up to Boston for drinks. You go to the apartment, get in and get out, and we'll be all set."

Mia is silent and impossible to read as she tilts her head and examines me. I really need her to say yes. If not, I'll call Kevin. I need help, and I can't let this get back to Cat. Mia is right; it will break her heart. Since the moment I found out she was Catherine James, I knew this day would come. But I've worked to be a better man. To be a man worthy of her. And I didn't go through all of that—and fall hopelessly in love with her—only to lose her. I promised her a future, and now it's time to make sure we have that.

"One night," she replies, her eyes holding mine.

"One night?" I question.

354

"Yes, that's my price. Give me one night with Cat, and I'll do it."

I jump to my feet and shout, "The fuck?"

"You get everything else, Jay." She folds her hands in her lap and tilts her head like her demand isn't fucking insane. "You stole it all from me, and now you want my help, so that's my price."

"She's not a fucking hooker, Mia. I don't bargain with her body." Spinning, I slam my fist into my desk. "What the fuck is wrong with you? You claim to love her, and then you do this? Fuck you. I'll take care of it."

She stands, eyes wild. "One night, or I tell her."

I squeeze my eyes shut and fist my hands so tightly my nails puncture the skin. I could kill her. I could literally strangle her right here. End this right now. All I see is red. "Get the fuck out of my office," I say through gritted teeth. I can't be held responsible for what happens next if she doesn't leave.

"Worried she'll want it?" she sneers. "That she'll realize you aren't enough?"

She hits on a nerve, but I stifle my reaction. If she knows how much she's getting to me, it'll be that much worse.

"So help me God, Mia, if you don't get the fuck out of my office, I will fucking kill you."

The door to my office swings open, and Kevin walks in, scanning the space. When his eyes land on Mia, he turns back to me with a scowl. "What the hell are you two screaming about? Your secretary asked me to come in because she was so nervous."

I turn and face the window, knowing I can't be trusted. "Get her out of my office. Now!" I bark.

"I'm leaving," she mutters.

Before she can make it out, I warn, "Two can play at your game, Mia. You talk, I talk...and your best friend will know exactly what you just tried to do. So keep your fucking mouth shut."

Her answering glare is powerful enough that I can feel it burning into

355

my back, but I don't turn.

Kevin slams the door shut. "What the fuck was that about?"

I run my hand through my hair. *Think. What the fuck can I say? What can I do?*

At a loss, I pivot and point to the bar cart in the corner. "I'm taking the afternoon off. I don't want to talk about it. Just drink with me or get the fuck out."

Kevin follows me to the cart and clinks his glass against mine after a heavy pour. "To not remembering."

KITTEN'S SONGS

Hours later, I'm three sheets to the wind when my phone rings. I grip it with all my strength, wishing I could actually crack it. As if ignoring her will fix things.

It won't. I have no choice but to answer because she holds all the cards now.

If she tells Cat, I lose everything. Because Cat *is* everything.

"What?" I growl, taking the phone outside so I can hear her over the bar crowd.

"Call Carter!" she hisses.

"What?"

"Call. Carter," she enunciates, still in a whisper. "I'm in his room, but someone just came in the front door. I'm in the closet. Call him and tell him to meet you before he catches me!"

"Fuck," I say. "Stay in that goddamn closet until I call you back."

I hang up without waiting for a response and dial Carter.

"Hey, Jay," he answers coolly.

"What are you doing?"

He laughs. "Just got home. Going to make dinner and head to bed. I'm beat."

"Come to Boston. Kev and I are at Pearl. Thought we'd hit up Rebel next." I dangle the carrot, hoping he'll take it.

He whistles. "Wow, you've been so busy this past month, I really did think you got a girlfriend or some shit, but Rebel..."

I can almost picture him scratching his chin as he considers the request.

"No girlfriend," I lie, tipping my face to the night sky, pleading with whoever's up there to forgive me for all my transgressions. It's for a good cause. So I don't lose the best part of me, a person I vow to be good to for the rest of my life. I'll take care of her, keep her happy, treat her better than anyone else could. Isn't that worth the stumbles I have to take to get there?

I run my hand through my hair. What is taking him so long to answer?

"Sorry, man. It would take me an hour to get there. Tomorrow night?"

I text Mia that she's shit out of luck. She better come up with another plan.

"Rebel, Carter. Fucking Rebel," I try again.

He laughs. "Tomorrow," he promises.

I agree, even though by then, I'll probably have been discovered. I don't even head into the bar. I call a cab and text Cat and beg her to meet me at home. She's working late with Sophie. And knowing this may be the last night she ever looks at me in that soft way of hers, I selfishly ask her to come to me for the night.

The next morning, while I lie in bed with the love of my life in my arms, the unraveling begins.

> Mia: I have the disk. You have two weeks to make a decision, and then I go to Cat with the proof, and we both lose her. Your choice.

357

51

HOW TO SAVE A LIFE BY THE FRAY

Jay

Allow a sociopath to touch my girlfriend? Or break my girlfriend's heart? Doesn't feel like much of an option. Killing Mia would be preferable.

Although jail time would also break Cat's heart.

"Motherfucker," I growl for the thousandth time since I received the ultimatum. "Who fucking does this?"

Uncovering my father's plan has now become my top priority.

When the two-week deadline comes and goes and nothing happens, I foolishly let myself relax a little. By week three, I'm convinced she was bluffing.

And then during week four, Mia walks into my office and upends my life.

"I'm pregnant," she says as she sits in the chair across from me, her eyes watering.

"You're what?"

"Pregnant. With child. Ya know? When two people have sex, the sperm—"

I slam a hand to the top of my desk, cutting her off. "I know what pregnant means, Mia. I just have no fucking idea why you're telling me."

"Because it's your fault," she says matter-of-factly.

I huff out a breath and lean back in my chair, steepling my fingers.

This should be good. "And how is it my fault?"

"You didn't get your best friend out of the apartment like I told you to, so I took matters into my own hands."

I stare at her, at a loss as to how any of this relates to me.

"Carter," she says, prompting my memory.

"You slept with Carter?" I shout, unable to hide my shock.

She sighs as if bored with the details and scans my office before turning her attention back to me. "Yes, Jay. What else was I supposed to do when he found me in his room?"

I roll my eyes to the ceiling and blow out a breath. Carter is so goddamn predictable.

"Why are you telling me?"

"You haven't taken me up on my offer—" she starts.

I hold my hand up to silence her. "You slept with her fucking brother, you psycho. I am not letting you anywhere near Cat."

She sighs. "I'm aware, asshole. My point is that I'm pregnant, and I need money. I—" She closes her eyes, as if this pains her to admit. "I don't want to be like my mom. Or yours." She looks past me, surveying the Boston skyline through the window behind me. "This baby deserves better than a fuckboy like Carter. But I can do this, Jay. This is my chance."

I roll my tongue over my teeth. She isn't necessarily wrong. And buying her silence isn't the worst idea. But I don't trust that I'll ever have her complete loyalty. "How much?"

"Ten million," she says without batting an eye.

I laugh. Fucking laugh. "You've lost your damn mind. Ten million dollars? That's extortion, not help for you and your child."

She shrugs. "You want the disk, and you want to protect her. You want to *keep* her," she reminds me. "Ten million, or I tell her the child is yours."

I spin away from her. I can't fucking look at her smug face. At this person I stupidly felt sympathy for only moments ago. She used my mommy issues to manipulate me. Remind me of our commonalities. And

I *almost* fell for it.

"Go for it, Mia. Fucking tell her whatever you want. She won't believe you. And when she finds out you slept with her brother—*and she will find out*—she'll hate you. Is that what you want? You pretend to care about her. You pretend her safety means something to you, and then you pull this shit. My only priority is her. So if she can't get over what I've done in the past, that's a risk I'm willing to take. I'm not putting her safety in your hands."

Mia's expression hardens, and her eyes go cold. "It's the mob, Jay. Your father's been funneling stolen money from the mob into the Jameses' bank accounts. *All* of them. You want to keep her safe? Pay me, and I'll give you the information. I care about her safety, but I have to think about me and my child first."

My heart stops, then drops into my gut. All this time, I knew my father was angry. And he's vengeful, yes, but I've always assumed he was stealing trade secrets or pushing James Whiskey into bankruptcy. I could tolerate those deceits.

Edward James stole my mother—she killed herself after what he did to her—I'd never forgive that. But the mob? Icy fear rushes through my veins, and my skin prickles at the thought of what this means for Cat.

"The mob?" I croak, stunned. How did he even pull this off?

Even as I ask, I know it's true. Dean. He's managed to do things for my father and me over the years that I'd rather not know about.

Mia just lifts her chin. She knows she's got the upper hand. There's nothing left to say.

I rub at my forehead, at an absolute fucking loss. Obviously, I need a plan, but I'm too bewildered by her revelation to think. In the meantime, I need to buy Mia's silence. "Fine. But if you so much as whisper Cat's name, I swear to God, Mia, I will send the mob straight to your door, hear me? Forget she exists. *Forget I exist.*"

Mia nods, then she stands and slides a piece of paper across my desk.

"As soon as the money hits the account, I'll have the disk delivered to your office." She shuffles to the door, but turns back, her hand on the knob. "For what it's worth, I really did love her."

I bark a humorless laugh. "Get the fuck out." And when she retreats, I grab the first thing I find and throw it at the window. The stapler slams against it hard and crashes to the ground. With no idea what to do, I put my head in my hands and scream.

52

I LOVE YOU ALWAYS FOREVER BY DONNA LEWIS

Cat

"Choose any seat you want, Kitten," Jay says, motioning around the plane with an outstretched hand.

I smile back at him and roll my eyes. "I've been on a private plane before."

He laughs. "But you haven't been on mine. And I'd bet money mine's nicer than any James plane."

Such a brat.

The damn things are practically identical. It's almost like our fathers bought the same model. But I keep that to myself. I'm sure it would enrage him to think my father had anything like his.

And this weekend is about us. Not our fathers, not our families. It's our own Christmas before he heads to London. The plan is for me to meet him in Paris the day after Christmas so we can spend the week together before my internship starts. But I'm dreading the time we'll have to spend apart before then. And I have no idea how I'll make it six months without him.

"Tell me again how often you'll come visit me," I beg as I settle into a seat. There are four chairs in our row: two here and two across the aisle, each with plenty of leg room. I groan when I sink into the soft leather. "I need the information on this leather." Rubbing the seat on either side of my legs and luxuriating in the way my body melts at the contact, I peek at him through my lashes. "Designers should use nothing but this fabric anywhere. I want this on my body. I want it everywhere."

Jay laughs and tugs at my hand, then waffles our fingers together. "I'll fly out every other weekend. You'll be sick of me. And I'll have my assistant get you the information about the leather. I'll have pants and a jacket made for you. Does that cover everything, Kitten?"

I smile as he presses a kiss to my knuckles. "I could never grow sick of you. You're my favorite person."

"Only you," he whispers as he leans over and grabs my seat belt, pulling it across me and tightening it as his eyes hold mine.

"You don't think I know how to buckle my own seat belt?" I tease.

Jay steals a kiss. "I take care of what's mine. And you're mine."

I close my eyes as I press my lips to his. "You know…I could give you another one of my firsts today," I whisper.

Jay's eyes dance. "You'll be happy to know that I plan to give you a first too."

"You've never had sex on a plane?" I almost shout, gripping both armrests and sitting up straight.

"You act like I'm a manwhore," he laughs.

I glare at him. "Before me, you were."

Jay shrugs. "I barely remember that person anymore."

"You don't miss it?" I probe, if a little hesitantly. We've only been together for a few months, so even though he's not sick of me yet, who's to say he won't eventually want what he used to have?

"Honestly?" he asks, one brow cocked, his eyes so bright the ice-blue color is almost azure.

The air between us crackles, and I swallow back the lump in my throat. It's one thing to ask for the truth, but it's another thing to hear it.

"Ye-yes," I stutter.

With a finger hooked under my chin, he tilts it so I can't look away. "The idea of anyone else makes me sick. The idea of someone other than me touching you, of someone other than you touching me …either scenario makes me want to hurt someone. I'm so fucking in love with you, Cat. I'd cut off my own hand before I'd betray you."

I suck in air, trying to keep my heart from seizing. The intensity of this man, of his love, of his devotion, is intoxicating.

The jolt of the plane speeding forward doesn't break our connection. "I need you," I whimper.

Jay chuckles, his easy smile returning. "Don't worry, Kitten. I'm going to spend the entire weekend making you come." His hand drops from my jaw, and he delves beneath my shirt, snaking up under my bra and tweaking my nipple.

"Jay," I pant, darting a glance at the flight attendant, who's doing her best not to watch us.

He gives me an easy smile before tipping his chin up and calling, "Nadia, do me a favor. Unless I call for you, stay up front."

Once she's out of sight, Jay continues his teasing. "Look out the window, Kitten," he whispers against my neck, then plants his lips there, searing my skin with hot kisses.

With the fingers of the hand not tangled up in my bra, he rubs me right where I need him.

"I can't—you can't," I whisper. "I, oh my God. I can't stay quiet."

I squirm against him, my words in direct opposition to the way my body reacts to his touch.

He covers my mouth with his, licking at my lips until I let him in, then he kisses me stupid. The kiss goes on and on, all while he rubs me over my pants and simultaneously explores my breasts as he moans into my mouth. When he pulls both hands away and undoes his seat belt, I almost lose it.

"Jay!" I whisper-shout.

"Relax, Kitten," he chuckles, "we're in the air. It's safe to move around." He waves toward the window.

"Wh-what are you going to do?"

"I'm going to have my in-flight snack," he says cheekily, dropping to his knees in front of me and shimmying my pants down my legs.

"Jay," I beg. Though I don't know what for. To keep going? To stop? My gaze is locked on the back of the brunette's head. She's sitting a few rows up but facing forward stiffly. I bite my lip. "She'll hear us," I whisper.

His blond hair falls to his forehead when he peers up at me between my bare thighs. "Good, let's see how long it takes for her to start rubbing herself once you start moaning."

"She wouldn't," I whisper.

He smiles. "Wanna bet?"

"Have you...?" I start, but I can't force the words out. Is that detail something he knows from experience?

Jay squeezes my thighs and rises a little higher on his knees. "I will never bring a woman I've fucked around. I promise you that. I would *never* do that to you."

I blow out a relieved breath. Why do I think the worst of him so often? I'm the one who still hangs out with Mia. I'd hate if he spent time with an ex. In that moment, I know that friendship is over. It's been on life support for a long time, and if anything, the friendship only brings me anxiety.

I nod and give him a small smile. I trust him.

He grins devilishly at me. "Can I eat now?"

I giggle and drop my head back against the seat. "Have at it, Mr. Hanson."

The first slip of his tongue makes me hiss, and in my periphery, Nadia jolts in her seat. Oh shit, Jay's right. She might just be into this. He slides a finger in, and I can't help but let out a moan. On cue, her head falls back, angling a bit more.

"Why is this so hot?" I whisper.

Jay's laughter against my sensitive lips makes me arch my back and

368

cry out again. "My naughty girl," he teases, licking right up my seam before dipping his tongue in and making my eyes roll.

"Fuck, Jay," I rasp louder than I mean to.

Nadia's head jerks, and she catches me watching, my lip caught between my teeth. I don't want her to look away. I want her to watch. What the hell is wrong with me?

Jay squeezes my thighs, pulling my attention back to him. "You want me to tell her to enjoy herself?" he asks.

"Like with us?" I ask, finally shifting my focus back to where he's situated between my legs.

He laughs against my thighs and licks me again. "No," he says darkly. "She can look, but she can't touch."

I squirm against him, and that's all the answer he needs.

"Nadia," he bellows from the floor. "If you'd like a better seat, the one across from Cat is open."

Without hesitation, she stands and practically stumbles down the aisle, her eyes trained on me. "Are you sure?"

I nod once, and with that, she drops into the seat across from us. I swallow. Hard. She's beautiful. Long dark hair pulled back off her face. Cerulean eyes. Dark skin. Jay doesn't spare her a glance.

"She won't mind if you touch yourself," Jay says drily.

I turn back to him in confusion, but he's talking to Nadia. With another silent nod, I watch in fascination as she slides a hand between her legs.

"Take off your skirt," I instruct, surprised by my own boldness.

Jay laughs. "See? I told you she wouldn't mind."

Euphoria surges through my veins when she obeys.

She slides her skirt and stockings to her ankles, keeping her legs at an awkward angle. I kind of like how she's locked in that position.

"Spread your knees wider," I murmur.

She studies me, a seductive smile on her lips. "What now, ma'am?"

Holy fuck. I'm going to come. "Suck on your finger."

Jay's gaze burns into me as he continues to lick. He's enamored. Proud. Turned on. And I love it.

Nadia slides her finger into her mouth teasingly, her attention still locked on me, and sucks. Her sounds mix with the sound of Jay sucking on my clit, sending increasing waves of ecstasy rolling through me.

I moan. "Now pull your panties to the side and let me see how wet you are for us."

"Is her pussy wet, baby?" Jay asks, never turning to look for himself. I almost feel guilty. Like I'm cheating on him. But he's all in, eagerly working me over. Listening to me control her, taking what I want from him, allowing him to do his favorite thing in the world, eat me—he loves it all.

"It's perfect," I say as she slides her finger back and forth. She knows the rules before I even tell her. She won't do anything until I say. "She's a good girl," I murmur. "I'm going to let her come."

"Let's see who can get off first."

I let my attention rake over Nadia's body until we make eye contact. Her pupils are blown wide, almost eclipsing her irises. Yeah, she's in. But I want her to go first. I want to win. "Deal. Nadia, be a good girl and fuck that pussy," I order.

Following my command, she slides in, arching her back. The euphoric expression on her face sends sparks of heat shooting through my core. I'm not going to lie; I want to taste her. I cry out as Jay distracts me with two fingers. He fucks me hard with his hand, his tongue working my clit, determined to win.

"Touch your nipple and circle that clit. I'm too close," I whine.

Nadia tweaks her nipple, never slowing her rhythm.

"Show it to me," I beg.

"Take your shirt off too," she says as she slips her top off one shoulder, then the next, exposing her hard dark nipples.

I strain against Jay, wanting to be closer to her.

He holds me down with an arm flung over my pelvis. "Just looking, Kitten," he growls. When my face falls, he smirks. "Unless you make her come first. Then…maybe I'll let you have a taste."

I practically cry in desperation. This is so wrong. I shouldn't want this. He's enough.

As if Jay can sense my thoughts, he squeezes my thighs. "I know, baby. Don't worry, I'm not upset."

When I slip my shirt over my head, leaving me in just my black bra, Nadia bites her lip and tips her head toward me. "Take it off," she whispers as she circles her clit again. She's bucking against the seat, and I'm slowly losing the battle.

"Oh fuck," I cry out as my orgasm takes me by surprise. I arch up into Jay's mouth and close my eyes as I ride wave after wave. When the spasms ebb, I open my eyes and watch Jay. He looks extremely pleased with himself, his eyes are brighter, almost the color of the Caribbean Sea, and he's smirking as he takes slow licks off my pussy, enjoying his prize.

He kisses my thigh softly. "Don't worry, baby. You can still make her come." He meets my gaze, his look intent. "With your lips if you want."

I suck in a breath and look back at her. Truth be told, the moment's over. I shake my head. "Words are enough," I rasp. "Nadia, show us how pretty you are when you come," I whisper.

Jay lays his head on my lap, turning his attention to her like he knows I want him to. I want him to enjoy this with me. But a second later, he stands in front of me and drops his jeans. I think my eyes pop out just as comically as Nadia's when he pulls his cock out of his boxers and presses it against my lips.

"Make us both come, baby," he whispers, his free hand pressed softly to my cheek.

I swallow him down, sucking and moaning around his cock while Nadia's moans echo around the cabin. Soon, my core is throbbing again, and I finger myself while sucking Jay off. Tears streak down

371

BRITTANÉE NICOLE

my cheeks, no doubt taking my mascara with them as I gag around him. My orgasm hits quickly. His cock, her sounds, my fingers—the stimulation is all too much.

When I cry out again, Jay's cock twitches. He growls "fuck I'm going to come" at the same moment Nadia sighs out "I'm coming."

When the cabin is filled with nothing but our labored breathing, Jay wipes at my cheek with his thumb and smiles. "Greatest flight of my life."

53

YOU ARE THE BEST THING BY RAY LOMONTAGNE

Cat

"**S**o," I deadpan as we disembark after saying goodbye to Nadia, "threesomes are kind of awkward."

Jay lets out a loud laugh, the sound carried away by the wind. "Fuck, you really are my favorite person."

I shrug, but my smile is big. "Didn't you find it a tad bit uncomfortable getting dressed right alongside her and then asking her to get you a drink? Like, the girl was staring at your ass while you came down my throat. *Awkward*," I sing teasingly.

He pulls me closer and kisses the top of my head. "It's fucking cold. You better have brought a heavy jacket if we're going to make it to the tree tonight."

I shake my head and grin at the way he changes topics like what just happened was completely normal. Maybe it is to him. But hell, I can't blame him for what happened on the plane. That was all me. I wanted it. Probably too much.

"We need to go to the hotel first," I say, squeezing his hand.

Jay shoots me a cocky grin. "Still horny?"

Is that really a question? I'm dying to get him alone. I want him to fuck me for hours. And besides, I brought a little surprise. "Yes."

He throws his head back and laughs. "My little virgin no more."

"Yeah." I roll my eyes. "I think we flew right past that milestone, Mr. Hanson."

"Eh, that ass still remains virginal." He slips a hand down my back and squeezes one of my cheeks.

I tense beside him. "Yeah, not happening. That area is for one thing only."

Jay's laughter lights me up inside. "Whatever you say, Kitten. If I had to bet, you'll be begging for me to fuck that tiny hole by the end of the weekend."

KITTEN'S SONGS

When we get to the hotel, Jay informs me we have dinner reservations across from Rockefeller Center, and he says we can't be late, so the sex has to wait. We're exchanging Christmas presents tonight since we won't be together for the holiday. Even the thought of celebrating without him makes my heart ache. But I force myself to ignore the pending goodbye and focus on our time together.

Strolling down the sidewalks of New York, we hold hands and enjoy the hustle and bustle of the city. It's so different from Boston. Louder, brighter, and the energy is heightened. Shots of Christmas spirit have been passed around the population, the holiday dripping down each building and seeping into the streets.

"One day I would love to live here," I admit.

Jay brushes a kiss to my hair. "We'll have an apartment here, Boston, and Paris. Anywhere else, Kitten?"

I smile up at him. "Planning our future already?"

Jay's smile fades, and his eyes turn serious, the glacier color going a steely blue. There's not a hint of teasing in his voice when he replies, "It's all I think about."

"Jay," I whisper, searching his face and seeing nothing but sincerity.

He stops our movement and, without warning, cups my upper arms and spins me so I'm facing away from him, though his hands still hold me tight. His strong body presses against my back, and his warm breath tickles my ear. "Merry Christmas, baby," he says softly, and there in front of me is the tree.

I drop my head back, resting it against his chest where his heart beats erratically. "I want everything you want. You want a penthouse in the city? Done." He runs his hands up and down my arms. "You want to live across the street from your brothers? I'll deal. You want a house? Tell me how big. Whatever you want, it's yours," he promises. He lifts my hair and presses a kiss to my neck. "Hold your hair for me, Kitten."

I follow his instruction, and he slides a necklace around my throat, pressing another kiss against my skin before connecting the clasp. "What is this?" I say, tucking my chin to get a look as he lifts up the pendent and leans over my shoulder.

"Our first kiss," he replies, as if that explains it completely.

The yellow stone sparkles in the lights of the tree. It's circular and has to be at least four carats. "Jay, this is—"

"A yellow diamond. The minute I saw it, I thought of you. Our first kiss. The song that was playing. If you were a color, you'd be yellow. You're my fall. My pumpkin spice. I can't write music, Kitten, but if I could, every song I'd write would be for you."

I spin around and loop my arms around his neck, gazing into his beautiful glacier eyes. "I love you."

"I don't deserve you, Catherine, but this necklace…it's my promise to you. That if you let me, I'll work to be worthy of you for the rest of my life."

I rub his jaw with my thumb, soaking in the feel of the clean-shaven skin. "You are worth so much more than you give yourself credit for. I've never met a more generous man. A more thoughtful one. A person who makes me laugh as much as you do."

He smirks. "So I'm worth more than all those orgasms?"

I bite his lip and then rest my head against his chest. "You're worth everything, Jay." I pull back and tip my chin so I can study him. "Only you," I whisper against his lips.

"Irrevocably. Completely. Head over *fucking* heels," he promises. He kisses me softly. "Now come on, Kitten. We've got a date right over there," he spins me around, "and we've only got it for a half hour."

My breath catches at the sight in front of me. I hadn't noticed until now, but the skating rink is empty. "You rented out the skating rink at Rockefeller Center?"

He tilts his head, giving me one of his *is this a serious question?* looks but doesn't respond.

I laugh. "Okay, money bags, let's go see how long you can stay up."

Jay waggles his brows, and I slap him in the stomach. "On the ice, Mr. Hanson! Mind out of the gutter."

He palms my ribcage on either side and tickles me. "I'm just joining you at your level, naughty girl."

KITTEN'S SONGS

Hours later, we're back at the hotel. Candles flicker, rose petals adorn the bed, and Jay sits in a chair, his arms tied behind his back and his chest bare, as I walk toward him, blindfold in hand, wearing only a pair of heels and my yellow diamond necklace.

"Fuck, Kitten. This is the best Christmas present I've ever received," Jay rasps, pressing forward, chest heaving, straining for me to get closer. "Just give me a taste," he begs, licking his lips.

Fuck, I really like it when he begs. It's going to my head. This entire day is. I'm drunk on desire. On the power he's given me by submitting completely. I dangle the blindfold above his head as I get close, and he nips at my nipple, sucking on it until I hiss. "You going to ride me while I'm blindfolded, Kitten?" he asks eagerly.

"That's the fun of the blindfold, Jay. You won't know what to expect. Won't know what's touching you, *how* I'm touching you. You just have to feel it."

Jay laughs dryly. "So the student becomes the teacher?"

I smile. "Something like that." I take one last moment to take in the way his beautiful eyes burn for me, then I kiss him and position the blindfold. Then I wrap my arms around his neck before securing it as I settle on his lap. The sight of him bound and blindfolded, his cock hard between us, is almost too much. In his ear, I whisper, "The ways I could take advantage of you right now…"

He chuckles, his voice deep and lust filled. "Please do. Have at it, Kitten. My body is yours to use for your own pleasure."

"While that sounds tempting, right now I just want to please you."

Palms flat against him, I glide them down his hard body and press my knees to the floor, pulling his legs apart and giving myself room to settle between them. Then I trail kisses up his thighs, like he often does to me. "Oh fuck, Cat," he growls.

Loving the sounds and the way his legs bounce in anticipation, I run my tongue right up his balls while still lightly scratching at his thighs. "Holy fuck. Where the hell—" he starts, but he loses his words when I suck his length into my mouth, taking him all the way to the back of my throat. He tugs against his restraints and growls again. "I need to touch you."

I don't let up. Continuing my mission, I suck him in and out of my mouth, all while he curses and groans and begs for me to ride his cock. With my desperation for him dripping down my thighs, I squeeze them together, but I don't give myself even one moment of release. I'm edging us both. When he's so close he's about to lose it, I squeeze him tightly, holding him there, and pull my mouth off him.

"Fuck!" he yells.

"Give it a minute, baby," I whisper, standing up and kissing him on the mouth. He's desperate for me, his tongue reaching out for me, trying to grasp me in any way he can.

"Please, honey, please ride my cock. Make me come," he begs.

He's so fucking gorgeous. His cock throbbing and wet, his chest rising and falling with heavy, uncontrolled breaths, his mouth searching for mine.

"I want you to eat me first," I demand.

He practically throws himself off the chair, landing with a thud on the carpet on his knees. "Get on the bed," he growls as he crawls on his knees in the right direction. I'll give him credit; either he can see under the blindfold, or he has a really good memory because he gets right up to the edge of it in no time. "Now," he grits, twisting in my direction like he knows I haven't budged.

"For someone who's tied up and blindfolded, you are awfully bossy," I tease.

"Catherine," he warns.

"Oh, the full name." I laugh but obey as the pulsing between my legs reaches a fever pitch. I need his mouth now. With three strides, I'm next to him, pushing myself to the very edge of the bed, in front of his mouth. With the slightest amount of force, I grab hold of his head, positioning him right where I want him. Even with the blindfold on, Jay is compliant. With his nose, he pushes my thighs farther apart, and then he leans in and licks.

"Fuck, you taste like heaven," he purrs between my legs.

I grip his hair and push him deeper. He doesn't fight it. He just feasts, his lips and tongue lashing at me until I'm coming apart at the seams.

"St-st-stop," I gasp, pulling back.

Normally, he holds me in place and doesn't let me squirm away, but with his arms tied behind him, he can't this time. I almost regret it. But I got too close to the edge. I want us to come at the same time. While he's buried deep inside me. And I want it to be the best sex of his life. Something he'll remember every night while we're apart.

"Take these off so I can fuck you properly," he growls.

I jump up and do just that. I need his hands on me.

When his arms are free, he tears the blindfold off and stares down at me, his eyes murderous and frenzied. "Bend over," he demands.

I fall to the bed without thought, spreading my arms and legs wide. His palm lands on my ass with a loud smack, pulling a yelp from me. At the contact, my body pulses, already on the edge of my climax.

"Please, Jay."

"Please what, Kitten?"

"Make me come," I cry, delirious now, just like he was.

He spanks the other cheek.

"You want to go to the edge, Catherine…then you wait," he grinds out before slapping me again, his voice is hoarse and hard and desperate, just like I feel. The spanks are in rapid succession, making it hard for me to catch my breath, but I get wetter with each one. Closer and closer to completely losing it.

"Please," I cry, full-on sobs racking my body with desperation for him.

The tip of Jay's cock presses between my cheeks, and I almost beg for him to fuck me there. I need his cock, and right now I'm so frenzied, so frantic, I don't care where.

"You want this?" he asks, pressing it farther.

So out of control with need, I grab for the sheets, gripping for anything, trying to find some sense of restraint. "Yes, please, anywhere. Please just give me your cock."

He laughs as he presses lower, sliding between my lips and pushing inside me, his chest and abdomen slamming into my back and his lips finding my neck. "Fuck, you feel so good," he whispers.

I can't breathe. I can't speak. My walls are already pulsing around him, tiny orgasms taking over before he's even begun moving.

"I can feel you working me over. Your body wants my cum so badly it's trying to squeeze it out of me. That what you want, Kitten? You want me to fill you up? Make sure this pussy knows it's mine and only mine?"

"Yes," I plead.

He pulls back, then slides forward again slowly. I'm delirious with pleasure, my brain foggy and my nerves on fire. Sweat drips down my back as he picks up speed and works me over, driving in and out at such a pace I can't catch a breath. His cock swells, an atomic orgasm edging closer in my core, and when it hits, I crash through the wave, my body electrified with aftershocks that pour through me and don't stop.

Jay's animalistic growl as he comes is the only thing that tethers me to this bed. To this place. When his cock stops twitching, he slumps over me and presses thousands of kisses against my skin. Each kiss blends into the next, no beginning and no end. His lips moving down my body, as if he's making sure he doesn't miss a spot.

I groan when I see the trail of mascara all over the duvet cover. "Oh shit," I whine.

Jay rolls over and pulls me onto his chest. "I love that I fuck you so hard that your mascara runs, that it stains the sheets." He kisses my forehead. "The evidence of us is there for good."

I smile up at my insane boyfriend. "I love you," I whisper.

"Only you," he whispers back.

54

I DON'T WANT TO MISS A THING BY AEROSMITH

Jay

Watching Cat leave me at the airport is the hardest thing I've ever done. She believes I'm heading to London. She thinks we'll reunite in Paris in a few weeks. I'd like to believe that's true. That I can pull off what I need to over the next few weeks. That I can keep her safe, convince my father to end this vendetta, keep Mia's mouth shut, and somehow convince her brothers that I'm the right man for her. That I can make her happy. But there are so many obstacles stacked up against us. I can't help but feel like I'm fighting a losing battle. One that will inevitably end with not only my heart in shambles, but likely the rest of my life too.

I won't walk away from her without a fight.

I won't walk away, period.

The only way we're ending is if it's by her choice.

I fly commercial so my father doesn't catch wind of my destination. I don't want anyone to track my trip.

Cat takes the private plane back to Boston. I made sure Nadia would not be the flight attendant this time around. There's no way I'm letting that woman anywhere near my girlfriend if I'm not there.

When I land, I rent a car under an alias. I drive the thirty minutes to the home I never imagined stepping foot in. As I pull up, parking in the circular driveway, the bay glimmering in the distance offering a false sense of hope, I fix my eyes on the only man in Cat's life who knows about us. He's waiting for me. Just as I suspected he would be.

Theodore James descends the front steps of his home wearing jeans, a cowboy hat, and a scowl. "You better have a good reason for all the secrecy, son," he says, tapping his cigar so the ashes float to the ground.

I blow out a breath. "You didn't tell anyone, right?"

He just stares at me. Not a man of many words, apparently.

"Right," I mutter, holding out my hand. "Good to see you."

He glares, then nods in the direction of the house. "Come inside. I have a feeling we'll need a whiskey for this conversation."

I follow him through the front door, immediately catching sight of a picture of Cat above the mantel. She's younger and just as beautiful as she was when I watched her walk away today. My heart twists at the image of her. But that photo is the perfect reminder of why I'm doing all of this.

He leads me to what looks like his study and points to two oversized chairs. "Take a seat," he instructs. "Whiskey?"

I shake my head. "No, thank you."

He pours two fingers into a lowball glass for himself and settles in the chair opposite mine. He leans back, crosses one leg over the other, takes a sip of what's surely James whiskey, and studies me. The weight of his stare is like an anvil on my chest. There are very few people in this world whose opinions of me matter. For years, it was only my father. Then Cat came into my life. And now her grandfather.

Am I good enough for her? Probably not. And he knows that.

"How's my granddaughter?" he asks with a slight tic of his lip.

Knowing that nothing has slipped by him, I go for the truth. "She was fine when I left her in New York, as I'm sure you're aware."

He nods once, confirming my suspicions that he keeps tabs on her whereabouts.

"But I'm afraid she's in danger."

His body goes rigid, and he sits up. "Danger?"

I fixate on a spot just over his shoulder, unable to say these next few words while looking at him. Because the truth is that I bear some responsibility for why the woman we both love is in this predicament.

I planted the disk. I aided my father in setting up their family. How can I even look myself in the mirror, let alone look this man in the eye?

"My father is out for revenge. I'm sure that's no surprise to you."

He remains stiff but gives a simple nod.

"Because of the affair," I continue. "And because of what happened after. Your son broke my mother's heart, and she killed herself…and my unborn brother."

For the first time since I arrived, emotion filters across Theodore James's face. His expression splinters, and he puts his drink on the side table. Then he stands and paces toward the window and back. He stops, regards me as if to say something, and then scoffs and shakes his head. With a few strides in the opposite direction, he's in front of the window again, looking out toward the bay.

When he finally speaks, his voice is low. "I met your mother, you know."

I clear my throat. "Did you?"

Turning, he shakes his head and smiles. "Your mother was a lot of things, but suicidal wasn't one of them." He closes his eyes for a long moment, and when he opens them again, a war wages within them. Then he tells me a secret that changes everything.

When he's done speaking, all I know is that nothing will ever be the same.

"I don't know what to do," I whisper. Tilting forward, I brace my elbows on my knees and drop my head, at a complete loss.

Theo taps on the glass with his knuckles. "That makes two of us." He chuckles, the sound full of torment. "I've tried to work it out over the last few weeks. How to deal with this development with you and Cat. I hoped it would be a passing thing. But…then I got your call. You love her," he says, his cobalt eyes finding mine. The lines etched across his face show his age, the stress he's endured. Likely because of my mother and Cat's father. His company and ours. Life. He wears the years on his face, and in this moment, I feel every one of them.

The only truth I know with every fiber of my being is one thing. "Yes, I love her."

He nods once and blows out another breath. "And she loves you?"

I dip my chin almost violently. "Yes."

"And she's in danger? Tell me everything."

He settles in the seat next to me, and I tell him everything I know, everything I've been able to dig up. And we formulate a plan. One I'm not sure we can pull off, but I take comfort knowing he can pull off his portion. He needs to protect his grandchildren. And the only way to protect them is to get them the hell out of Boston so this can't touch them. I just have to hope that one day I can join them.

As I open my car door, ready to head back to the city, my heart heavy with the knowledge of what's still to come, I look up at Theo with only one request. "If things don't go how they're meant to…please don't tell her. Let her think I didn't care. That I walked away. Don't let her mourn me. Us. Just…" I take a deep breath, knowing I need him to do this. "Make sure she moves on. Make sure she's happy. That's all I ask."

Theo frowns, but he doesn't fight me. "You have my word.

55

SPARKS BY COLDPLAY

Jay

I storm into my father's penthouse, rage boiling beneath my skin. It's dark, and if not for the shadow the moon casts over his figure in the living room, I'd think the house was empty.

"What took you so long?" he mutters.

Panting, I halt and suck in a deep breath, trying to calm my nerves before I give away everything in one fell swoop. This is not time to confront him about the bank accounts. I'm only here because I need to know where my mother is. Need answers about what happened all those years ago. Does he know the truth?

Of course he does, I scoff, annoyed by my own naivete.

"Expecting me?" I ask, my voice surprisingly even.

"Been expecting you since I saw you with Catherine James on your arm at the Halloween Ball," he replies to my utter shock.

"Catherine Bouvier," I correct.

He laughs and angles forward, shadows slicing his face in half, a fitting dichotomy in this moment. For so long, I believed he was the victim. That Edward James was the devil. Now I wonder who this man even is.

"Don't tell me she fooled you into believing she wasn't a James."

I growl. "Don't fucking say her name. Don't even think it. Understand?"

My father's face disappears again as he settles back in his chair. "Pathetic."

"I'm pathetic?" I bark. "You're the one sitting in your ivory tower by yourself. You've destroyed every relationship you have. Pushed us all so far that none of us want to be near you. Not even your own wife. Where is she, Dad? I know she didn't kill herself. Is she even dead?"

My father's voice is low. "Oh, she's below the ground, all right."

I run my hand across my face, the horror of his words bleeding through me. "What did you do?" I whisper.

A glass flies by my head, and I duck. It crashes to the floor, breaking into shards as my father howls. "What did I do? What did I fucking do? *She* had a fucking affair! You caught her! Don't you remember? You walked in on her with another man. You told me about the affair! *You!* Don't come in here on your high horse and pretend it didn't happen that way!"

The horror of his admission, of what I know he'll tell me, the knowledge that he's right—that I'm the one who set it all in motion—makes my stomach bottom out. "No," I whisper.

My father's shadow grows as he stalks toward me. "Go. You've made your choice. And you chose wrong."

I suck in a breath. "Dad, what did you do?"

"Don't *Dad* me," he shouts. "You went to fucking Edward James's house. You're *fucking* his daughter! You know, for a moment, I thought you were using her, and I was proud. *I was fucking proud.* But that night, I saw the truth. The way you looked at her. Kept her from me, She's not part of our revenge. You fell for her, you *stupid* fool."

Fuck. He knows too much. But maybe I can still get through to him. So I beg, my voice breaking. "Please, Dad. I love her. Keep her out of this. I'll help you take down Edward James. But leave her out of it."

He laughs as he takes another step closer. "I have the disk." The whiskey on his breath beats me down. His eyes are dilated, his cheeks sallow. "You should leave. My friends are on their way to collect the proof. Wouldn't want you to get your hands dirty," he mocks.

"But how?" I ask, desperate to understand.

He shakes his head. "Such a disappointment. After I saw you with her, I had your office bugged. I'm always a step ahead for a reason. Your pathetic friend wanted ten million, and you didn't even wire the money. I gave her twenty," he grits out.

Fucking cunt. I ball my fists, racking my brain, but my thoughts race and jumble. I can't grasp a single one that makes sense.

"Dad, there's no going back once you do this. The James kids are innocent. They had nothing to do with the affair. This is fucking insane," I say, pulling at my hair and pacing, talking more to myself at this point. He paid twenty million dollars for evidence he plans to turn over to the mob so he can get back at a man who slept with his wife. *And Mia fucking took it.*

As the ground sinks below me, I grab for his shirt. "You can't do this. I won't let you."

He pushes me back and reaches into his pocket. "Keep your hands to yourself, Jonathan." When he pulls his hand out, he's gripping a handgun. "I brought you into this world, and I have no fucking problem taking you out."

I hold up my hands and step back. He's fucking lost it. How long has he been this delusional?

A knock sounds, and my father glares at me before sticking the gun into the back of his pants. He walks toward the door, flicks on the lights, and turns toward me. "Keep your mouth shut while they're here. I'm serious, Jay. They'll kill us if they know the truth. You may care about your sweet Catherine, but you won't live to see another day if you open your mouth in front of these men."

Grinding my molars, I look away from him. I can't stand the sight of him. He takes the reaction as a tacit agreement and opens the door.

Two men step inside with ease, arms swinging casually. They move toward the center of the room, not waiting for my father to actually invite them in. Their presence fills the space, their chests puffed and their faces hard, the weapons on their hips unhidden. When the taller of the two spots me, he smacks his friend's arm. The shorter guy smiles when he takes me in. At my feet, the broken glass draws their attention.

"You having a party?" one says as he looks from me to my father.

My father shakes his head. "It's just my son. He's leaving." He nods toward the door.

I should take his advice. Get out of here and warn Theo. Make sure he gets everyone out of town quickly.

But part of me still wonders if I can stop this.

I suck in a breath. "I'll clean this up before I head out," I say, gesturing to the glass.

My father rolls his eyes. "Come with me," he says to the two men. "I have the disk in my office." With a glare, he stomps past me, the men following him. "In here," he says, pushing his office door open. "I'll grab drinks." If my father is nervous, his voice doesn't give anything away. But when he turns, his eyes are wild. He pushes his gun into my hand. "If you hear anything…"

My mouth drops open. "You just threatened me with this, and now you want me to save you if your deal with the mob goes sideways?"

His eyes harden and his jaw tenses. "We rise together, or we burn together. Choose the right side, Jonathan." He presses the weapon into my hands. "Your mother did this to us. Remember that. The James family and your mother. It's you and me against the world. It always has been."

I can't keep up with his words. But his eyes, they're the same ones that comforted me when I was a kid. The man who taught me everything I know about our business. The man I spent every holiday with. The only parent I've ever really known. I just need time to get him to realize that this is a devil's errand. That he won't be happy even if the James family ceases to exist. He's still heartbroken over my mother's death.

Even if he was likely the cause of it.

I take the weapon, though, and watch him stalk into the office and shut the door, my mind spinning. What the fuck do I do now?

I take out my phone and stare at the picture of Cat and me in front of the tree at Rockefeller Center. Her eyes are lit up with pure joy, and my expression matches hers. I'd do anything for her.

I type out a quick text as I make up my mind. I'll protect Cat or die trying.

> Irrevocably. Completely.
> Head over fucking heels.
> It always has been and
> always will be only you.

Resolutely, I prowl toward the closed office door, gun in hand, side chosen.

"As you can imagine, this can't get back to me," my father says.

"The boss just wants his money back. And to take care of those responsible," the shorter man says.

I listen beside the door, waiting for more information about what my dad obtained.

"The proof is in my safe. But I have the names," he replies.

With that, I know. I open the door and stare him down. He meets my glare with a depraved smile on his face, winking at me before turning back to his guests.

"Dad, don't," I plead.

He opens his mouth to speak. I don't think, only act, as he clears his throat, stands a little straighter, and says, "Catherine—" On autopilot, I aim the gun and fire, shooting my father straight in his open, lying, deceitful mouth. The blowback from the shot knocks me on my ass, and the shouts from the men as they descend upon me are the last thing I hear.

56

ONLY YOU BY CHEAT CODES

Cat

It's been two weeks, and I haven't heard a word from Jay. For the first twenty-four hours, I chalked up the lack of communication to him being busy with travel and seeing his brothers. But it's been radio silence since. I have no idea how to reach him other than through calls and texts. I'm about ready to fly to fucking London and storm into his house.

I don't even know where he's staying.

This is complete insanity.

My calls and texts go unanswered. My emails. My fucking rants to the sky.

I'm supposed to be enjoying Paris with my family for Christmas. Everyone is here. They helped me move into my apartment. We've visited the popular tourist spots. The Louvre, the Eiffel Tower, even a trip to Versailles. And through it all, I've hidden my sulking, but I'm at my wits' end.

"How's Jay?" I ask my brother, clearly giving up completely.

Carter shrugs. "Haven't talked to him."

"You didn't text him at all over the last week? It's Christmas. Don't you exchange happy holidays?"

My brother surveys me, his eyes narrowing. "You didn't?"

"Didn't what?" I scoff.

He throws his head back and guffaws. "Oh, you did? You so fucking did. Ugh, Cat, gross. He's a manwhore."

I swallow thickly, reining in the words I want to shout in defense of him. "I have no idea what you're talking about."

He shakes his head and picks up his phone. "I'm going to fucking kill him."

I don't even care that we've been outed. Maybe he'll respond to Carter. Although, if he does, then what does that say about us? Has he been ignoring me?

"Fuck," Carter mutters, staring at his phone, his eyes wide and his mouth agape.

"What?" I ask, snatching the phone from him, expecting to see a message from my boyfriend. My boyfriend, who has been ignoring *all* of my calls.

Instead, I find a text from Cash. It's an article with a shocking headline. Cash comes storming into the living room of our apartment, crossing in front of the picture window with a perfect view of the Eiffel Tower. "Did you see my text?"

"Warren Hanson Murdered," I whisper, the words not making sense. "What? When?" My heart jolts. "Is Jay—"

My grandfather walks into the room. "He's fine, Cat. He's okay." He glares at my brothers and pads toward me. "He's taken over the company, so he's been busy."

I can't hide my confusion. Why would my grandfather know how Jay is? If he's fine, why hasn't he called me?

"Pa?" I ask, aware that my brothers are both gaping now.

My grandfather waves a hand, motioning for them to leave, but Carter stands tall. "I want to know what's going on."

"It's not your business," my grandfather grits out.

Cash eyes me, but I can't meet his gaze, my hands tremble as I wait for them to leave.

"Say it," I whisper to my grandfather once we're alone. "Whatever you know, just say it."

My grandfather's face falls. "He got Mia pregnant."

I shake my head. "No."

My grandfather reaches for me, but I pull back. "No! It's a lie. He wouldn't do that to me."

Tears stream down my face as my heart cracks wide open.

"Sunshine, he fooled you. He fooled us all. He's just like his father. You're better off." My grandfather stands resolute, but his words lack resolve.

"What aren't you telling me?" I cry, wiping at my cheeks.

He presses his lips together and glances out the window. "Enough. You don't want your brothers finding out you were involved with him. I'll take them out. Cry it out and move on. He's not worth it." My grandfather looks back at me, his eyes swimming with devastation and his face drawn. He's not telling me the truth. This *can't* be true.

But my phone calls to Jay remain unanswered. As do my texts.

KITTEN'S SONGS

SIX MONTHS LATER

"Honey, I'm home," Sophie sings as she walks into the apartment carrying a paper bag filled with groceries.

As she pulls out the bottle of wine, a loaf of bread, and an assortment of cheese, I can't help but laugh. "You are so basic."

She beams at me. Laughs and smiles are hard to come by, if I'm being honest. Her chest rises and falls as she takes a deep breath. Then she's reaching into the bag again, her eyes downcast. She slides the magazine spread across the table without looking at me.

"What's this?" I ask, my hand falling to my stomach subconsciously.

"Cynthia wanted to give you a heads-up before it runs. It's going in this month's edition."

I press my lips together. There's only one thing she'd want to run by me. Only one thing everyone has danced around for months. I watch out the window, refusing to look at what Sophie's placed in front of me. "I'm sure it's fine," I mutter, standing to get a closer peek of the scene before me. A man and a woman walk down the street with a little girl between them, swinging her exuberantly. A couple holding hands heads in the opposite direction. As they pass, the woman looks back at the family wistfully. Three men in business suits chat animatedly, probably heading out for drinks or dinner after work. An entire world before my eyes. *Paris.*

"You should call him," she says softly, closer now.

I frown. "I have called him. A hundred times. Probably more. He never picks up. What am I supposed to do, take out an ad in the paper?"

She sighs as she slides the magazine in front of me again. "He kind of did."

When I finally look, my heart drops to my stomach. There, printed on the glossy page, is a picture of Jay with a woman on his arm. She's looking up at him adoringly. I huff out a breath. "There's certainly no point in telling him now, is there? I'm giving up the baby. I'll live in Paris, and he'll live in the US. He'll never have to know. Clearly, he's already moved on…" My voice cracks as I cradle my swollen stomach with one arm and point to the article with my free hand. "With her," I mutter. "Grace Winters."

WONDERING WHAT HAPPENS NEXT?

SIGN UP HERE FOR A SNEAK PEEK INTO THE FUTURE.

HTTPS://BOOKHIP.COM/ZFTJCFH

AND DON'T FORGET TO PRE-ORDER EXTRA DIRTY NOW.

HTTPS://GENI.US/EXTRADIRTYDUET

ACKNOWLEDGEMENTS

Thank you for reading this book even though you knew I would crush you. Thank you for loving this crazy whiskey world just as much as I do. It a dream to write these characters, to torture you with their heartbreak, and to lift you up with their joy. The Boston Billionaires Series changed my life last year, taking writing from a hobby that I loved to a business that I enjoy more than anything else I've ever done. So thank you from the bottom of my heart and I swear you will get all the answers and your happily ever after in Extra Dirty. I promise the pain is worth it.

To my team, I could not do this without you. Sara, you are in my head at all times and while sometimes it's scary I wouldn't want anyone else by my side. I appreciate you and your dedication to these characters, especially Jay. Brittni, I say it all the time, you make my stories better and now you make my life better, too. Looking forward to great things this year as we continue to grow together. Mo, once again you've outdone yourself with the beautiful formatting. Having you and C2C by my side since day one was my best decision. Jen, thank you for all the hard work, especially helping scour the internet for hot men. It's a tough job but someone has to do it. And to Beth, my wonderful editor, I swear I'm sending you the next book so you'll not be on edge anymore! Thank you for loving these characters and giving them better words than I could have. And grammar. Thank you for that.

To my incredible and wonderful street team, you are the reason I sell books. End of. Thank you for putting food on my table. No seriously, you ladies are my sounding board day in and day out, you keep me grounded and I just adore you.

And to my author besties, Jenni, Elyse, Swati, and Daphne, I couldn't do this without you.

Seriously. Thank you for your unwavering support, your friendship and your rants.

And my OG's that have been there since people first started reading me, who have been shouting at people to buy my books and when they didn't you were sending them to them anyway, Amy, Amy and Anna, your support and friendship is unmatched.

Last but certainly not least, my family. I love you. Thank you for your support.

If you are wondering what is coming next, follow me on Instagram, join my awesome Facebook group, sign-up for my newsletter and follow me on TikTok. Much love to you all!

OTHER BOOKS BY BRITTANÉE NICOLE

BRISTOL BAY SERIES

SHE LIKES PINA COLADAS
KISSES SWEET LIKE WINE
OVER THE RAINBOW
LOVE & TEQUILA MAKE HER CRAZY
A VERY MERRY MARGARITA MIX-UP

BOSTON BILLIONAIRES

WHISKEY LIES
LOVING WHISKEY
WISHING FOR CHAMPAGNE KISSES

DIRTY TRUTHS

STAND ALONE ROMANTIC THRILLER

DEADLY GOSSIP

COMING SOON

EXTRA DIRTY

Printed in Great Britain
by Amazon

45475574R00225